MAGGIE CHRISTENSEN

Safe Harbour in Pelican Crossing

Dedication

To my granddaughter, Lara, a marine biologist who loves sharks

Also by Maggie Christensen

Oregon Coast Series
The Sand Dollar
The Dreamcatcher
Madeline House

Sunshine Coast books
A Brahminy Sunrise
Champagne for Breakfast

Sydney Collection
Band of Gold
Broken Threads
Isobel's Promise
A Model Wife

Scottish Collection
The Good Sister
Isobel's Promise
A Single Woman

Granite Springs
The Life She Deserves
The Life She Chooses
The Life She Wants
The Life She Finds

The Life She Imagines
A Granite Springs Christmas
The Life She Creates
The Life She Regrets
The Life She Dreams

A Mother's Story

Bellbird Bay
Summer in Bellbird Bay
Coming Home to Bellbird Bay
Starting Over in Bellbird Bay
Christmas in Bellbird Bay
Finding Refuge in Bellbird Bay
Escape to Bellbird Bay
Second Chances in Bellbird Bay
Celebrations in Bellbird Bay
Happy Ever After in Bellbird Bay

Pelican Crossing
The Restaurant in Pelican Crossing
Secrets in Pelican Crossing
A New Dawn in Pelican Crossing
A Christmas Surprise in Pelican Crossing

One

Erica Masters looked down at her granddaughter lying peacefully in her pram, the niggle of unease coming to the forefront of her mind again. When she returned to her home here in Perth four months earlier, she was looking forward to picking up her old life again. Geoff, her abusive husband, was dead. He couldn't control or hurt her anymore. She fully intended to find a nursing position and enjoy the life she'd been forced to give up when she married Geoff and moved with him to his native Perth in Western Australia. But her daughter-in-law Briony's difficult pregnancy, coupled with her son Kieren's request for her help had forced her to change her plans.

Now, although still living in what had been her marital home, she was beginning to wonder if all was well in her son's marriage. Her thoughts were further complicated by the delay in finalising Geoff's estate. It should have been simple. When she and Geoff married, they'd made wills in which each was the beneficiary of the house and bank accounts when the other passed away. The business had come later, and Erica didn't know how Geoff had left it, but assumed it would go to Kieren who had worked with his dad in the car yard since he left school.

Each time she'd asked Kieren for information, or an explanation of why it was taking so long, he'd managed to avoid answering, only muttering about difficulties in the yard taking up his time. She had a vague recollection of some talk about invoices before Geoff died. At that time, she had been concerned her husband intended to harm her, so hadn't paid attention, but now she wondered if he'd been involved in some dodgy dealings that Kieren was now trying to resolve. It wouldn't surprise her. The man she'd fallen in love with, the handsome, smooth-talking guy who'd promised her the earth and whisked her off to Western Australia, away from all her friends and family, had proven to be a controlling bastard. But it had taken her years to recognise it, then admit it to herself, and for him to finally hit her once too often and force her to leave him.

'You okay, Mum?'

Erica looked up at her daughter-in-law and smiled. She loved that the young woman called her Mum. Briony was looking tired, her blonde hair pulled back in an untidy ponytail, her tee-shirt stained with smears of the chocolate she snacked on when Kieren was at work. Erica remembered what it had been like for her when Kieren was a baby, the broken nights, the worry that she'd make a mistake. She hadn't had anyone to help her. She'd managed. She'd had to. And Kieren had survived, survived to become so like his dad it sometimes scared her. He didn't look like Geoff. He took after her side of the family in that regard, resembling her brother, Joe, as a young man. It was a pity he didn't take after Joe in personality too. She sighed.

'I'm fine, Briony. How about you? Are you getting enough sleep?'

'Not really.' The younger woman dropped onto the bench beside Erica. 'Ava wakens a lot, and Kieren never gets up in the night. He says he needs his sleep as he has to go to work every day. As if I sit around doing nothing. Men!'

Erica patted her arm sympathetically. 'Ava's asleep now. You sit here and rest while I make us a cup of tea, and there's some of the lumberjack cake I made yesterday. How about a slice of that too?'

'Oh, that would be lovely. Thanks, Mum. I don't know what I'd do without you.'

That was part of the problem, Erica thought, as she went into Briony's kitchen to prepare the tea, the kitchen that was now almost as familiar to her as her own, she spent so much time here. It was a pleasant house with views across the city, but it wasn't her home.

Briony had become too dependent on her, on knowing she was there to help, to take care of Ava, to step in when Kieren was too busy or too heartless to be there for his wife. It had been okay when they'd all returned to Perth for Geoff's funeral. Erica had been too confused to think of herself, happy to support the pregnant Briony, to make meals, help with the housework, spend time with her while Kieren sorted out matters at the yard.

But she'd never intended it to continue. Now it was time for Briony to take more responsibility, for Kieren to step up to help his wife. Erica knew the local hospital was crying out for more staff. They'd be delighted to offer her a position. Then her life could go back to some form of normality. She'd still help out with babysitting, of course. She wanted to be part of little Ava's life, but not on the everyday basis she was at the moment. She'd speak with Kieren on the weekend, she decided, ask about Geoff's estate, suggest it was time for her to go back to work, for them to make plans for Briony to become more independent.

*

'Thanks, Mum. Great dinner.' Kieren leant back in his chair, his posture so like his father's, Erica winced.

'Thanks, son.' Erica knew lamb roast was his favourite. It was why she'd cooked it tonight. 'Why don't we take our coffee through to the living room? I want to talk to you about something.'

'I'll check on Ava, then clear up while you two talk,' Briony said.

'No, Briony. What I want to say involves you too. We'll wait till you make sure Ava is asleep.'

A concerned expression clouding her pretty face, Briony went off to the bedroom which Erica had set up for her granddaughter, turning what had been Geoff's study into a nursery fit for a princess.

'What's this about, Mum?' Kieren asked, when all three were seated in Erica's living room. It still held the furniture she and Geoff had chosen together and which she loved too much to part with, despite the unpleasant memories many of the pieces held for her.

'It's about your dad's estate… and my future. Why is it taking so long to settle? I know you said you're busy, but surely it's all straightforward? And…' Erica glanced across at Briony, '… it's time I went back to work. I was speaking to one of the nurses, and they're looking for staff.

I've been happy to help you out with Ava, Briony, but I can't do it for ever. I have my own life to lead, and I need to work.'

There was a stunned silence. Then Kieren cleared his throat. 'It's not that simple, Mum. Dad… he… Hell, there's no easy way of putting it. The business is in a mess. We're going to need to sell this house to keep the car yard afloat.'

Erica's heart sank. 'But it's my house.'

'No, Mum. Dad left it to me, he left everything to me.'

Erica stared at him, her stomach churning. 'When?' she managed to utter.

'A few years ago. He said he'd spoken to you about it, that it would simplify things when…' His voice trailed off.

'He never said a word. We agreed we'd leave everything to each other, though I expected you to get the business.' *What was this going to mean for her?*

As if she'd spoken aloud, Kieren continued. 'It's not a problem, Mum. You can move in with us. We can build a granny flat, and you can share with Ava till then. It'll make things easier for Briony too.' He smiled at his wife.

'No!' The word exploded from Erica without her volition. A granny flat! She was not yet fifty. She wanted to reduce the time she spent helping Briony, not to move in with her and Kieren, to give up her independence. Erica swallowed. 'How bad is the business?'

'Pretty bad. I'm still trying to unravel some of Dad's deals, work out who he owed money to. This place will have to go.' He gazed around the house he'd grown up in, as if calculating its value. 'I'm sorry, Mum,' he said as if it was an afterthought, 'but what do you need with a big place like this, when you can move in with us? And you haven't worked as a nurse for as long as I can remember. Dad always said you weren't cut out to be a career woman, that you couldn't be trusted to look after yourself. Briony needs you. Ava needs you. Can't you see that?'

Briony opened her mouth to speak, but Kieren put his hand on her arm, squeezing it tightly, and gazed at Erica as if he could see what she was thinking and bend her to his will.

Erica felt a shiver run down her spine. The expression on Kieren's face was so like the one she'd seen on Geoff's, usually when he was determined to get his way. She didn't doubt his evaluation of the business – it was just like Geoff to leave it in a mess – but Erica didn't intend to give up her newly found independence for anyone, not even her son, daughter-in-law and her beloved granddaughter.

She didn't say any more then and forced herself to act as usual when she bid the young couple farewell. But later, lying in bed, the moonlight streaming in through a gap in the curtains, she thought again about Kieren's words. If what he said was true, Geoff had managed to screw her from the grave, to force her to be dependent on the good will of her son, the son who only saw her as a glorified nursemaid, who'd believed what his dad said about her. If she stayed here, she'd lose the independence she'd hoped for.

Erica thought back to the time she'd spent with Joe in Pelican Crossing, in the town where she'd grown up. She knew what she had to do. With a sense of déjà vu, she picked up the phone to call her brother.

Two

Life was good. Jamie Whittaker stared out at Pelican Crossing harbour and counted his blessings. Only two months earlier, his younger son's girlfriend had presented him with his first grandchild, a son to carry on the Whittaker name. Mandy was a sweet girl, if a bit of a livewire. She and Gary made a good couple and between her personal training business and his dive school and kitesurfing school, they had much of the local outdoor industry sewn up. The only fly in the ointment was their failure to marry before the child was born.

But they were soon to remedy that. The wedding was to be held in two weeks' time. It would be a small gathering, given the new baby, only the two families in attendance. On Mandy's side, that meant her mother with her new partner, the editor of the local paper, her sister and brother-in-law, her half-sister and fifteen-year-old niece and, of course, her grandmother. Gary's relatives were fewer – Jamie himself, plus brother Rory. There was some doubt as to whether Gary's mother, Jamie's ex, would attend, but Gary told his father he'd invited her.

This should have been another reason for concern for Jamie. He hadn't seen Cindy since she'd left him when the boys were in their teens, angry at the demanding hours he spent on the fishing boat he'd inherited from his dad. It was the only life he'd known, and he'd loved it, loved setting off at the crack of dawn and heading out to sea, returning with nets filled with fish for the market. But Cindy had hated that he was never home, and she claimed he always stank of fish when he returned.

Now, all these years later, he could understand her anger and disappointment, how she'd resented his devotion to a life which didn't allow much time for her… or their family. The irony was that, left with two teenagers to take care of, he'd sold the fishing boat and now owned a fishing charter and boat hire business.

These days Cindy lived in Melbourne. She'd kept in touch with the boys, and they visited her from time to time, always seemingly glad to get home. Neither were fans of the city. Jamie had expected her to visit when little Archie was born, but Gary reported she was on a cruise. Surely she'd be here for the wedding, wouldn't she?

Jamie drained his coffee and rinsed the mug. There was no point in wondering about Cindy's intentions. He had given that up years ago, long before they parted ways. The local girl he'd fallen in love with in his twenties had become an enigma to him, just as he'd been a disappointment to her. He had a busy day ahead. He was booked to take a group of Sydney businessmen on a fishing trip and knew from experience how demanding such groups could be. Despite his no alcohol rule, they inevitably managed to squirrel away a bottle or two which they'd slug when they thought he wasn't looking. They didn't have a clue about fishing and were only interested in posting photos of themselves on the internet with the big fish they caught, blaming Jamie if they failed to snare one.

Dressed in his usual work gear of a pair of cut-off khaki pants and black tee-shirt emblazoned with the outline of the big fish which was the emblem of his business and the words *Whittaker Fishing Charters*, Jamie headed out, glad the harbour was only a short walk away. He'd bought this place when the boys moved out, first Rory, then Gary, and he found himself rattling around in the family home. The two-bedroom cottage was one of a row of old fishermen's shacks which had been renovated over the years and was perfect for his needs.

Jamie loved his walk to work, the scent of the ocean, the cries of the seagulls circling overhead, and the sight of the pelicans perched on the bollards by the water, hopeful of being tossed fish from the few fishing boats which still set off from the harbour each morning.

There were various rumours as to how Pelican Crossing got its name, and Jamie preferred the one about pelicans crossing the road to the fish restaurant for their daily scraps of fish. But it was more likely the town's name came from the nearby Boodalang River, boodalang being the Aboriginal word for pelican and which had been anglicised by the early settlers. Whatever, it was a good name, and Jamie was proud of his town.

Gary's dive school was located in the building next to Jamie's office, and his son was standing in the doorway.

'Morning, Dad.' Gary grinned. The tall young man wearing a pair of board shorts and a tee-shirt with the dive school logo, his blond hair tied back in a ponytail, his chin and cheeks peppered with stubble, reminded Jamie of himself at that age.

'You're having an early start.' Gary didn't normally arrive at the dive school till after eight unless he had a dive organised, but there was no sign of him readying the dive boat.

'Archie kept us awake again.' He rubbed his chin. 'Mandy's taking care of him, so I thought I might as well get a start on the day.'

'How is the little one?'

'He's good, apart from the fact he keeps us awake. But I wouldn't be without him. Why don't you drop over for dinner tonight?'

'Can do, if it's not too much for you both.'

'We'll get a takeaway. It's easier these days.'

'I can bring one, and a couple of beers.'

'That would be great, Dad.'

'Won't be long now.'

'Two more weeks. I can't wait. I guess we should have done it sooner, but...' He shrugged.

'No worries. I'm looking forward to it.' Jamie had been delighted when Gary and Mandy teamed up. It was good to see his younger son so happy. If only Rory could find a partner too. But thinking of his sons' happiness, only reinforced his own solitary existence. There hadn't been a woman in his life since Cindy left, partly because of lack of opportunity, partly because he didn't trust himself to make a good choice. He'd thought he and Cindy were the perfect match and he'd been wrong. The only other woman he'd ever been interested in had been Erica Harris, his teenage sweetheart. But she'd left Pelican Crossing as soon as she finished school and broken his heart.

There had been a time, late the previous year, when she'd returned to the town, and he'd had hopes... but her brother proved to be very protective of her – something about her marriage – then she was gone again.

'One thing, Dad…' Gary said, as Jamie was about to open his office door. 'Mum called. She's coming to the wedding.'

Three

Once she had decided, Erica lost no time in making plans. She would be sad to leave Perth, but the *For Sale* sign which had appeared on her front lawn was all the incentive she needed. Within a week she had packed all she'd require for the next few months and booked her flight.

'I wish you would stay, Mum,' Briony whispered as they said goodbye, after she'd spent her final evening with her and Kieren and given little Ava one last hug.

'I'll come to visit, and you can visit me in Pelican Crossing.'

Briony's face brightened. 'I'll do that,' she said. 'I'm going to miss you.'

'I'll miss you too.' Erica hugged her and for a moment wondered if she was doing the right thing. But one glance at her son's expression confirmed her decision. It was so like his father's. She hoped Briony would never know the torment she'd experienced with Geoff, that she was the only victim of Kieren's controlling behaviour. But she couldn't be sure, and her subtle questioning of her daughter-in-law elicited only a vague response. Maybe, if Briony did keep her promise to visit Erica in Pelican Crossing, she could find out more.

With one last look at the house she'd called home for so many years, Erica got into the taxi and was whisked off to the airport. Then, a day later, after spending a night in Sydney where she enjoyed the peace and quiet, as well as the many exciting thoughts of what her future might hold, she walked into another airport terminal to see Joe waiting for her.

It was strange being back here again. But this homecoming was different from her last one when she was fleeing from Geoff. This time she wasn't beset with fear. Instead, she was filled with enthusiasm about new possibilities. She'd already been in contact with the local hospital, who'd responded that they'd be delighted to have her back. Her previous employment there had been so brief, and she'd left so suddenly, she'd been unsure of her welcome.

'Welcome back, sis.' Joe gave Erica a warm hug. 'Good to see you again. You're looking so much better.'

'Thanks.' He was referring to the last time he'd picked her up here. Then, she'd been a shadow of her former self, worn down by Geoff's continual criticism and her futile attempts to please him, her body broken and bruised from his attacks. 'You're looking good too. Things going well with Gill?' she asked, aware of his relationship with the local divorce and family law solicitor who had helped protect her from Geoff. The relationship had been in its early stages when she'd returned to Perth.

'Very well. In fact…' Joe blushed, '… we're thinking of moving in together. The only challenge is that she feels uncomfortable about moving into my place with its memories of Barb, and her apartment is too small for Coco.' Joe's chocolate labrador, Coco, had been his sole companion after his wife died, until first Erica, then Gill, came on the scene. 'We've been looking around for something to buy,' he added. 'But don't worry. There's no rush, and I may not sell the old place.'

'Wow!' Things had certainly moved fast. Erica had only been gone a few months.

Joe blushed again. 'We're neither of us getting any younger and we've both been on our own for some time. When you know, you know.' He grinned, looking like he had in his teens when he'd won a game of cards.

'I'm pleased for you, Joe. You deserve to be happy. And Gill's a great lady.'

'Yeah. Thanks. Coco likes her too,' Joe said as if this was the final accolade. Perhaps it was.

Back at the house, Coco gave Erica a rapturous welcome. It was good to be back, but she was very conscious that this was Joe's house.

Joe took Coco for a walk while Erica unpacked and had a shower.

Changing from her travel outfit into a pair of white pants and a multicoloured top she felt like a new person.

'If you're not too tired, do you fancy going out to dinner to celebrate your return?' Joe asked when he returned and had fed Coco and filled her water bowl. 'I can check if we can get a table at *Crossings*,' he added, naming Pelican Crossing's premier restaurant.

'I'd love that and I'm not too tired. The air here seems to have energised me already.' Erica laughed, feeling a sense of freedom she hadn't anticipated. '*Crossings* would be wonderful.' Erica remembered eating there on her previous visit. The restaurant, which had begun life as a fish and chip shop before becoming a fish restaurant, then being transformed into its current incarnation by Poppy Taylor and her late husband. Now it brought tourists to Pelican Crossing from all over Australia, thanks to its having being promoted in magazines and on television.

When they walked into the restaurant, Erica was assailed by a sense of familiarity. Although she had only been here once with Joe, there was something about the atmosphere that made her feel welcome, as if now she'd really come home. Glancing around, she caught sight of Poppy on the other side of the room, but didn't think she'd seen them. There would be time enough to catch up with the woman who'd been kind to her and had recommended a solicitor to her – the solicitor who was now her brother's partner.

After studying the extensive menu, they decided to share a dozen oysters followed by nasi goreng for Erica and chilli crab spaghettini for Joe, all accompanied by a bottle of prosecco because – as Joe said – they were celebrating.

'You're spoiling me, Joe,' Erica said, when the waiter had filled their glasses, and they toasted each other and the future, which now looked rosier than ever to Erica.

'I want to get my own place,' Erica said, while they were waiting for their meals.

'There's no need.'

'I know, but I'll feel better if I do. I'm here to stay this time and I want somewhere to call my own. I have a bit of money I managed to squirrel away and I'll be earning a good salary. Something small would suit me. Perhaps one of those apartments overlooking the marina. I'll rent until I can afford to buy.'

'It's a relief to see the old Erica back again. I was worried she had disappeared for good. It must have been a wrench to leave your granddaughter.'

'Yes, it was.' Erica gazed into space, remembering the feel of Ava's warm body, her soft skin, the scent of milk and baby powder. 'But Briony has promised to visit. It will do her good to get away for a bit. I'm worried about her.'

Joe raised an eyebrow. 'Kieren's not…?'

'Not as far as I can tell, and Briony isn't giving anything away. But he's so like Geoff, Joe. It worries me. I can only hope he's treating her well… And now there's the baby…'

'He wouldn't hurt his own child.' Joe sounded shocked.

'No, but Ava's a girl. It's not like it was with Kieren. Geoff always treated him like a mate, someone he could mould in his own image. It'll be different for Kieren with Ava. I hope I'm wrong.'

*

Next morning, when Joe had gone to work, Erica took Coco to the beach. It was wonderful to feel the sand beneath her feet and to smell the scent of the ocean again. She hadn't realised how much she'd missed this. She was looking forward to getting back into the water. Last time she'd been here, she had joined a group of wild swimmers, mostly women, who braved the ocean at the crack of dawn. It was amazing to be out there just as the sun was rising. She couldn't wait to do it again.

Erica had been so lost in thought, she hadn't noticed that Coco had run off to join another dog at the edge of the water. The spaniel was accompanied by a woman Erica recognised. Old Agnes was an institution in Pelican Crossing. Erica had met her on her previous visit, though didn't remember her from when she was growing up there. She was of indeterminate age and with her wild mane of white hair and long skirt trailing in the water, looked like an aging hippie. Erica knew she managed a pelican rescue centre by the river, and had heard that she was renowned for her words of wisdom, but hadn't had much to do with her herself.

'It's Erica, isn't it?' Agnes said, when Erica drew close. 'You're Joe Harris's sister. Good to see you back. The city didn't agree with you?'

'Not exactly.' Erica was unsure how to reply. She didn't want to reveal her reasons for leaving Perth, even though she had the distinct impression Agnes would understand, maybe even offer advice. Erica wasn't ready for advice.

'Then you're in the best place,' the old woman said with a smile, bending down to ruffle Coco's ears. 'You have a great day,' she added, before calling her dog and walking away.

'Thanks, you too,' Erica called after her.

On the way back to Joe's, she stopped off to gaze in the window of the local real estate office, disappointed to see few available rentals which would suit her needs. Most were large homes and beyond her budget. With a sigh, she returned to Joe's.

Erica ensured Coco had water and gave the dog a treat, before making herself a cup of lemon and ginger tea, glad Joe still had some of the teabags she'd bought when she was here before. Then she took her tea and phone out to the yard and called Briony.

It felt strange to be talking to her daughter-in-law while she was sitting here in Joe's back yard, Coco snuffling around the edge of the garden, difficult to believe that only a few days ago, she was in Perth, cuddling her granddaughter. It was as if she was in another world.

Four

Jamie was ready for a beer when he walked into the old hotel opposite the harbour. *The Grand Hotel*, known locally as *The Grand*, had been there for as long as he could remember. It was where he'd ordered his first beer – when he was still underage – where he'd celebrated his twenty-first, then his bucks party, and it hadn't changed much over the years. There had been the time when a new owner wanted to change the name, but there had been a local outcry, so *The Grand* it had remained. There was nothing grand about it, the hotel having retained its original frontage and décor which the locals all accepted and loved. The only difference was that in recent years, in addition to serving the familiar brews which Jamie loved, it had added a selection of craft beers from a local brewery owned by a couple of young guys of his sons' generation.

Looking around, he caught sight of his old mate, Cam, standing at the bar and headed towards him. He and Cam Mitchell had been at school together and, although Jamie hadn't been part of the tight clique of four Cam belonged to, they had remained friends over the years. Now Cam managed the marina next to the harbour and owned *Pelican Marine*, a boat sales and chandlery business. Like Jamie, he'd divorced, but was now remarried to another old school mate, Poppy, who owned the restaurant *Crossings*. The pair often met for a beer after work.

'Your usual?' Cam nodded to the brimming glass sitting on the counter, its sides dripping with condensation. 'I got one in for you.'

'Thanks.' Jamie took a long swallow. 'Boy, that tastes good.'

'As bad as that?' Cam grinned and took a gulp from his own glass.

'You couldn't read about it.' Jamie wiped his mouth with the back of his hand. 'A group of self-satisfied Sydney businessmen who were hungover when they arrived and managed to smuggle a few bottles of whisky on board. Then they had the hide to complain when they could barely stay upright to catch anything.' He shook his head.

'Wishing you were back on the fishing boat?'

'Almost. But it's not always like that. Most groups are well behaved, grateful if they end up with a couple of fish, happy to have had a day out on the water. How was your day?'

'Pretty average. Your Rory is proving to be a valuable offsider. I can see him wanting to take over one day, though not just yet. I still have a few more years in me, even though Poppy is on at me to slow down.'

'Good to hear the young chap is doing well. He and his brother gave me more than a few sleepless nights after Cindy left. I never expected to be left with two teenagers.'

'Me neither. Though luckily Lachlan never caused me any worry.'

'You were lucky.' Cam had been left to care for his son when his wife left town with a teaching colleague. Jamie might complain about bringing up his two boys on his own, but he didn't know how he would have coped with knowing his wife preferred another woman to him.

'Fancy having a bite to eat? Poppy's deserted me tonight for some women's thing, and I don't fancy going home to an empty house. Odd how quickly I've got used to having a woman around the place.'

'Sure.' Jamie couldn't stifle the stab of envy he felt at the mention of Cam's relationship with Poppy. Not that he envied him Poppy. He wasn't sure he could cope with someone as feisty as she was, but it would be nice to have someone to come home to after a busy day.

'How's the new grandson?' Cam asked, when they were settled at a table with plates of steak and chips and a second glass of beer.

'Archie?' Jamie smiled, relaxing at the thought of the little fellow he doted on. 'Doing well. We'll have him out on the water before much longer. But I have a bit of catching up to do with you and Poppy. How many is it?'

Cam laughed. 'Four at last count, with Amber's twins, but I know what you mean. I feel the same about Lachlan and Scarlett's boy,

Taylor. There's something special about knowing your name will carry on when you're gone.'

'Hey, less of that. I hope we're good for a few more decades yet.'

'I'll drink to that.'

The pair chuckled and no more was said until they had finished their meal.

They were about to leave when Cam said, 'I hear your old flame's in town again.'

Jamie stopped in his tracks. There was only one person who'd fit that description, one person he'd dated before Cindy. Erica Harris – Masters now, he remembered – had been staying with her brother last year. But she'd returned to Perth after the death of her husband. And he'd barely managed to meet her when she had been here. Her brother had made sure of that. 'Erica?' he asked, his voice sounding odd, even to him.

'Who else? Poppy said she and Joe were in *Crossings* the other night. I guess she's here on a visit. You're not still…?' He peered at Jamie intently.

'What? No, of course not. I'm just curious. Last time she was here, it was all very mysterious, as if Joe wanted to keep her under wraps. He sometimes likes to keep everyone guessing.'

As Jamie farewelled Cam and made his way home, the news Erica was back in town was going round and round in his head. Was this just another visit or was she back for good? He intended to find out, and this time, he determined he wouldn't let Joe stop him from contacting her.

Five

It was so good to be back in the water. Erica couldn't believe how she'd all but forgotten the exhilaration of being out in the ocean as the sun was rising.

Once out in the bay, Erica turned on her back to float, as she'd seen the others do, and watched the sun's rays change the sky to pink and gold, a sense of peace enveloping her.

When, at dinner the previous evening, Gill had asked her if she intended to join the group again, she'd been quick to assure her she did, ignoring Joe's negative comments. Erica had been back in Pelican Crossing for three days now and it was time to get back into good habits. She'd already contacted the hospital and was due to start the following Monday.

'Glad you made it,' Gill greeted her, as they picked up their towels together. 'It's such a great way to start the day. Pity I can't persuade Joe.'

The two women laughed at the idea of Joe joining them. Although the group consisted mainly of women, there were a couple of men who sometimes made an appearance. But Joe was never one of them.

'What are your plans for today?' Gill asked, as they walked back to their cars – fortunately the second-hand Mazda Joe had purchased for Erica on her last visit had still been sitting in his garage. 'Livvy's still away, isn't she?'

'Yes.' Olivia Grace, who had been one of Erica's best friends throughout school, and who had been instrumental in her joining the wild swimmers, was on an extended visit to England. 'But Rhana Black's still here. The three of us did everything together as teenagers. It was good to catch up with them again last year. I'm having lunch with Rhana today.'

'Enjoy!'

By this time, they had reached the car park, and Gill pressed the key to unlock her car. 'See you soon,' she called through the window as she drove off.

Erica watched her go before getting into her own car to drive back to Joe's.

This morning, knowing Erica would be going out, Joe had taken Coco to the office as he often did, and the house seemed very quiet without the dog's snuffling. It was a big house, too big for one person, Erica thought. She was glad Joe intended to sell it. She knew he had hung onto it because of all the memories it held of his late wife, Barb, but it was time for him to move on with his life, time for her to move on too. Perhaps Geoff had done her a favour in leaving everything to Kieren. She'd been angry at the time, but there was a sense of freedom in having to start over, and Pelican Crossing was a good place to do it.

Back at the house, Erica showered and changed before making breakfast. She took her coffee and two slices of sour dough toast topped with mashed banana out into the courtyard, along with a book she'd found on the bookshelf. It was by Sarah Morgan, an author she wasn't familiar with, and she was enjoying it. She seemed to remember Barb had belonged to a book club, the same one Gill was a member of and which Livvy had urged her to join. Maybe this time she would. It would be good to meet another group of women, and she loved to read.

On her last trip to Pelican Crossing, Erica had been so worried about Geoff following her, so intent on setting up the apprehended violence order recommended by Gill, that she hadn't been able to relax and enjoy all that Pelican Crossing had to offer. This time it was different. She was here to stay. There was no Geoff. She was free.

Engrossed in her book, time passed quickly, and it was soon time to leave for Rhana's. Rhana, who'd always loved animals, had never married. She now lived out of town on a small acreage and bred spaniels, seeming to enjoy her solitary existence and preferring her dogs to people.

Erica smiled when she came to the gate on which there was a metal sign with a picture of a spaniel and the words *Spaniels Live Here*. She'd only visited once before, that time with Livvy, and had been surprised at how little her old friend had changed from the untidy teenager she remembered. Tall and heavily built, Rhana had never bothered with fashion or makeup, always saying people would have to take her as she was. Despite her sometimes abrupt manner, Rhana had been a good friend, and Erica was looking forward to renewing that friendship.

Once through the gate, Erica drove up the dirt driveway to where a house nestled among a mixture of palms and pandanus. A volley of barking greeted her as she stepped out of the car and, alerted by the noise, Rhana appeared in the doorway wearing jeans and a tee-shirt bearing a picture of a spaniel.

'Welcome back!'

Erica found herself enveloped in a warm hug, while a wet tongue tickled the toes which were peeping out of her sandals. 'Thanks, Rhana. It's good to be here.' By this time another two dogs had joined the one at Erica's feet. She looked down at them and smiled. 'Another litter?'

'Yes, these are Bonnie's and are all spoken for. They'll be gone in another week. Then it'll be more peaceful around here for a bit. Let me put these three back with their mum, and you can come inside.'

Erica followed her friend into the farmhouse kitchen which looked as if a bomb had hit it.

'Sorry about the mess,' Rhana said sweeping a pile of newspapers off the scrubbed wood table and moving a bag of dogfood to the floor. 'It's been a bit hectic these past few days.'

'But you love it.'

'I do. I like to keep busy. Tea or coffee?'

'Coffee, thanks. I hope you haven't gone to a lot of trouble…' Erica could see a pot of soup on the stove and there was the aroma of freshly made bread.

'It's good to have someone to cook for. When I'm on my own I live on bread and cheese, though I do always bake my own bread. There's nothing like it.'

'Your mum did too.' Erica remembered. Mrs Black had been a wonderful cook and the three teenagers had often enjoyed her freshly baked bread liberally spread with homemade jam… and her cakes.

Rhana paused for a moment, as if remembering her mother who had now passed away. 'I'm nothing like Mum. I couldn't take time for all the kneading and proving of dough. I let my bread maker do the work.' She gestured to the white machine sitting on the kitchen bench beside the newly baked loaf.

'It does smell delicious,' Erica said.

Maybe she'd try making her own bread too. Geoff had always insisted she buy his favourite brand, but now she could experiment. It was a heady sensation to have no one to answer to. For so long she'd lived in fear, with the need to keep to the rigid guidelines her husband set for her, it was odd for all that to have changed. Even last year, when she'd left Geoff and come to stay with Joe, the thought of her husband was never far away, preventing her from living life to the full.

By the time Rhana served up the vegetable soup – made from vegetables she'd grown herself – and bread, liberally spread with her home-made hummus, she'd managed to elicit Erica's reason's for returning to Pelican Crossing.

'It sounds as if your daughter-in-law might be in trouble,' she said. 'You say she feels okay about how your son treats her?'

'I may be imagining it. She may be fine. But he's so like his dad, I worry for her, and…'

'There's nothing you can do. Sounds as if you've already done what you could. You were wise to leave when you did. I can't imagine what it could have been like for you if you'd stayed.'

'Mmm.'

'And you're living with your brother again?'

'For the moment. I want to find my own place. Joe has his own life, and now he and Gill are together he's planning to sell. I don't want him to delay his plans because of me.' Erica picked at a crumb on the table. 'I've never been totally independent, Rhana. It's time.'

'I can't argue with that. I've lived alone since Mum died, if you can call living with a pack of dogs living alone,' she chuckled.

'I've been looking around but there doesn't appear to be anything suitable available. I guess I'll just have to keep looking.' She sighed.

Rhana didn't immediately reply then she said, 'What about Livvy's place?'

'Livvy's place? What do you mean?'

'Well, as you know, when she left she only intended to be gone for a month She gave me a key in case anything went wrong – a flood in the kitchen or something. But now she's still there, I wonder...'

'You mean...?' Erica felt a bubble of excitement. Was Rhana suggesting...?

'Why don't you email or WhatsApp her and ask if you can stay there till she gets back? I bet she'll agree. It's not good for the place to be sitting empty. A house needs someone to take care of it.'

Erica pictured Livvy's home, the renovated fisherman's cottage, one of a row on the other side of the harbour from the town. Like many such buildings in Pelican Crossing, the house had gone through several makeovers, the original small rooms opened up to make one large living/dining area with floor-to-ceiling windows which during the day let in lots of light. She visualised herself seated in one of Livvy's deep armchairs, gazing out at the view of the beach. It would be perfect.

As soon as she got back to Joe's, she'd email Livvy.

Six

It was Gary's wedding day, and Jamie was excited for his son. Mandy
was a lovely girl and Jamie was glad Gary was making an honest woman
of her, although he knew it was an old-fashioned way of thinking.
The young couple had chosen to have a beach wedding, on the less
populated beach opposite Jamie's cottage, with lunch at the yacht club
afterwards. Before Archie was born, Mandy had worked there part-
time and had been able to get a good deal on the meal.

Dressed for the occasion in a crisp pale blue shirt and cream
chinos, his short greying hair neatly brushed, his skin tingling from
the unaccustomed application of an aftershave Gary had given him
for Christmas, Jamie crossed the road to the beach. When he stepped
onto the beach, his feet, inappropriately encased in a pair of dress
shoes, sank into the soft sand. He cursed inwardly, wishing he'd worn
sandals.

Most of the others were already there, standing beside a flowered
arch together with an unfamiliar figure. Jamie guessed she was the
marriage celebrant.

'Hey, Dad!' Rory greeted him.

Jamie noticed his eldest son had come more casually dressed,
his multicoloured shirt, white pants and sandals more suited to the
conditions. The groom was similarly dressed, though his shirt had a
white background and his feet were bare. His long hair, so like Jamie's
had been at his age, and often tied back in a ponytail, was neatly tamed
into a bun.

Jamie went up to his sons. 'Well, Gary, this is it,' he said. 'No backing out now.'

'As if,' Gary said with a grin. 'Mandy would kill me.' He chuckled, then looked around warily as if to see if anyone was listening.

Jamie's eyes roamed around the rest of the group. There was Mandy's mother, Liz, and grandmother, Joan, with the pram containing little Archie. Standing beside them was Liz's partner, Finn Hunter, along with the daughter who had arrived in town only a year earlier and *her* daughter who was still a teenager. Next to them was… Jamie blinked, then looked away. It couldn't be… but it was. Standing there with a smile on her face, arm-in-arm with a guy who looked as if he'd stepped out of the pages of *MEN* and wouldn't look out of place in a boxing ring, was Cindy, his ex-wife.

Although Gary had warned him she'd be there, he really hadn't expected her to turn up. He glanced over again to see her stare at him, then whisper to her companion. Jamie flinched. He could guess what she might be saying about him. It would be nothing complimentary. He remembered her last scathing comments before she'd left him for good. He looked away to where Mandy and her older sister, Tara, were approaching from the pathway to the beach, accompanied by Tara's husband, Mark.

As they drew nearer, the sound of music which had been muted, grew louder. It was the same tune which had been played at his and Cindy's wedding. He felt like he was travelling back in time as the chords of *Sweet Caroline* sung by Neil Diamond drifted across the beach.

Suddenly the music stopped, and everyone's attention was focussed on the couple standing under the arch. Mandy looked beautiful, dressed in a loose white dress, her feet bare like Gary's. Jamie felt a lump in his throat as the pair spoke their wedding vows, promising to love each other for the rest of their lives. They exchanged rings then gazed into each other's eyes with such love Jamie had to look away to hide the moisture in his eyes.

It was almost thirty years since his own wedding, since he and Cindy had made similar vows. Mandy's mother was divorced too. She'd have done the same, filled with hope and anticipation for the future. He hoped Gary and Mandy's marriage would last longer than their parents' had, that they'd have the happy ever after they deserved. But, as he knew, life was a lottery, as was marriage, and no one could predict the future.

The music started up again, this time it was *Your love keeps lifting me higher* sung by Jackie Wilson, and everyone joined in. It was a joyful occasion, and Jamie determined not to allow the presence of Cindy and her new man to spoil it for him.

'Congratulations,' Jamie said, going up to Gary and hugging him, then turning to hug Mandy and kiss her on the cheek. 'Welcome to the family, Mandy,' he said. 'I hope the pair of you will be very happy together.' Then he moved away as he saw Cindy approaching.

The formal part of the proceedings over, everyone made their way to the yacht club where a large table had been prepared for them. Since it was early, they were the only ones there.

Fortunately, Jamie was seated at the opposite end of the table from Cindy, next to Liz and Finn, so he was able to enjoy the meal and the conversation which revolved around Mandy and Gary and little Archie, who had slept through the ceremony and was still asleep. As was usual at the yacht club, the food was delicious, a seafood meal comprising oysters, then lobster served with potatoes dauphinois and broccolini. This was followed by a delicious dessert of tiramisu, and all washed down with a chilled pinot grigio from South Australia.

When the meal was over, and everyone had been served with glasses of champagne, in the absence of a father of the bride, Jamie rose to toast the newly married couple and give the speech he'd spent the last three nights preparing. He cleared his throat. Unused to public speaking, he was more comfortable on the deck of his boat than standing here, even though he knew everyone present. And he was conscious of Cindy's jaundiced expression. As he'd planned, he spoke of Gary's heritage, his father's life on the sea, his own history as a fisherman, and his pride in Gary's move into the diving school. Then he talked of Mandy's entrepreneurial skills in establishing her personal training business, how Gary and Mandy had met, finishing with the birth of their son and his best wishes for their future happiness. Finally, with a sigh of relief, he asked the group to join him in a toast to the bride and groom, glad to be able to sit down again.

To Jamie's surprise, Rory took his place, giving his own short speech, followed by Liz, then Tara. By then, other guests were arriving in the restaurant. It was time for the wedding party to leave.

As she walked past his chair, Cindy brushed against him. 'Same old Jamie,' she said in a sneering voice. 'I made the right decision.'

Jamie was stunned. Their marriage had been over for years. She was in a new relationship. There was no reason for her continued bitterness. He opened his mouth to reply, then thought better of it. It was neither the time nor place to get into an argument with his ex-wife.

'Okay, Dad?' Rory asked.

'All good.'

Outside the club, everyone went their separate ways. The young couple had decided against a honeymoon and were returning to the apartment they'd moved into together a year earlier.

Jamie found himself alone.

As he walked back home, he reflected on the events of the day. The wedding had gone well, his speech probably could have been better, but he'd got it over. The only awkward note had been Cindy's comment at the end.

Back home, Jamie made himself a coffee and took it into his front yard. He could see the ocean from here, hear the roar of the waves. It was almost as good as being at sea.

He thought again about the day, the ceremony, the words of the marriage vow Gary and Mandy had chosen. Marriage was a serious commitment, one he valued. Despite the failure of his own marriage, he'd seen enough happy ones to hope that, maybe, one day...

He'd been sorry when his marriage fell apart, felt responsible. But had it been his fault? Over the years he'd pondered on that question, failing to come to a conclusion.

Seeing Cindy today had emphasised how different they were. Although like him, she'd grown up in Pelican Crossing, she'd always hankered for a life in the city. Now she'd moved on with her life, whereas he'd remained here, still tethered to the sea which was part of his heritage.

His thoughts moved to Erica, to the young girl she'd been when, as teenagers, they'd sworn their undying love. He'd been heartbroken when she left, but it wasn't how it had been with Cindy. He and Erica had been too young, and she wanted to pursue a nursing career. At the time, he'd imagined she might come back, work in the local hospital. He sighed. But she was back now. He remembered the last time he'd seen her, on his fishing boat with her brother a year earlier. She had changed, but he suspected the girl he remembered wasn't far beneath the surface and he was excited to discover if he was right.

Seven

Erica put the flowers she'd bought in a vase and placed it on the table by the window. She'd been living in Livvy's cottage now for a week and already it felt like home. Her friend had replied to her email immediately, grateful to have someone look after the place, and Erica had wasted no time in moving in, despite Joe's attempt to persuade her otherwise.

It felt good to have a place to call her own, even if it wasn't really hers, and now she was working at the hospital again, she was earning an income. After a busy week on the ward, it was good to have Saturday to relax. She'd invited Joe and Gill for dinner – Coco too, of course – and had spent the morning shopping for food. The flowers were an impulse buy, when their scent drew her into a florist on the way to her car. They looked good, brightening up the room and filling it with a delightful fragrance.

Erica's only regret was that she didn't have more of her own things around her. They were all still in Perth, in her old house. Kieren had promised to have everything shipped to Pelican Crossing when the house sold, arguing that it would be more attractive to buyers if it was still furnished.

It wasn't the only thing they'd argued about. When she'd revealed her plans to leave, Kieren had first tried persuasion, then had lost his temper, ranting and raving in a way that scared her and made her glad she was going to the other side of Australia. Briony's reaction was different and more difficult to cope with. She had burst into tears and pleaded with Erica not to go, saying how she couldn't manage with Ava on her own and wouldn't it be wonderful for Ava to have her grandmother living with them. At one point, she almost wore Erica down, but she remained adamant. She didn't want to stay and become a glorified housekeeper and babysitter for her son and daughter-in-law. For the first time in her life she was free, and she intended to make the most of it.

After unpacking her shopping, Erica made herself a cheese and tomato sandwich for lunch with some sourdough bread she'd bought from the bakery, followed by a crisp apple. Then she started to prepare the spicy chicken dish she intended to cook for dinner, mixing the marinade and pouring it over the chicken thighs before covering the dish and putting it into the fridge. That done, she took her book out into the small courtyard, enjoying the unfamiliar feeling of having no one to please but herself.

Closing the book with a sigh, Erica stared into space for a few moments. She had related to the character in the book, who had set out to start afresh, though her husband hadn't died, but left her for another woman. But, unlike the woman she'd been reading about, Erica had no intention of becoming involved in another relationship. The saying, *once bitten, twice shy*, came to her. After Geoff, she'd never be able to trust another man – or trust her own judgment. When she and Geoff met, she'd been sure he was the one for her, that they'd live happily together for the rest of their lives. When he'd swept her off to Perth, away from all her family and friends, she'd had no inkling of what lay ahead, of the months and years of coercive control, until she'd had enough. Then, when she *had* left him, come to Pelican Crossing, her fear he'd follow her. The shock of his sudden heart attack then death when he did, still haunted her dreams.

Erica took the book inside and checked the time. It was still afternoon. She had plenty of time for the walk on the beach she'd promised herself, before she needed to start cooking dinner. Pulling on her sandals and popping a hat over her short, dark hair, frowning at the sight of more grey streaks and wondering if she should visit a hairdresser, she set off.

The pathway to the beach was across the road from the row of old fishermen's cottages, of which Livvy's was one, another plus about the location. As soon as she stepped onto the sand, Erica took off her sandals, and, with them dangling from one hand, made her way down to the edge of the water and dipped her feet into the waves lapping on the shore. *This was heaven*, she thought, as she wandered along, the sound of the ocean and the salty scent of the sea taking her back to her youth, to her teenage years when everything seemed possible, and to the boy she'd dated. He'd been older than she was, one of Joe's friends. But, luckily, by then Joe was so wrapped up in Barb, he scarcely noticed what his younger sister was doing or who she was with. Erica was lost in a dream of the tall, brown-haired youth who'd captured her teenage heart before she left town to study nursing in Sydney. It was where she'd met Geoff and her life changed for ever.

The sound of music interrupted her thoughts. Startled, Erica looked up to see a cluster of people some distance away. She stopped, not wanting to interrupt, as she realised a wedding was taking place right here on the beach. As she watched, the young couple embraced, and the music became louder. A beach wedding. How romantic. As a teenager, Erica had wanted her wedding to be like that. Instead, she and Geoff had married in a Sydney registry office, his choice, perhaps a sign of what was to come. She hoped the bride on the beach would have a happier married life than she had but couldn't help but feel cynical. It was true that Joe and Barb had been happily married for over thirty years, but they had been the exception. Look at Gill, Joe's current partner, who had recently settled a lengthy and acrimonious divorce and spent her life arranging divorces for others. Not many marriages survived. It wasn't a route she'd ever travel again.

*

By the time Joe and Gill arrived with an excited Coco, Erica had forgotten all about the wedding on the beach.

'This is nice,' Joe said, gazing around the room and walking over to the tall floor-to-ceiling window which looked out onto the ocean, Coco padding behind him. 'What do you think, Gill? Could you handle something like this? It's very different from your apartment.'

Gill walked across the room to join him, putting her arm around his waist. 'Hmm. Different in a good way. I could maybe get used to it. But I don't expect Livvy's interested in selling.' She raised an eyebrow in Erica's direction.

'I doubt it. As far as I know, she does intend to return. She's only extended her stay. She hasn't moved away for good.'

'Pity,' Joe said, as Erica handed both him and Gill glasses of white wine, 'but there's a whole row of them. They've been here for as long as I can remember, and not all of them have been renovated. I'd be willing to bet some are still with the original family. Maybe…'

'Listen to him,' Gill said affectionately. 'Once your brother gets a bee in his bonnet, there's no stopping him.' She chuckled.

Erica smiled. Gill was good for Joe. He'd lucked out twice, unlike her. She remembered the wedding on the beach. 'I saw a wedding on the beach today,' she said. 'Just out there.' She pointed out the window.

'That would be Mandy Phillips and Gary Whittaker,' Gill said. 'Mandy's mum, Liz, is a friend of mine. They already have a small baby – a boy, I think. Liz wished they'd married before the birth, but young people…'

'How is Freya?' Erica asked. Gill was no doubt thinking of her own daughter.

'She's good.' Gill's face lit up. 'She's loving the university and life in Sydney, planning to be back at the end of the month for Easter.'

'How lovely.' Erica knew how pleased Gill had been when her daughter accepted a position at Sydney University after working overseas for many years. She wondered what it would be like to have a daughter, someone to share things with. She'd never been able to share things with Kieren. He'd always been his father's son, and now… he was in danger of turning into him.

Then Gill's earlier comment struck her. Last time she'd been here, she'd met Gill's friend, Liz, had dinner with her and her partner, the editor of the local paper. She'd thought her kind, but perhaps a tad interfering. Then the name of the bridegroom. Gary Whittaker. Could he be related to Jamie Whittaker, the boy she'd been daydreaming about on the beach?

Eight

Jamie gazed out the window to the beach where a group of young people had set up a net for beach volleyball. It looked very different from what it had yesterday with the floral arch and the bridal couple. It was as if the wedding had never happened. For the first time in his life, Jamie felt lonely, saw the passage of years stretching before him, every day like the one before.

Was it seeing Gary married, seeing Cindy again? Whatever the reason, Jamie knew he didn't want to spend the day alone, so instead of making his usual Sunday breakfast, he set out to walk into town.

When he reached *The Blue Dolphin Café* he stopped, seeing Cam and Poppy sitting at one of the outdoor tables as they did every Sunday.

'Morning,' he said.

'Morning, Jamie.' It was Poppy who spoke. 'Here for breakfast? Why don't you join us? You can tell us all about the wedding.'

Jamie hesitated, unwilling to intrude, but when Cam nodded his agreement, he pulled out a chair. He'd be glad of the company. Cam and Poppy were two of his favourite people, and he might be able to learn more about Erica. 'Thanks,' he said.

'Well?' Poppy said, when Jamie had ordered breakfast, choosing a breakfast wrap along with a macchiato, and leaning her elbows on the table.

Jamie felt uncomfortable. He drew a finger around the inside of his collar – he was wearing the same shirt as he had the day before but today it was teamed with a pair of cargo pants and sandals. 'It was a wedding,' he said.

Poppy laughed. 'We know that, Jamie. What were the bride and groom wearing? Were there any surprises, any disasters? How did your grandson behave?'

Jamie stared at her, stunned.

'You'll have to excuse Poppy,' Cam said with a grin. 'She loves weddings, and all of ours are already married, so she has to make do with hearing about other people's.'

'Oh! Well…' Jamie racked his brains, trying to recapture the event, but only seeing Cindy's smirking expression at first. Then his mind cleared, and he had a clear picture of the happy couple. 'It was good. All went according to plan. It was what you might call a perfect beach wedding. A small group, family only. Mandy was wearing something white and loose, Gary was in white too, both barefoot. There was music and we all joined in. Little Archie slept through it all. I guess that's it.' He paused. 'Then we had a meal at the yacht club. Phil did us proud,' he said, referring to the owner of the club.

'And…?' Poppy asked, as if she'd recognised the reason for his initial hesitation.

'Cindy was there.'

'Oh! I did wonder if she'd turn up. It's been a while…'

'Fifteen years,' Jamie said, unable to keep the bitterness out of his voice. 'It was good she made the effort for Gary's sake.' He could see Poppy was about to ask more about Cindy, so was glad when his breakfast arrived at that point.

By the time the waitress had left, Poppy seemed to have forgotten what she was going to say about Cindy. Instead, she said, 'Did you know Erica Harris is back in town? I heard she's back for good this time. Didn't you and she…?'

Jamie almost choked on his coffee.

'Poppy!' Cam said.

But Poppy affected an innocent expression and grinned. 'I seem to remember one summer…' she said. 'She was a few years below us in school and… what?' she asked as Cam glared at her. 'I'm only asking.' She gazed at Jamie, waiting patiently for his reply.

Jamie cringed. He'd been hoping to learn more about Erica, about what she was doing here, how long she intended to stay. He hadn't expected to be the subject of an interrogation on their teenage relationship, though perhaps interrogation was too strong a word. Poppy was just being Poppy. She was always interested in other people, but in a nice way, concerned for them. 'We dated for a bit,' he said, 'before she went to uni in Sydney.'

'See, I was right,' she said, turning to Cam. 'I remember the two of you looking very happy together.'

We were, Jamie thought. Had he ever been that happy since, even with Cindy in the early days? Maybe when Rory, then Gary was born, when his fishing charter business began to take off. But there had been nothing like the heady exhilaration of his first love. 'It was all a long time ago' he said. *But sometimes it feels like yesterday.*

*

Erica had had a quiet morning. She'd enjoyed pottering about in Livvy's back yard and had now turned her attention to the front garden which was showing signs of neglect since Livvy had been gone. She was pulling up a particularly vicious weed when she heard someone on the other side of the fence.

'Erica?'

Turning so rapidly she almost fell over, Erica found herself staring into a pair of familiar brown eyes. She gazed wordlessly at him, her heart pounding, then, 'Jamie!' she said, too surprised to say more.

'What are you doing here?' he asked, gesturing to the cottage behind her. 'I thought Olivia was still overseas.'

'I'm looking after the place for her… until I find somewhere of my own.'

There was an awkward silence, during which a new and unexpected warmth flowed through her.

'Amazing,' Jamie said. 'I live a few doors along.'

'Oh!'

A warning voice whispered in her head, memories of their teenage passion filling her mind. The last thing she wanted in her new life was to be reminded of what life had been like before she met Geoff, what it could have been like if only… 'I'm sorry, I have to go.' Erica picked up her garden implements and hurried inside. As soon as the door closed behind her she stood against it, her breath coming in gasps. It was foolish, she knew, but the sight of Jamie Whittaker, looking every bit as handsome as she remembered – even better than he had on that fishing trip the previous year – had sent her heart racing.

Taking a deep breath, she went through to the kitchen. She dropped the tools she was carrying on the table and turned on the electric jug, before taking a packet of camomile tea out of the pantry and a mug out of the cupboard.

A few minutes later she was sitting outside with her tea, thinking about what had just happened. Jamie Whittaker was a neighbour. He lived in the same row of cottages as Livvy! Had she known? Had Rhana known when she'd suggested Erica move in here? Of course they had. They both knew about her history with him. All three had been friends back then. They had shared everything. Erica felt a wave of anger erupt. She picked up her phone.

'Rhana!' she said when her friend answered, 'How could you?'

There was a pause, then she heard her friend chuckle. 'You've met, then?'

'You knew, you and Livvy. Did you plan this together? Was this your idea of fun?' She remembered how they used to play pranks on each other, but this was no prank.

'Calm down. I'd forgotten Jamie lived there when I suggested you talk with Livvy, then she reminded me and we thought… Oh, Erica, it's perfect. You were so good together back then. We all thought you'd stay together, that you'd come back to Pelican Crossing when you graduated. I bet he thought that too.'

Erica winced. There had been a time when she had planned to come back, then she'd met Geoff, and he'd swept her off her feet. It was only much later she realised how he had quickly isolated her from Pelican Crossing and all her friends and family.

Rhana was still speaking. 'Now you're both single, Livvy thought… maybe…'

Erica was shocked. 'You thought we could get back together, just as if the past thirty-odd years had never happened?'

'Not exactly, but…'

'I can't believe you could be so stupid. I've just lost my husband, come out of an abusive relationship. The last thing I need is to get

involved with another man... especially someone like Jamie, who...'
Erica's voice broke. She knew Jamie was nothing like Geoff, but she
was no longer the naïve young girl who had been flattered by the
attention of the boy who was one of her brother's friends and local
lifesaving champion.

Nine

That didn't go well.

Jamie stared at the closed door through which Erica had fled as if she couldn't get away from him fast enough. He'd been on his way to the office to catch up with some paperwork when he'd seen her in Olivia Grace's garden, scarcely able to believe his eyes. Erica had been on his mind so much in recent days, it was as if his subconscious had conjured her up. He'd had to blink to make sure she was real.

She was and living just three doors along from him. But if Jamie had expected her to be pleased to see him, he was wrong. She'd barely said a word to him before heading inside and slamming the door behind her.

Jamie carried on to his office, set on the edge of the harbour. A couple of pelicans were perched on the bollards by the water, no doubt hoping for food. The days when they could rely on the fleet of fishing boats coming in with their catch were long gone, only a few still making the trip out to sea each morning to return with fish for the markets, their crew exhausted.

He didn't miss those days when he'd risen before dawn to set out in all weathers, but there had been something satisfying about it, about pitting oneself against the elements to provide food for local families and businesses. It had been good enough for his father who had died in harness, leaving Jamie to carry on... until Cindy left him with two teenagers to care for.

Jamie sometimes wondered if she'd have stayed with him if he'd sold the boat sooner, then he'd remember how she'd always talked about Melbourne, the restaurants, the shops. She'd spent a holiday there as a teenager and loved it. In retrospect, it was amazing she'd stayed in Pelican Crossing with him for as long as she had.

Once in the office, Jamie made himself a coffee and fired up his computer. But although he stared at the screen, he couldn't concentrate on checking his bookings or updating his files. He couldn't get Erica Harris out of his mind – he couldn't think of her as Erica Masters, another man's wife, now his widow.

His mind went back to when they first met. He could remember it perfectly. It was at a party at Joe's. All of their crowd were there to celebrate something which he'd now forgotten – a birthday, a lifesaving carnival, a rugby game? Maybe even the end of the school year. Erica hadn't been at the party. She was two years younger than Joe and his mates, only sixteen. But she had a habit of hanging around them when they congregated at Joe's place, as they often did.

That particular night, Jamie had been coming back out to the yard from the kitchen with a fresh supply of beer when he'd caught sight of her. She was tall and dark like her brother, but the likeness ended there. Erica was all woman, her curves beginning to become apparent, her dark hair curling around her face and falling to her shoulders. Their eyes met. He'd stopped in his tracks as if he was seeing her for the first time. His breath caught in his throat then, 'Want one?' he asked, holding up a beer.

'Yes please, but don't tell Joe,' she'd said with a grin.

Jamie smiled at the memory. He'd never made it back to the others, instead joining Erica and spending the rest of the evening with her. After that, they'd been inseparable. It was lucky Joe had started dating Barb, so wasn't too interested in what his little sister got up to. It had been a halcyon time, a summer of love. But Erica had been determined to study nursing and at the end of school had enrolled in a course in Sydney while he was destined to work on his father's fishing boat.

They'd corresponded at first, her letters full of her new life in Sydney, his with boring accounts of life in Pelican Crossing and the fishing, then her letters had become less frequent before stopping completely. He'd heard from Joe that she was getting married, then that she'd moved to Perth. He started dating Cindy, and the rest was history.

Joe sighed and fixed another cup of coffee. He couldn't sit here lost in the past. He had work to do. His phone rang. It was Gary.

'Hi, son, tired of married life already?' he joked.

'Ha, ha, Dad. I'm calling to invite you to dinner. Mandy and I thought it would be nice to get together again tonight at our place. It was all a bit formal yesterday. Not really our scene. I'll throw a few steaks on the barbie, and we can kick back and relax over a couple of beers. Mandy's mum and Tara are going to bring along some salads.'

'Sounds good.' It was just what Jamie needed to take his mind off Erica, but… 'Your mum?' he asked, his stomach churning. He didn't think he could take another evening in Cindy's company, listening to her sniping.

'She's gone. Headed back to Melbourne on the first plane this morning, couldn't wait to shake the dust – or should I say sand – off her feet.' He laughed, but Jamie detected a note of bitterness underneath the laugh. Cindy had let her son down again.

'Okay, I'll bring a slab of beer. What time?'

'Come when you're ready. We'll probably kick off around seven, once the little one's asleep. Come earlier if you want to see him awake.'

'Okay. Will do.'

The call finished, Jamie felt energised and by the time he left the office to go home and change, he'd updated the schedule for his fishing charter and got everything ready for business next day.

*

On his way to Gary's, Jamie stopped at the bottle shop to collect the beer he'd promised, then continued on to park outside the young couple's apartment close to the river.

It was lovely in this part of Pelican Crossing at this time of day. The sun was just beginning to set, sending streamers of gold and pink across the sky. A trio of pelicans landed on the grassy bank of the river close to where a family were packing up from their picnic. Seemingly unafraid, the birds waddled close to the group, their enormous beaks making them look top-heavy. Then, when one of the children started to run towards them, as one, they took off into the air, wings flapping, to land again on the water where they settled to watch what was happening on the shore.

Jamie chuckled at their antics. Those birds never failed to entertain him. He could watch them for hours.

When he walked in, Gary and Mandy's apartment seemed to be bursting at the seams. Fortunately, it was on the ground floor, and they could spill out into the small courtyard. The kitchen was filled with women – Mandy, her mother, sisters, grandmother and niece. When he had greeted them all and cuddled his grandson, he joined Gary, Rory, Finn and Mark by the barbecue and dropped the beer into an esky which was sitting there.

'Good to see you, Dad,' Rory said, slapping him on the shoulder. 'Pity Mum had to leave.' He winked.

Jamie smiled at his eldest son's sardonic remark, knowing there was no love lost between him and his mother. She had refused to accept her son's sexual preference and pretended the reason he wasn't in a relationship with a woman was simply because he hadn't met the right one. She wasn't wrong about that, but it wasn't a woman Rory was looking for. Jamie hoped one day Rory would find someone special too.

In typical Australian fashion, it was the men who manned the barbecue, enjoying their beer while the women remained inside, only joining them when Archie was asleep and the steaks were almost ready.

It had turned dark, and the air was filled with the loud chirping of cicadas and the scent of the citronella candles, lit to repel the mosquitos. When they all sat down to eat, the men perched on kitchen stools due to the shortage of chairs. Gary and Mandy hadn't anticipated such a large group when they furnished their home with cast-off pieces of furniture from family and flat-packs from IKEA.

Jamie was enjoying the evening, joking around with Rory and Gary, talking boats with Mark who was considering buying one for weekend sailing, and chatting with Finn about local events, when he heard a comment from Liz.

'Did you know Joe Harris's sister is back?' she asked the group at large. 'She's living in Olivia Grace's place. That's near you, isn't it, Jamie?' she said, bringing him into the conversation.

Everyone turned to look at him.

'Oh,' Liz's mother said, 'in one of those lovely old cottages. I always wanted to live in one of them,' she said, a note of regret in her voice. 'Is she back for good this time? I seem to remember hearing something about her husband. Didn't he die in the local hospital? Then she went back to… wasn't it Western Australia?' she looked at Liz.

'That's right, Mum. I don't know all the details, but at lunch last week… I meet three friends for lunch regularly,' she said, glancing around the group to ensure everyone was listening.

Jamie winced. He knew of Liz's reputation as a gossip and while he was eager to know more about Erica, he hated to hear her life being bandied about in public. 'Excuse me,' he said, pushing his chair back and going inside.

Once there, he stood for a moment, staring into space, before heading to the toilet as an excuse for leaving the table.

When he got back the conversation had moved on, and they were discussing plans for Easter which was the following weekend.

'It was last Easter we went on the dive trip,' Mandy said gazing lovingly at Gary, 'when we…'

'And when Julie and Tilly arrived in Pelican Crossing,' Liz said, looking across at the daughter and granddaughter who'd suddenly appeared in her life.

'We need to do something special,' Liz's granddaughter declared.

Gary and Rory looked uncomfortable. 'We were planning a fishing weekend,' Gary said. 'Sorry, Mandy.'

'There's going to be a special Easter event at *The Haven*,' Joan said warily, referring to the over-fifties resort where she lived. 'I don't suppose…'

'Probably not. Mum,' Liz said. 'How about we arrange to have breakfast on the beach on Good Friday, then everyone can do their own thing for the rest of the weekend?'

Her suggestion seemed to gain everyone's approval, and Jamie sighed. He wouldn't need to be involved and could get the boat ready for the fishing trip he had planned with his sons, unaware of any special anniversaries needing to be celebrated. It had just been him, Rory and Gary for so long, he'd forgotten what it was like to be part of a large family. But he supposed with Gary's marriage to Mandy, he was now part of Mandy's extended family. It was a bizarre thought but not an unwelcome one.

Jamie was wrong in thinking he was off the hook with Liz. Mandy and her grandmother were clearing away the plates, and Gary and Rory were arguing with Mark about some footie game, when Liz turned to Jamie and said, 'You and Erica were an item for a while at school, weren't you? I was fairly new to Pelican Crossing, in the same year at school, and she was close friends with Olivia Grace and Rhana Black – you bought Sandy's spaniel from her, Finn,' she added, turning towards him. 'I admired the three of them so much, but they were a tight group. And I seem to remember you and Erica…' She peered at Jamie. He felt she could see right through him.

'We dated… yes. Then she left to study in Sydney.'

Liz nodded. 'And now she's back,' she said, her voice loaded with meaning.

All the way home, Liz's voice reverberated in Jamie's head, the words *Now she's back* going round and round and making him dizzy.

Ten

Erica awoke to the realisation that today was her birthday, and she didn't need to go into work. She stretched luxuriously, then the memory of seeing Jamie the day before broke into her consciousness. Jamie Whittaker was her neighbour.

She let the thought percolate for a few moments, blushing at the memory of her rudeness. There had been no need for her to rush off inside and slam the door. He was only being polite. It must have been a shock for him too, to see her there in Livvy's garden. Last time they'd met had been on the fishing charter Joe had organised. He'd been busy, and there had been little time to talk… but she'd noticed him, noticed him noticing her. Her stomach churned at the memory. Nothing had been said. Probably Joe hadn't seen anything, but Gill would have. Women noticed these things.

So, what now? He was a neighbour, and a friend of Joe's. They'd be bound to meet again. She'd need to make it clear that she wasn't… But what if his interest in her was all in her imagination? Was she being paranoid, thinking that any man who spoke to her had intentions of…? This was Jamie, she told herself, the boy she'd been in love with when she was sixteen. She was fifty today, a long way from that young girl, and had learnt to be far more cautious. She'd never trust a man again or give way to her emotions.

Giving herself a shake, Erica rose, showered and dressed, choosing to wear a pair of beige pants with a pink blouse. She had arranged to meet Joe for breakfast at *The Blue Dolphin Café*, then she planned to spoil herself with a shopping spree before the dinner Joe and Gill were treating her to at *Crossings*. It was going to be a perfect day, and she didn't intend to spoil it with worrying about something that was unlikely to happen.

When Erica arrived at the café, Joe was already seated at one of the outdoor tables, with Coco lying at his feet. The dog rose to greet her.

'Hello, Coco,' she said, ruffling the dog's ears. 'Good morning, Joe.'

'Happy birthday, sis.' Joe rose and pulled her into a warm hug. 'I can't believe my little sister is fifty.'

'Believe it,' she said with a laugh. 'Half a century. Where has the time gone?'

'I just need to look in the mirror and I can see,' Joe chuckled, pointing to his greying hair, so like her own. 'Gill sends her best wishes. She has a full schedule today, but she'll see you tonight. In the meantime… this is from both of us.' He handed her a brightly wrapped package.

'Oh, Joe, thank you!' Erica hadn't expected anything. When Barb had been alive, there had always been a gift in the mail, but since her death, Joe hadn't seemed to notice the date. She supposed it was different now she was living here… and Gill would no doubt have chosen it. She pulled off the wrapping to reveal a set of headphones. 'Wow! How did you know?'

Joe grinned. 'Gill said she'd heard you complaining about the free earpods which came with your phone, and I know how you like to listen to audiobooks and that meditation stuff.'

'Thanks. They're perfect.' Erica leant over to place a kiss on his cheek. *That meditation stuff* he referred to, was a hypnotherapy programme Livvy had recommended to her. She knew Joe had no time for what he called mumbo jumbo, but it helped her relax and was exactly what she had needed to help with the stress she'd experienced after leaving Geoff, and his subsequent death. She'd continued to use it afterwards, the twenty minutes of enforced relaxation helping her adjust to her new sense of freedom.

'What'll you have for breakfast?' Joe asked picking up a menu. 'My treat, remember.'

Erica didn't need to check the menu. She knew what she wanted. 'I'll have the brekkie wrap with a flat white,' she said. 'Thanks, Joe. I think this may be my best birthday since…' Her eyes filled, remembering her childhood birthdays when her parents had spoiled her, then those when she was married to Geoff who'd believed celebrating birthdays was an unnecessary indulgence after turning twenty-one. She'd secretly slipped gifts to Kieren, then to Briony too, without his knowledge.

'I'm sorry,' Joe said, patting her arm, his kindness almost bringing her to tears.

'Two brekkie wraps, a flat white and a macchiato,' Joe said to the waitress who had appeared at his side, allowing Erica time to pull herself together.

'How are you finding being back?' he asked.

'It's good. I'm loving being able to work again, and living at Livvy's…'

'About that…' Joe shifted in his seat. 'I should have told you, but… One of your neighbours is Jamie Whittaker. I wanted to tell you before you found out for yourself.'

'Too late, Joe. I met him yesterday. I was in the front garden when he walked past.'

'Hell, I'm sorry, Erica. When you were here last year… He asked about you. I didn't tell you then, because I knew you were distraught about Geoff. You didn't need an old boyfriend looking you up. I hadn't realised you two were close back when…' He coughed.

'When you and Barb had no eyes for anyone else?' She chuckled. 'It suited me… us… at the time. I doubt you'd have approved of your little sister dating one of your mates.' An image of her teenage self with Jamie flickered behind her eyes. She dismissed it. She didn't want to remember those carefree days before her life changed.

'Probably not. Jamie's a good guy but you were only sixteen, Erica. We were older.'

'Two years.'

'Two years is a lot when you're sixteen and eighteen. Not so much these days. As I said, Jamie was asking about you. Would you ever…?'

'No! Don't even think about it, Joe. I'm never going to let myself be fooled by a man again. Once is enough for me. I know you found love a second time around, and I'm glad you did. I love Gill. You're good together. But it doesn't work for everyone. I could never trust myself to make the right decision. I thought I had with Geoff and look how wrong I was. And I worry that Kieren has inherited much of his father's nature. I only hope…'

'Surely not!' Joe looked shocked. 'Not Kieren.'

'I hope I'm wrong, but the way he wanted to take over my life, the speed with which he put the house up for sale. He expected me to move in with him and Briony as if…' Erica shook her head, too upset for words, reliving her Facetime call with Briony before she left home.

Her daughter-in-law had called to wish her happy birthday, little Ava gurgling happily in her arms. It had been lovely to see them both, to receive the birthday wishes, but there had been something about Briony, about her wariness, as if she was afraid Kieren would walk in and discover her speaking to Erica. She knew Briony might have been worried about something else, but Erica couldn't help feeling anxious.

Eleven

Jamie awoke on Easter Saturday to find a gale blowing. There would be no fishing trip today. He sighed and turned over in bed but was unable to fall asleep again. Yesterday had been good. The breakfast on the beach had gone without a hitch, and he'd spent the rest of the day with Rory and Gary preparing for the three-day trip up the coast they'd planned. It wasn't often the three of them were able to spend time like this, and he silently cursed the unexpected change in the weather.

Rising and going through to the kitchen, his eyes fell on the large chocolate Easter egg. Mandy's mother, Liz, had presented everyone with one saying it wasn't Easter without Easter eggs. It was a long time since he'd had an Easter egg. When the boys were small, the house had been filled with them, and he could remember their excitement as they hunted for the eggs the Easter Bunny had left for them. But Cindy had never been a fan, too worried about her weight to indulge in chocolate, unlike…

Jamie's mind went back to one particular Easter, when he and Erica had been a couple. They had given each other Easter eggs which they'd eaten on the beach after spending the morning surfing. The chocolate had begun to melt, coating their hands and faces. They'd kissed, becoming even more covered in chocolate before jumping into the sea to wash it off.

As he brewed coffee and made his morning toast, Jamie's eyes kept straying to the egg, the memory of Erica sparking an idea. She'd loved chocolate, and he was willing to bet she still did. She'd clearly been shocked to see him that day. It had been a surprise to him too. But now she'd had time to recover, perhaps it was up to him to take the first step, to make an overture of friendship. After all, they were neighbours. She couldn't ignore him for ever. And they had been friends… more than friends… all those years ago. A lot of water had flowed under the bridge since then. They'd both married. He'd had children, probably she had too. And what better time than Easter to renew their friendship? The more he thought about it, the better the idea seemed. He'd go to visit Erica and take her the Easter egg.

Jamie tidied up the kitchen then showered and dressed, pulling on a pair of jeans and a tee-shirt, one which Gary had Mandy had given him for Christmas and which was smarter than those he wore for work. Checking himself out in the mirror, he wondered how he looked to Erica. The thirty years they'd been apart had taken its toll. Whereas she had kept her looks, only becoming more elegant over the years, his hair had more than its share of grey and the time he'd spent on boats had weathered his skin, adding a network of wrinkles and sunspots, some of which had been removed by the skin specialist he visited every six months.

Finally, he was ready. He could delay no longer. Taking a deep breath, he picked up the egg, locked up, and walked along till he came to Olivia's cottage.

It was quiet at this time in the morning, the only sounds the roar of the ocean and the squawking of the seabirds overhead. Jamie made his way up the path to the bright blue front door with its stained glass panel and knocked. There was no reply. He didn't know why it hadn't occurred to him that Erica might not be at home. He stood confused for a few moments, then placing the Easter egg on the doorstep, turned to return home.

*

Erica opened her eyes and stretched. Seeing the sun streaming through the window, she realised she'd slept longer than usual. It had been late when she arrived home the night before after a long shift in the Emergency department. It had been a typical Easter Friday. Busy all day with a variety of minor injuries and complaints due to the GPs being closed on the holiday – a holiday for everyone but the medical and nursing staff at the local hospital. Things had begun to taper off in the late afternoon, only for the victims of a car accident to be brought in, sending everyone into a flap which only eased when all the casualties had been treated and dispatched either to surgery or to a ward. It had been close to nine o'clock before she arrived home, and she'd fallen into bed without taking time to eat.

Erica had always loved these long shifts as it meant she got more days off between them, but she was glad to have a change in the next week. At fifty, she didn't have as much energy as she used to, and she was finding the long hours more difficult to handle.

Now, after a good night's sleep, she felt re-energised, and it was Easter. She had always loved Easter and everything associated with it. As a child, she and Joe had hunted for Easter eggs, then as a teenager, too old to believe in the Easter Bunny, she'd gone surfing with her friends, but she'd still enjoyed seeing a chocolate egg at her place on the breakfast table. The memory of an Easter spent with Jamie Whittaker and the chocolate eggs they'd eaten on the beach flitted into her mind, to be immediately quashed.

She jumped up, showered and dressed in a pair of three-quarter pants and a favourite tee-shirt, thinking as she did, how much Geoff would have hated this casual look. It gave her a sense of satisfaction to know she could now dress as she liked.

After a breakfast of bacon with scrambled eggs on toast washed down with a cup of lemon and ginger tea, Erica pulled out her phone to Facetime Briony. As Ava was too young for an Easter egg, she'd sent her a soft pink bunny and wanted to make sure it had arrived safely – as well as wanting to check in on Briony who she called each week.

This morning, Erica was surprised to see Kieren's face appear on her screen.

'Hi, Mum,' he said. 'Happy Easter. Briony's just getting Ava up. We had a difficult night with her. Briony thinks she's started teething.'

'Oh dear! I remember when you were that age. It's no fun.' It sounded as if Kieren was being more of a help to Briony than Geoff had been to her. Perhaps everything was fine with them, and she'd been worrying needlessly. 'How's everything?' She felt a sense of guilt that she had barely spoken to her son since leaving Perth.

'I've been meaning to contact you. I have an offer on the house, not as good as I'd hoped, but I intend to accept. If you let me know where to send everything, I'll make arrangements to have it shipped.'

'Thanks. I haven't checked out storage here yet, but I will do and let you know. Everything else okay?'

There was silence for a moment, then, 'I don't know. I'm still trying to figure out some of Dad's paperwork – or lack of it. I don't know what he was up to, Mum. There are so many debts.'

'Oh!' Erica didn't know what else to say. 'Your dad never shared anything with me about the yard. You don't think…' She couldn't bring herself to say what she suspected – that Geoff had been involved in something illegal.

Kieren said it for her. 'I hate to say it, Mum, but I'm afraid Dad might have been dealing with some dodgy characters. I think I may have to get the business audited before tax time.'

'You know best, Kieren.' She hoped he did, and that he didn't get himself embroiled in whatever Geoff had been up to.

'Here's Briony,' he said, and Erica saw the phone being handed over.

'Happy Easter, Mum, and thanks so much for the bunny. Ava loves it, don't you honey?' She turned the phone to show Ava holding the pink toy.

'I'm so glad. Happy Easter to you too. Sorry I couldn't call yesterday. I was working all day.'

'Not a problem. I knew you had to work. Kieren was working too. He seems to spend all his time at the yard. I hope it's all sorted soon.'

Erica winced at the despondent note in Briony's voice. She hoped so too and wondered if she'd been too hasty in leaving Perth. Then she remembered that if she'd stayed, she'd have been sharing Ava's room. She'd have been the one whose sleep was disturbed, and it would have been even more difficult to leave.

By the time the call finished, Erica was in a state of confusion. She missed Briony and Ava. She wished there was something she could do to help them, to help Briony with Ava, to help Kieren sort out the mess Geoff had left him. But she knew she'd made the right decision in leaving, in coming back to Pelican Crossing.

She needed to clear her head so, taking her hat from the hook behind the door, she headed out and crossed the road to the beach. Once there, with the sand between her toes, the roar of the waves in her ears and sniffing in the salty tang of the sea, she felt her cares fall away. It was gusty this morning, and she had to hold onto her hat to stop it from blowing away, but it meant she had the beach to herself. No one else was foolish enough to venture out in this weather, but Erica found it bracing as she leant into the breeze. It was as if it was blowing away any regrets she might have about leaving Perth, Briony and Ava. Strangely, she felt no concern about leaving Kieren. He'd cope. He was like his dad in that respect, though hopefully not Geoff's complete counterpart. Briony had seemed less anxious this morning. It was a good sign.

Finally the wind became too much for her, and Erica turned to walk back to the cottage she now thought of as home. She hoped that, by the time Livvy returned, she'd be in a position to buy a place for herself, but had no idea when that might be. Her mind on future possibilities, Erica was at her front door before she noticed something sitting on the doorstep. It was a large Easter egg. She picked it up and looked around, but there was no one to be seen.

Twelve

Erica stared at the Easter egg which was now sitting on the kitchen bench. Who could have put it there? The only people who knew where she lived were Joe, Gill, Rhana and… Jamie Whittaker. She immediately discounted Rhana. Her friend rarely came to town and certainly wouldn't come unannounced to leave an Easter egg. She picked up the phone to call Joe.

'Hey, sis, happy Easter,' he said when he answered the phone. 'I was about to call you.'

'Happy Easter,' she said. 'So, it wasn't you who snuck over and left me a chocolate egg this morning?'

'Not guilty. Must have been the Easter bunny,' he chuckled.

'Ha, ha.' But if it hadn't been him or Gill, it must have been… Erica's stomach churned. 'So, why were you going to call me?'

'I know you were working yesterday, but thought you'd be free today. We've decided to a have a barbecue, just a few friends, and we'd love it if you could join us.'

'I'd love to.' This was one of the benefits of having come home to Pelican Crossing, the impromptu gatherings which were a feature of the small town, and which she'd always loved. 'Can I bring something?'

'Maybe a salad? But don't go to any trouble. It'll be very casual. Gill and I are only calling around a few people now, and I guess some of them will have other plans.'

'Okay.' As Erica ended the call the thought struck her that Jamie might be one of the people on Joe's list to call. He was one of his friends. She wasn't sure how she felt about the possibility of meeting him again after the way she'd reacted last time. It would give her the opportunity to thank him for the egg. It must have been him who left it, but why?

Erica turned on the radio to the local channel and sang along to some old favourites as she put together the roasted sweet potato and feta salad that was one of her favourites, before putting it into the fridge. Then, with the afternoon to kill, she decided to make a start on the book for the book club which was due to meet the following week. Now she was planning to stay in Pelican Crossing, Gill had persuaded her to join, and it was lucky her shifts had changed so she'd be able to attend, but it didn't give her much time to read the Elin Hilderbrand title the group had chosen. *The Perfect Couple* had recently been adapted for Netflix and evidently some members of the group had watched the series and wanted to compare it to the book. Erica had neither read the book nor watched the series, but had loved other books by the author so was looking forward to an enjoyable read. But she found it difficult to concentrate, the image of Jamie Whittaker appearing on the pages as she snacked on the Easter egg while she read.

*

Erica dressed in a blue and white calf-length dress with half sleeves and a heart shaped neckline, and applied her makeup with more care than usual, telling herself she was *not* making an effort in the hope of impressing Jamie. It was a long time since she'd cared what a man thought of her, but she regretted that she'd been without makeup, her hair a mess, and wearing her old clothes when Jamie had surprised her in the front garden.

As she brushed her hair into its usual sleek style, Erica couldn't help but remember how it used to be, how her long curls had streamed out from under her helmet as they sped along on Jamie's motorbike. How angry her parents would have been if they'd known, not to mention Joe. But she and Jamie had managed to keep their friendship a secret from them, even though all her friends knew and envied her. At first, that's all it had been – friendship. She'd been flattered to be singled out by her brother's friend, to be chosen by him as his companion on those wild rides and their surfing adventures on less populated beaches, where they were unlikely to meet Joe. But it had soon become something more, morphed into those moments when they sought to be alone, when she'd known the thrill of being in his arms, of the kisses which she never wanted to stop. But Jamie had always been conscious she was his mate's little sister. He had never taken advantage of her innocence. Unlike Geoff, she thought, who'd had no such compunction.

Erica heard the buzz of conversation when she knocked at Joe's door before pushing it open to be greeted by Coco. 'Hello, old girl,' she said, patting the dog with her free hand and balancing the bowl of salad in the other, her bag over one shoulder. She walked through the house to the kitchen where most of the noise was coming from.

'Oh thanks. Yum,' Gill said, when Erica handed her the salad. She gave her a warm hug.

Erica returned the hug. She'd come to know Gill very well the previous year, even lived in her apartment for a time when she was hiding from Geoff, fearful he'd come looking for her. It had been out of character for the solicitor to mix her personal life with her professional one and to invite a client into her own home, but Gill had done it as a favour to Erica and Joe, and it was something Erica would never forget. Besides that, the two women had discovered they had many things in common, not least a love for Joe. Erica was delighted her brother had found someone to make him happy again after losing his wife to cancer.

'Don't blame me,' Gill said, nodding to the group of people spilling out of the kitchen into the back yard where Joe was presiding over the barbecue, surrounded by a bunch of other men. Erica's heart seemed to skip a beat as she saw Jamie standing alongside her brother.

'Anything I can do to help?' she asked, seeing that most of the women in the kitchen were busy fixing salads or pouring drinks, while they chatted among themselves.

Gill looked around, seemingly distracted, then said, 'Would you be a dear and take the steaks out to Joe? They've been marinating for hours, and I don't imagine any of the guys out there will have given it a thought.'

For a moment Erica hesitated. She'd been hoping to avoid Jamie for as long as she could, not be forced into contact with him as soon as she arrived. She took a deep breath. 'Sure. Where are they?'

'Thanks a bunch.' Gill handed Erica a large platter covered with Gladwrap and containing enough steaks to feed what Erica now noticed were only ten people. Besides Gill and Joe, there were Gill's three special friends, Poppy, Liz and Rachel, along with their partners, Cam, Finn and Luke. With a shock, she realised she and Jamie were the only two unattached people there. She gave Gill a pained glance, but the other woman didn't blink. *Whose idea had it been to invite both her and Jamie? Had it been Gill or Joe who had suggested it? Or was she being paranoid?*

Forcing a smile on her face, and followed by Coco who was excited by the scent of the meat, Erica carried the platter out to where the men were drinking beer and chatting. Joe seemed to be the only one tending the barbecue. 'Here you are,' she said, carefully placing the platter on a bench at the side of the barbecue and avoiding looking in Jamie's direction, though conscious of his eyes on her.

'Thanks, sis,' Joe said. 'Glad you could make it.' He gave her a peck on the cheek.

I'll bet, she thought, but said nothing. She recalled his comments about Jamie when they'd had breakfast on her birthday. If he thought he could throw them together and… he was wrong, so wrong.

Returning to the kitchen, Erica accepted a glass of wine from Liz and soon became involved in the conversation. It seemed that Rachel, who Erica hadn't met before, had become carer to her four-year-old granddaughter when her son had arrived from overseas and left the little girl with her. As a new grandmother herself, Erica's heart went out to her, but it appeared Rachel had three other granddaughters too. The topic of the conversation revolved around the fact that Rachel's son, who was called Alexander, had seemed interested in Liz's partner's daughter and it was Rachel's fervent hope that something might come of it. The complexity of it all was beyond Erica. She was only relieved they weren't trying to match her up with Jamie, but it reminded her how the gossip mill worked in the small town.

There was another knock on the door, and an attractive, tall woman with short auburn hair appeared in the kitchen. 'Sorry if I'm late,' she said, looking embarrassed. She handed Gill a bottle of wine.

'Not at all. Everyone, this is Kate. She works with Joe at the council as town planner. She's only been in Pelican Crossing for a few months, and Joe thought it would be good for her to meet a few more people.' She proceeded to introduce everyone to Kate, but Erica barely heard her. She was so relieved to discover she wasn't the only single woman there.

Since everyone else had known each other for years or, in the case of Luke and Finn, was attached to someone who had, it was only natural for Erica and Kate to gravitate together.

Once the steaks were cooked and the salads had been taken outside, Erica chose a seat beside Kate and as far away from Jamie as possible, though she knew she couldn't avoid him for ever.

She and Kate soon discovered they had several things in common – they both loved outdoor sports, especially swimming and surfing, were avid readers and favoured natural remedies over prescription medicine. There was something else about Kate that caught Erica's attention, a cloudiness in her eyes, an apparent unwillingness to speak of her past, all of which made Erica feel sympathetic towards her. She had no desire to talk about her past either.

'Everyone here seems to be part of a couple,' Kate said, when the conversation stalled. She glanced around. 'What about the good-looking guy over there?' she gestured to where Jamie was sitting talking with Joe.

To her surprise, Erica felt a stab of jealousy, which she quickly attempted to stifle. But the feeling refused to go away. She might not want Jamie herself, but she realised she didn't want him to hook up with Kate either. Mentally chastising herself for being a spoilsport, she replied, 'That's Jamie Whittaker. He and Joe went to school together, along with Cam and Poppy. He runs a fishing charter and boat rental.'

'Hmm.' Kate glanced over at him again.

It was later, and Erica was about to leave. She was in the kitchen washing the bowl in which she'd brought the salad when she became aware of a presence behind her.

'Why do I get the impression you're avoiding me?'

Erica turned quickly, almost dropping the bowl, to see Jammie standing there. She looked around, but they were alone in the kitchen. 'I... I'm not,' she stammered. 'It was you who left the chocolate egg on my doorstep, wasn't it?'

Jamie looked uncomfortable. 'It was an impulse. I remembered how much you like chocolate…'

A picture of her and Jamie leaping into the ocean to wash off the remains of chocolate forced itself into Erica's mind. She wondered if he remembered too. She glanced at him. *Of course he did.* 'Thank you,' she said. 'It was a kind thought.' Maybe now he'd leave. She turned back to the sink and made a show of washing the already spotless bowl.

'Erica,' Jamie put his hand on her shoulder and turned her round to face him, 'Word is you're back for good. I think we need to talk.'

Thirteen

Jamie had been waiting for an opportunity to speak to Erica, watching her sitting at the other side of the yard, seeming to have chosen a spot as far away from him as possible. Now he'd managed to catch her alone. When he put his hand on her shoulder, he felt her tremble beneath his touch. 'We need to talk,' he repeated. 'I'm your brother's friend. We're neighbours. We're not exactly strangers. Can we be friends again?'

Erica stared at him for a moment, her body tensing. Then she shook off his hand. 'I can't do this now,' she said.

'Everything okay here?'

Jamie turned to see Joe in the doorway, Coco at his heels. Before he could reply, Erica said, 'Fine, Joe. Jamie was about to leave.' She scowled at him, her eyes wet with tears.

'Sure,' Jamie said, putting up both hands defensively.

'I'll see you out.' Joe accompanied him to the door. 'Sorry,' he said when they reached it, 'I don't know what's got into Erica. Did you two have an argument?'

Jamie shook his head. He had no idea what he'd done wrong. 'I thought she'd like the Easter egg I got yesterday. She wasn't home, so I left it on the doorstep. When I went into the kitchen, she thanked me politely, then seemed to freeze when I said we should talk.' He left out the bit about her trembling and the tears. Her brother didn't need to know that. Jamie wondered how much Joe knew about their teenage relationship.

'I'm sorry, mate.' Joe sighed. 'I think Erica may be finding it difficult being back. It's not long since she lost her husband… I don't know how much you've heard about that. He was a cruel bastard, and the way he died…' He shook his head. 'Anyway, seems things didn't turn out the way she expected when she returned to Perth, so she's back here again, for good this time, I hope. But it's not easy for her. I think she misses her daughter and granddaughter more than she expected and…'

'And?' Jamie asked.

Joe sighed. 'I was going to say she doesn't miss her son so much. I get the impression he's a lot like his dad. I've heard you and she were an item back when…' he cleared his throat, '… around the time Barb and I got together. It's none of my business, and I know I shut you down last year when you asked about her. But things are different now. I'd love to see her settled and happy. I'm not going to play the heavy big brother and ask what your intentions are. We're both too old for that nonsense. But I would suggest, if you have any feelings for her at all, to be cautious, to go slowly and work to gain her trust. I think she may have lost faith in her own judgment where men are concerned. A bit like Gill when we met,' he said chuckling.

'I appreciate that. Thanks, mate.' Jamie said. As he walked off he reflected that it was good to have Joe's approval, but it didn't get him any further with Erica who seemed to want nothing to do with him.

*

'You all right?' Joe asked Erica who was standing at the kitchen sink lost in thought, Coco lying at her feet. 'Jamie's gone.'

'Thanks, Joe. I'm glad you appeared when you did.'

'Will you tell me what's going on?' he asked. 'When I walked in, I could sense the atmosphere. It was icy. Jamie's a good guy and I believe you and he were once…'

'Oh, Joe!' Erica was close to tears.

'Come here, sis.' He pulled her into a warm hug. 'Let me make you a cup of that herbal tea you like – I think there's still some in the cupboard – and you can tell me all about it.'

A few minutes later, her hands wrapped around a mug of camomile tea, Erica was sitting in Joe's living room with him and Gill, Coco's head on her lap as if the dog knew she needed comforting.

'Now,' Joe said.

'Is it okay for me to be here too?' Gill asked. 'I could take Coco for a walk.'

'No, it's fine. You may understand better than Joe.'

'Okay.' Gill took Joe's hand and squeezed it, making Erica wish she had someone to comfort her too, someone other than her brother. 'I know you may find it difficult to speak about what's worrying you, but it's often good to talk about your concerns. It can help clarify things in your own mind.'

Erica didn't respond immediately. She wondered if Gill was speaking as her solicitor, or as her friend and her brother's partner. She was right, whichever perspective she was speaking from. Erica didn't want to talk about her emotions, which were all over the place right now, had been since she saw Jamie in her front garden. But both Gill and Joe were staring at her with such concerned expressions, she felt obligated to say something, to share some of her worries.

She put her mug down on the coffee table and stroked the skirt of her dress. 'When I came back to Pelican Crossing, it was as if I was starting a new life, a life free from all the stuff that had happened to me. Everything was falling into place – my job at the hospital, Livvy's cottage. I started swimming again.' She gave Gill a grateful look. 'Then Jamie appeared in my front garden, and it was as if the past had risen up to haunt me, to remind me… You seem to know now,' she glanced at her brother, 'but at the time you were too wrapped up in Barb to pay attention to what I was doing, who I was seeing. Jamie and I were close. If I hadn't met Geoff…' She gazed into space. 'But I did, and he managed to sour me for all men. I can never trust a man again, never trust my own feelings. I was so wrong before. How do I know I won't make the same mistake again?' She picked up her mug and took a long swallow, overcome by a sense of despair. She'd never doubted her own judgement before Geoff.

'I know you may not believe me, but I do know how you feel, Erica,' Gill said. 'I see so many unhappy women every day, women like you who have suffered through an unhappy marriage. Then I had a similar experience. Max wasn't violent but he refused every reasonable settlement in our divorce proceedings and, as you know, I almost lost my daughter in the process. It soured me for all men too. I vowed never to become involved with one again. Then I met your brother.' She smiled at Joe and squeezed his hand again. He smiled back at her.

Erica felt a twinge of envy at the sight of their overt expressions of affection. 'Joe may be the exception,' she said. 'And, even if he isn't, I can't trust myself to be able to differentiate between someone I can trust and someone I can't. I'm still trying to come to terms with Geoff's death,' she finished, knowing it wasn't quite true. Geoff's death had been a relief, an end to her suffering. Then Kieren had started to exert *his* control over her.

'Just remember, there *are* some good men out there. Don't tar them all with the same brush as your late husband. It took me a long time to realise that, but I'm glad I did.' She smiled at Joe again with such love Erica had to look away.

'We're just asking you to have an open mind, Erica, not suggesting you rush into anything,' Joe said, breaking his silence. 'I'd hate to see you ruining your life because of the way that bastard treated you. Gill knows what she's talking about.'

Erica exhaled. 'Thanks for your concern, guys. It's good to know you've got my back. But I'm okay, really... or I will be. You don't need to worry about me.'

Joe and Gill looked at each other, then Joe said, 'Okay, sis. But we're here if you need us, if you need to talk... anytime.'

'Thanks,' Erica said again, glad the conversation seemed to be over.

'What are you doing on Monday?' Joe asked. 'We're going sailing with Cam and Poppy. There's room for one more.'

Erica experienced a flicker of disappointment. She'd have loved to join them, spend a day out on the ocean, the wind in her hair, but... 'I'm sorry. I'm working. Easter weekend is always busy in Emergency, and I'm starting a new shift. Maybe next time.' *If there is a next time.*

Erica hugged Joe and Gill goodbye, promising to see them soon. On the drive home, she reflected on the barbecue and the two conversations afterwards. It was kind of Joe and Gill to be concerned about her, but she didn't need their concern. She was doing all right without it, she thought, despite the little voice that reminded her how flustered she'd become when Jamie found her in the kitchen. And she couldn't help wondering what he wanted to talk to her about.

Fourteen

To Jamie's relief, on Easter Sunday the sun was shining and there was only the hint of a breeze, a perfect day for the start of their fishing trip. He called Rory and Gary, and they were both raring to go, Gary saying it would be good to get some relief from Archie's crying. Before Jamie could suggest it might not be fair on Mandy, his son added that he had it covered. Mandy's mum was planning to spend the day with her, and her niece, Tilly, had offered to stay overnight.

Jamie had spent a restless night, reliving his conversation with Erica, wondering what he might have said to have it go differently, the memory of how she had trembled, then almost burst into tears tearing him apart. Then there had been Joe's attempt at counselling him, advising him how to treat his sister. As if Jamie would rush into anything. He was well aware of her recent bereavement, that there had been some upset with her husband, something so traumatic it had driven her to seek refuge with her brother in Pelican Crossing. But now she was back, and it seemed as if she was prepared to make a fresh start. He wanted so much to be a part of that fresh start, but knew he had to treat her gently.

Both Rory and Gary arrived at the harbour a few minutes after Jamie, and they were soon off, heading out to sea with the prospect of two days fishing ahead of them. As they made their way out of the bay, Jamie had no time to wonder about Erica, busy steering the vessel until they were out in the open sea.

It was a glorious day. They fished, ate and drank – on this trip, Jamie had relaxed his normal rule and allowed the two younger men to bring along some beer, which they used to celebrate their catch. As night fell, they remembered previous trips, recounting their experiences which grew more and more exaggerated as the night went on. Then, as their eyes began to close, they snuggled down in sleeping bags ready to waken at dawn and do it all again.

Next morning, Jamie was awake first, glad to see it promised to be another lovely day. He looked down at the sleeping figures of his two sons, remembering how he had done the same when they were little and sleeping in their tiny beds in the house he and Cindy had shared. Now they were grown men, both taller than him and would be able to best him in a fight. It was incredible to think they were part of him, living beings he and Cindy had created together and brought into this world.

'Hey, Dad!' Rory opened his eyes, and Jamie's image of him and Gary as children disappeared to be replaced by the reality of the grown versions.

'Good morning. Ready for breakfast?'

As if on cue, at the sound of the word *breakfast*, Gary's eyes opened too.

While Jamie put the kettle on, Rory unwrapped a packet of ham and cheese sandwiches and shelled three boiled eggs, and Gary took out his phone, and went over to the side of the boat to call Mandy.

'All good?' Jamie asked, when Gary returned.

'All good. It seems the little lad slept right through the night. Mandy suggested I should go away more often. Not really.' He chuckled. 'But it looks like the tooth that was bothering him has come through.'

'Rather you than me,' Rory laughed. 'But I have to admit Archie is pretty cute, for a kid who has you as his dad.'

Jamie listened to their teasing and grinned. Nothing much had changed since they were kids themselves. But despite the teasing, the frequent arguments, they were the best of mates. He had worried about them for a time after Cindy left, when they'd gone through a difficult stage, getting into trouble at school, often fighting with each other at home. But they'd come good and he was proud of them. If only Rory could find a partner too...

It was almost lunchtime, and they were pulling in their lines when

Jamie let out a yell followed by a string of colourful expletives.

'What's the matter, Dad?' Gary asked, still holding his rod tightly.

'I've… I think I have a hook in my hand,' Jamie said, trying to remain calm when all he wanted to do was curse loudly again. 'The darned thing has got caught in the soft tissue between my thumb and the palm of my hand and it's giving me hell.' He screwed up his face, feeling dizzy.

'Let me see. Maybe I can pull it out.' Rory headed towards him to examine the injury. 'Wow!' he said, staring at the barb which had forced its way into Jamie's hand. 'Looks bad. At least I can cut off the line.' He drew out his penknife and proceeded to do that. 'You'd better sit down, Dad.'

Jamie was grateful for Rory's help as he led him to a bench seat. He was worried he might faint with the pain. By this time, Gary had joined them.

'It's pretty deeply embedded, Dad,' Gary said. 'I think we need to take you to hospital. If we try to get it out, we could cause more damage.'

'No, I can…' But, as his head continued to spin, Jamie knew Gary was right. It was his right hand. He needed to be able to use it. He couldn't risk either Gary or Rory trying to remove the hook, and he certainly couldn't do it himself.

The trip back to the harbour was agony for Jamie, his hand throbbed with pain and he continued to feel dizzy and nauseous. Rory had wrapped a towel around his hand to stop the blood from dripping onto his clothes, but it did nothing to ease the pain. He was glad when they reached the harbour, embarrassed to have to be helped off the boat and onto the wharf like an old man.

'I'll take Dad to the hospital if you finish up here and take care of our catch,' Rory said to Gary before bundling Jamie into his car and setting off for the hospital.

*

It had been a busy morning in the Emergency department, and Erica was ready for a break. But the arrival of a young boy who, along with his e-scooter, had been dragged under a car reversing out of a driveway had put paid to any thoughts of lunch.

When the boy had been taken off to surgery, she managed a quick break, just enough time to eat a sandwich and swallow a few mouthfuls of coffee, before returning to the fray. What was it about holiday weekends, she wondered. It was as if people lost their sense of caution and, with their GP closed, ended up here.

Her attention was caught by the sight of two men walking through the door, one supported by the other. This was nothing new… apart from the fact that she knew the older one. Jamie Whittaker's face was white, and his right hand was wrapped in a towel. They took a seat, and the younger man picked up a copy of the form which had to be completed by every patient.

Before she saw any more, Erica was called away to treat another case. She had almost forgotten the sight of Jamie, when he and the younger man she assumed was his son, were ushered into the cubicle where she was stationed.

'Fishing hook injury,' the doctor said. 'We get a lot of them at this time of year.'

Jamie winced. He was clearly in pain.

Following instructions, Erica carefully removed the towel and cleansed the wound, watching while the doctor administered a local anaesthetic and used forceps to grab and advance the barb through the surface of the anaesthetised skin. Then he clipped the point and its barb off, before backing the remaining, barbless hook out of the skin.

'Should be fine now, if you can cleanse and dress the wound, nurse,' the doctor said. 'You'll need to have the dressing removed in forty-eight hours,' he said to Jamie. 'Do you have someone at home who can do that for you?' He looked at the younger man whose face had lost its colour.

For some reason she'd have to work out later – and would probably regret – Erica found herself saying, 'We're neighbours. I can do it.'

The doctor gave her a strange look, though not as strange as the one Jamie was sending her. 'Excellent. Thanks, nurse. And…' he glanced at Jamie's paperwork. 'I see it's some time since you had a tetanus shot. We can take care of that before you leave. 'Nurse?' he said to Erica, who, having pre-empted him, had the tetanus shot ready to administer.

Jamie winced as Erica swabbed his upper arm and gave him the shot, trying to be gentle. 'Try to avoid using the hand where possible,' she advised.

'Thanks, Erica,' Jamie said, as he rose to leave, taking Rory's arm. His voice sounded weak and he seemed a little wobbly after the procedure he'd been through, but there was a twinkle in his eyes. 'You know which cottage is mine?'

'I do.' Erica felt her face redden at the admission she'd gone out of her way to discover that he lived only three cottages along from Livvy's.

'Okay, Dad?' Rory said, clearly eager to leave.

'Okay, son. So, I'll see you in a couple of days' time then,' Jamie said to Erica, his attempt at a grin barely hiding the pain he must still be feeling.

'You will,' Erica confirmed, part of her wishing she'd never made the offer.

Fifteen

'Who was that, Dad? I thought I knew all your neighbours,' Rory said as they made their way to the car.

'Erica Harris, sorry, Masters. She's staying in Olivia Grace's cottage while Olivia's overseas. She's Joe Harris's sister.' There was no need for Rory to know he and Erica had history. He'd been delighted, but surprised, when she offered to remove his dressing and guessed she was now regretting it. He thought of the state of his cottage. He wasn't the tidiest of people and with his right hand out of commission, how was he going to clean it up before Wednesday?

Gary was waiting for them at the gate. 'Everything's done and the fish are in the cold room in the dive centre, Dad. How are you?' he asked, seeing Jamie stumble from the car.

Rory answered for him. 'The doc took out the hook and he had a tetanus shot. He has a course of antibiotics to take, and one of the nurses who lives nearby is coming to remove the dressing on Wednesday.' Rory took his arm. 'I think you should probably lie down now, Dad, and…'

'Don't fuss!' Jamie hated this feeling of having to rely on anyone else, especially his sons. It should be the other way round, usually was. Was this what it was going to be like as he got older? They could shoot him before he got to that stage.

'Sorry, Dad.' Rory stepped back.

Gary held the door open for them, then Rory's words seemed to hit him. 'Your own private nurse, hey? Who is she? I presume it's a woman.'

Rory answered for him again. 'Joe Harris's sister. She's evidently living just along from here.'

Gary thought for a moment. 'I didn't know Joe had a sister but… she must have grown up here. Did you know her back then, Dad?' He winked.

Jamie chose not to respond.

Once inside, Jamie realised he was weaker than he'd anticipated. He was glad to agree to lie down, and grateful when Gary brought him a mug of hot chocolate – it had been what he and Cindy made for the boys when they were sick as children. He'd forgotten how comforting it could be.

'How're you going to manage, Dad?' Rory asked when he and Gary were ready to leave. 'It'll be difficult for you to do much with one hand.'

'I'll manage. I'm not in my dotage yet,' Jamie said testily, though he was grateful for their concern.

'I can ask Mandy to pop in tomorrow,' Gary said. 'She can help tidy up and maybe cook you something.'

'She doesn't need to bother. She has young Archie to take care of. She doesn't need to look after me.'

'She can bring him along.'

Jamie calmed down. It would be good to spend more time with his grandson. He was normally too busy with… He suddenly remembered the fishing charters he had booked for the rest of the week. 'One thing you could do for me… You or Rory.'

'Yes?'

'Your clients,' Rory guessed. 'I can do that. I just need to check with Cam, but I'm sure he'll be happy to give me the time off.'

'Thanks, son.' Jamie was sure too. Cam, as well as being Rory's boss, was a good mate and would know that, if the boot was on the other foot, Jamie would be the first to offer to help. 'I'll send you the information when I can get to my computer.'

'There's no need, Dad. Just give me the key to your office.'

Jamie fumbled in the pocket of his pants with his left hand and tossed the key to Rory, feeling as he did so, that he was giving away his independence. He knew Rory would do a good job, but he wasn't ready to hand over his business just yet.

Finally, Rory and Gary were gone, and Jamie was left in peace. He'd given in to Rory's suggestion that he lie down, but had chosen to do it on the sofa rather than go to bed in the middle of the afternoon like an invalid. As it was, they'd covered him up with a throw Cindy had bought in a fit of refurbishing, and which he'd forgotten he still had. But he had to admit it felt comfortable.

As the trauma he'd experienced began to take its toll, and the antibiotics began to take effect, Jamie's eyes closed, his last waking thought that at least one good thing had come out of this. In two days' time, he'd see Erica again.

Sixteen

Erica was glad the day was over. She was looking forward to attending the book club meeting this evening, but first, she had to visit Jamie to remove his dressing. As soon as she made the offer she'd regretted it, seeing the way his eyes lit up. But it had been too late to change her mind, and surely it couldn't be too bad. She'd go in, remove the dressing, check the wound and leave. If she treated it like any other professional contact, there wouldn't be a problem. But she knew it wasn't so simple. This wasn't just another patient, it was Jamie, who'd been her first love, who still had the power to make her tremble at the memory of those days, and who seemed determined to rekindle the past.

Still dressed in her nurse's uniform and carrying her first-aid kit, Erica made her way along the row of cottages till she came to the one which was Jamie's. She'd recognised it straight away. With the anchor in the front yard and the model of a fishing boat in the window, it couldn't belong to anyone else. She remembered how they had often talked about the house they would have – in those far-off days when anything seemed possible, and they couldn't imagine a future with anyone else. Even back then, boats and fishing had been his life. Jamie had worked on his dad's fishing boat, aiming to take over when his dad retired. She was surprised he'd sold the boat, set up his fishing charter business, but supposed it might have become too difficult to maintain after Cindy left. Cindy! Erica had been shocked when Livvy had written to tell her they'd married. Erica had already been married to

Geoff by then and pregnant with Kieren, so it shouldn't have mattered to her what Jamie was doing. But she remembered Cindy who had been a year below her at school and had always seemed too flighty for someone like Jamie. Well, it appeared she had been. The marriage hadn't lasted and, according to what Rhana had told her, Cindy now had a new life in Melbourne.

The letter about Jamie's marriage had been one of the last she'd received from her friend. Geoff had kicked up such a fuss about her receiving news from Pelican Crossing, it had been easier to let the friendship lapse. It had been such a bonus to meet Livvy and Rhana again when she was here last year, and to pick up her friendship with the two women who had been her best friends when she was growing up. And now she was staying in Livvy's cottage, and Jamie lived only three doors away.

After an initial hesitation, Erica took a deep breath, pushed open the gate and walked up the path bordered with bright flowering plants. She knocked at the door, to hear Jamie call, 'It's open. Come in.'

Once inside, Erica had to adjust her eyes to the dim light in the hallway, before following the sound of music and heading through to the back of the house where she found Jamie seated in a cane chair in the glassed conservatory.

The music stopped and she realised it had been the radio. 'Hello, nurse,' Jamie said, the amused twinkle in his eyes telling Erica he'd guessed why she'd chosen to come dressed in her uniform.

'Hello, Jamie. I won't take up much of your time,' Erica said, trying to keep her voice calm and hoping he couldn't detect her embarrassment… or her unease at being alone with him. She could remember the last time they'd been alone together. He probably could too. It had been the night before she left for Sydney to study nursing, the night when they'd almost… But he had pulled back at the last moment, saying he didn't want their first time to be on the beach. Looking at him now, his chin covered with stubble, no doubt because he'd been unable to shave, his hair longer than was fashionable for a man of his age, though not as long as it had been when he was eighteen, Erica wondered if her life would have been different if he'd had fewer scruples. He was still a fine figure of a man, his tee-shirt strained across shoulders which were broader than she remembered, his hair showing just enough tinge of grey to give him a distinguished appearance, his eyes still the same dark brown she had fallen in love with. She realised she was staring.

'Let's have a look at your hand,' she said briskly. 'Any problems?'

'No, it's been good.'

Pulling up a small stool, Erica sat on it, took Jamie's hand and removed the dressing. The wound was healing perfectly. 'How does it feel?' she asked as he tried to flex it. 'Still a bit tender?'

'Yeah, but better than it was. Can I test it out by making you a coffee?'

'Oh… I…' About to refuse, Erica realised it would be churlish. 'Thanks, Jamie,' she said, 'but I can't stop for long. I'm going to a book club this evening. It's my first time, and I don't want to be late.'

'And I'm guessing you won't be going dressed like that.' Jamie gestured to the dark blue pants and tunic with her nametag pinned to it, making her wish she'd changed before coming here. It had been a silly attempt at trying to put some distance between them, and it hadn't worked, as was clear from his next remark, 'Though it's a pretty snazzy uniform. I bet you get a few admiring glances in it.'

Erica blushed. She put her hands up to her face as if she could hide her red cheeks. *What was wrong with her?* She never blushed these days, though she had done at one time. Jamie had always been able to get under her skin.

She followed him into the kitchen, surprised to see the modern appliances sitting on the benchtop, looking incongruous in the otherwise old-fashioned space. Jamie really had changed from the young man she'd known who would have been happy to make do with something he'd picked up at the tip or in a second-hand shop. It was over thirty years ago, she reminded herself. People changed. She'd changed. She was no longer the happy-go-lucky girl she'd been back then. Life had left its mark on her. It should be no surprise that Jamie had changed too.

'I'm sorry,' he said, and when Erica glanced at him, she saw he was fumbling to fill the coffee machine, 'I'm not quite as able as I expected.'

'No, *I'm* sorry. I should have realised. Let me.' Erica took over the coffee making. 'How have you been managing?'

'Mandy has been coming over. Gary's wife,' he explained. 'She's been a great help, but it'll be good to be independent again.'

Erica remembered Gill telling her about Gary and Mandy's wedding, the wedding on the beach she'd been at pains to avoid. 'I understand,' she said. She valued her independence too. It was why she had wanted to move out of Joe's house, to have a place of her own.

Over coffee, which they took out into Jamie's backyard, Erica was surprised not to feel awkward, even though she was careful to avoid mentioning anything personal or harking back to the past, their past.

She was amazed how quickly the time passed, suddenly discovering she'd have to rush to make it to the book club in time. 'I'm sorry, I need to go,' she said. 'I'll take the cups in and…'

'I can do it,' Jamie said, rising to join her. 'It's been good to see you again, to talk properly.'

'Yes.' Erica realised it had. She'd enjoyed their conversation, and Jamie had made no attempt to be anything other than a good friend and neighbour.

'Can we do this again?' he asked. 'I sometimes get lonely of an evening, and I suspect you may too. Perhaps we can have a glass of wine together. No strings,' he added, as Erica's expression changed to one of caution.

'Perhaps,' she said, feeling uncomfortable. She wasn't sure she was ready to spend more time with Jamie, to drink alcohol with him. She couldn't dismiss the memory of what Geoff had been like when he'd been drinking. But Jamie wasn't Geoff, a little voice in her head reminded her.

'Can I call you?'

'I guess.' Erica entered her number into the iPhone Jamie held out. 'Now, I really must go. Be careful with your hand. It's still healing, so don't try anything too strenuous for the rest of the week. It should be fine after that,' she said, reverting to her nursing role.

'Aye, aye, nurse,' Jamie said chuckling.

Erica was chuckling too as she walked back home. Maybe they weren't so different to what they had been like all those years ago after all.

*

The book club was being held in Gill's apartment, so Erica felt quite at home when she arrived. But when she walked in to see the group of strangers all staring at her, her first instinct was to flee. Then Gill came forward to greet her, and she saw her new friend, Kate, was one of the group. She relaxed.

'This is Erica, Joe's sister,' Gill said, before introducing the other women to her.

Erica smiled, took her seat and glanced around. Nothing had changed since she spent time here the previous year. Gill's spartanly furnished apartment was so different from Joe's comfortable home which had reflected Joe and Barb's taste, and from Livvy's cosy cottage. Fleetingly, Erica wondered whose taste would prevail when Gill and Joe set up house together. It would be interesting to see.

Her attention was drawn back to the group, as Gill introduced the book by asking how many had watched the Netflix version. Two women indicated they had, while the others shook their heads, one saying she always liked to read a book first then decide if she wanted to watch the movie.

Saying they'd discuss the film later, Gill started the ball rolling by giving her thoughts on the book, which started with the death of the bridesmaid hours before the wedding. This led to a discussion of other wedding mishaps and disasters before the others gave their views, finishing with Erica, who found there was little left to say. Then the two women who had viewed the Netflix version provided their impressions of it. Although they had enjoyed it, they expressed disappointment at the inevitable changes to the plot and characters, with even the name of one of the main characters being changed.

As the discussion drew to a halt, Gill rose. 'Time for tea and coffee,' she said.

'Can I help?' Erica rose to join her and they made their way to the kitchen, where Gill had already set out plates of small cakes and a platter of biscuits and cheese.

When Erica returned to the living area carrying a tray of food, the conversation had switched from the book to stories of the women's own weddings. As she listened, Erica realised hers had been very different. Whereas most had been married in white, in a church with a large audience of friends and family, hers had been a hole-in-the-corner affair in a registry office in Sydney with witnesses drawn in from the office. She was too ashamed to describe it.

Finally, the evening was over, but before they left, it seemed there was one more item on the agenda. 'We need to choose the book for next month,' Gill said. 'I think it's your turn, Kelly,' she added, turning to one of the women who had watched the Netflix version of this month's book, and who Erica had learned was a potter, and one of group of women who owned and managed *The Mousehole*, a tiny shop she'd admired and promised herself she'd visit.

Everyone stared expectantly at Kelly, while Erica hoped she wouldn't choose something too literary, but one she could snuggle up with.

'I've chosen the latest by Nicci French, *Has Anyone Seen Charlotte Salter?*' Kelly said. 'A bit more of a thriller than this one. I think you'll all enjoy it, and it should give us lots to talk about.'

Erica was pleased. It was a few years since she'd read anything by the husband and wife team who wrote as Nicci French, and she'd always loved their books.

After helping Gill clear up and thanking her for introducing her to the book club, Erica drove home. She'd be glad to get to bed. It had been quite a day. She'd enjoyed the discussion about books, meeting a new group of women… and there had been the encounter with Jamie. She was grateful he hadn't asked her anything about her marriage, but as she turned into her parking spot, she wondered if she'd been too quick to agree to seeing him again.

Seventeen

It was now almost two weeks since he'd injured his hand, and Jamie's life was slowly getting back to normal. He'd been grateful for Rory's help with his fishing charters but was pleased to go solo again. Also, it was high time he made contact with Erica.

Jamie had thought a lot about the time she came to remove the dressing on his hand, suspecting her decision to arrive in her uniform indicated her insecurity and her desire to be totally professional. It had been a bonus when she agreed to have coffee with him, almost like old times, though he'd noticed how she'd shied away from any mention of them. The main plus had been when she didn't refuse his offer to meet again for a drink, and sensing her reluctance he hadn't followed up immediately.

He glanced over at his passengers as he steered into the harbour. They had been a good group today, no alcohol sneaked on board and no arguments when only two of the group managed to catch something. But he'd be glad to get in and home for a beer, or maybe he'd head to *The Grand*, see if Cam was there for a yarn. He hadn't felt like going to the hotel when his hand was still a tad weaker than normal, when he might have found it difficult to lift a glass of beer. He automatically flexed his right hand at the thought, glad there was no residual weakness.

As he passed *The Grand* on his way home, Jamie saw Cam go in, so instead of going straight to the cottage to shower and change, he followed his friend into the hotel.

'Hey, Cam,' he said, joining his mate at the bar. 'How's tricks?'

'Jamie!' Cam gave him a wide grin. 'I heard about your injury. Bad luck. You've recovered?'

'Good as gold.' Jamie held up his right hand. 'But it stopped me in my tracks for a bit. If it hadn't been for Rory and Mandy…' He shook his head. 'Thanks for giving Rory the time off.'

'That's what friends are for, and I was happy to help. I know you'd do the same for me. Let me buy you a beer.'

'I should be buying you one,' Jamie said, as Cam went ahead to order for them. 'The next one's on me, but it won't be today. One's my limit while I'm still on antibiotics. Probably shouldn't even have one, but I had the last tablet this morning.'

'I hear you had a private nurse come to remove your dressing.'

'How…? Oh, Rory.'

'Erica Harris,' Cam said. 'Didn't you and she…?'

'That was a long time ago, another lifetime,' Jamie said, hoping that would be an end to it.

Cam gave him a strange look, but said no more about Erica, instead asking, 'Did you hear about the proposal to expand the sports centre to incorporate a venue for live music?'

This prompted a discussion about the pros and cons of such a proposal and memories of Cam and Jamie's own youth when they had spent long summer nights on the beach, singing and dancing to the music of guitars which many of the young guys played.

The memory was still with Jamie as he made his way home. It seemed like yesterday, but it had been over thirty years ago when he and Erica had danced to the music of Jimmy Barnes, Midnight Oil and Tina Arena. They hadn't always joined the others on the beach, preferring to find a quiet spot where they could play the music they'd recorded from the radio on Jamie's cassette player. It was a world away from what kids did nowadays.

Erica was still on Jamie's mind when he walked into the cottage. It was time. He took out his phone to call her.

*

Erica was in the shower when she heard her phone ring. It had been another busy day in Emergency, and she was relishing the sensation of the hot water cascading over her. She debated letting it go to voicemail, but the sense of responsibility her mother had drilled into her made her turn off the water, wrap a towel around herself and go into the kitchen to pick up her phone. She caught it just in time. 'Hello?' she said.

There was a pause then, 'Erica, it's Jamie.'

Erica wished she hadn't answered. Even though she knew Jamie couldn't see her, she was very conscious of being half-naked and dripping water onto the tiled floor. Since it had been almost two weeks since she saw him, and he hadn't called, she'd thought – even hoped – he'd decided not to contact her.

'Jamie! How's the hand?' Maybe she could pretend this was a professional call.

'It's good, almost back to normal.' There was another pause. 'I'm very grateful you went out of your way to visit me at home.'

'No worries. It was on my way.' She still didn't know why she'd done it, but it had gone well, she remembered.

'About that drink I owe you. I wondered if you were free on Saturday. Maybe we could meet.'

There was another pause, this time while Erica tried to work out a response. Did she want to have a drink with Jamie, to open up the possibility of rekindling their past? Or was she making too much of this? It was only a drink with an old friend, and she didn't have too many of those. Geoff had seen to that.

'Okay,' she said warily. She realised it wasn't an enthusiastic response, but she didn't want to sound too eager.

'Great,' Jamie said, sounding relieved.

Had he expected her to refuse? Maybe she should have. She remembered what Gill had said. It was true. All men weren't like Geoff, but…

Jamie was speaking again. 'How about the yacht club… or we could try the new wine bar that opened recently. I'm not sure what it's like…' His voice trailed off.

Was Jamie as unsure about this as she was? 'The wine bar sounds good. The yacht club will be busy and…'

'… there will be people there who know us,' Jamie finished. 'Right, the wine bar it is. How about I pick you up at seven? I think they may have food if we want to eat…' His voice trailed off again.

Erica had a sudden urge to reassure him. This wasn't the confident, assured Jamie she remembered. What had happened to him over the years? She supposed a divorce could do that to someone, sap their confidence. She knew all about that, and Jamie had been left with two teenagers to look after. Or was his apparent lack of confidence her fault? Had she been less than enthusiastic? 'I'm looking forward to it,' she lied.

'Great,' he said again. 'See you at seven on Saturday.'

What had she done? She'd just made a date with Jamie Whittaker, with the boy she'd fallen in love with when she was only sixteen, the boy who, at one time, she'd thought she'd marry. She must have lost her mind.

Eighteen

The next day was busy at work, two traffic accidents using up all their resources and leaving the staff exhausted, making her poor company for Joe and Gill at dinner in the yacht club. Looking around the busy restaurant, Erica was glad she'd opted for the wine bar for her date with Jamie. It wasn't a real date, she told herself, only a drink with an old friend. But she knew it would look like a date to anyone else. She deliberately hadn't mentioned it to Joe and Gill, afraid of their comments. She hoped Jamie hadn't told anyone about it either.

On Saturday, feeling an unexpected sense of anticipation – it was so long since she'd been out with a man other than Geoff – Erica dressed in a pair of black slacks and a white sweater and took more care than usual with her makeup before brushing her hair into its customary style. She completed the look with a pair of high-heeled black sandals.

When Erica heard Jamie's knock at the door, she quickly slipped her arms into a red jacket, grabbed her bag and answered it, giving him no opportunity to step inside. She wasn't sure why, but she wasn't ready for him to access what she considered to be her private space, even though it did belong to Livvy, and he might have been inside before now.

'Ready?' Jamie was looking very smart in a pair of grey pants teamed with a navy sweater over a blue and white striped shirt. Tonight he was closely shaved and the scent of a familiar cologne wafted towards her, reminding her of the past she was at pains to forget. It shocked her he was still using it. She had changed her perfume several times over the years, always in an attempt to please Geoff. Now, she was wearing Calvin Klein's Obsession, which she had chosen for herself. She loved its fragrance which was a mix of floral and spicy and made her feel feminine. It was very different from the light floral scent she'd favoured in her teens.

'Ready,' she said, stepping out and closing the door behind her.

The wine bar was located behind Main Street and close to *Books and Coffee*, a combined bookshop and café Erica had discovered on her last visit to Pelican Crossing and which she loved to pop into to browse the books and grab a quick coffee and one of the delicious cakes. The wine bar was a new addition to the town and, from the noise emanating from it, was a popular one.

Jamie pushed open the door under the sign *Number 96*, which was the name of the wine bar as well as the street number, and they entered a dimly lit room which appeared to be filled with young people. A young man was playing a guitar in the far corner.

Seeming to sense Erica's uncertainty, Jamie steered her through the crowd to an empty table at the opposite end of the room from the musician, and which was somewhat protected from the noise of the other patrons. 'White or red?' he asked.

'White, thanks,' Erica said, curling her legs around the high stool and glad she'd worn pants.

While she was waiting for Jamie to return, Erica checked out the other patrons. As she'd expected, most were in their twenties or thirties. She guessed she and Jamie were the oldest ones there. But instead of feeling awkward, it gave her another taste of the freedom she'd been experiencing since she was back in Pelican Crossing. Geoff would have hated this place.

'Here you are.' Jamie placed two glasses of white wine on the table along with a platter of cheese, olives and biscuits. 'I thought we might want something to nibble on too,' he said with a smile.

'Thanks.' The food did look inviting, and Erica hadn't taken time to have a proper meal before she left. She placed a piece of cheese on a biscuit and bit into it, then took a sip of wine.

'Why don't you tell me a little about yourself,' Jamie said. 'I know you married and went to West Australia, then your husband died when you were here last year. What have I missed?' He raised an eyebrow.

Erica flinched. She didn't want to go into the whole sad story of how she'd made such a mistake in marrying Geoff. Instead, she said, 'That's right. I have a son and granddaughter back in Perth too.'

'So, what brought you back to Pelican Crossing?'

It was a reasonable question, but Erica didn't answer immediately. She twisted the stem of her glass and took a sip. 'It's complicated,' she said at last. 'When Geoff died… he didn't leave his estate the way we'd planned. Everything went to Kieren… our son. The business – a car yard – was in trouble and the house had to be sold. I could have stayed with Kieren and Briony, but…' She gazed into space, picturing again what her life would have been like.

'I can't see the Erica I knew settling for that.'

How little he knew. He could never guess what her life had been like with Geoff, and she could never tell him. That part of her life was over, best forgotten, though she would never forget. 'I'm not the Erica you knew anymore, Jamie,' she said, a break in her voice. 'I've changed.'

'We both have. It's been over thirty years, Erica. It would be strange if we hadn't. No one stays the same. Marriage changes us. I know it changed me… and when Cindy left…' He shook his head. 'She left me with two teenagers. It was no picnic, I can tell you.' He shook his head again. 'But I coped. We have to, don't we? We have to deal with what life presents us with, no matter how hard it is at times.'

Erica exhaled. He understood. Life had thrown him a challenge too, different to hers, but perhaps just as shocking. She nodded and took another sip of wine, unsure how to respond.

The music became louder, as did the voices of the other clientele as they tried to make themselves heard above it.

'Let's get out of here,' Jamie said, draining his glass, 'unless…' He gestured to the food which they'd barely touched.

'Fine.' Erica's head was beginning to ache from the noise. She finished her wine too and grasped the hand Jamie held out.

Once outside, Jamie released her hand, and they looked at each other and laughed.

'Perhaps not the best choice of venue,' Jamie said. 'I guess it's a sign we're getting older.'

They laughed again.

'It was okay at the start,' Erica said, 'but perhaps you're right. The yacht club might be more our scene.'

'Next time.'

Erica stared at him. Was there going to be a next time?'

'It's a lovely evening. Why don't we go for a walk along the beach?' Jamie said, then looked down at her flimsy sandals.

'I can take them off,' Erica said, the prospect of a walk on the beach sounding attractive after the noise of the wine bar.

Erica was relieved Jamie didn't make any further attempt to hold her hand as they walked along past the harbour towards the row of cottages and what she had begun to think of as *her* beach. It was Jamie's too.

As they stepped down onto the sand, she took off her sandals and looked up. The stars were shining brightly in a clear sky, the full moon sending a golden glow across the water. It was a perfect evening, and one she suddenly realised she didn't want to end.

Nineteen

Jamie couldn't believe his luck when Erica agreed to a walk along the beach. The wine bar had been a mistake – too many people, too noisy to talk much, and he should have anticipated the crowd would be younger.

But now they had the beach to themselves. It was a beautiful evening, the full moon providing the perfect romantic atmosphere. Jamie glanced at Erica. Despite the grey streaks in her hair, she hadn't changed much from the teenager he'd fallen in love with. But he knew that not all changes were visible to the naked eye. He hadn't lied when he said his divorce from Cindy had changed him, and he suspected there had been things in Erica's marriage that had changed her, things she wasn't willing to share, not yet, anyway. He hoped that in time, she might feel able to confide in him.

'What a lovely evening,' Erica said, gazing up at the stars.

'A bit different to the big city.'

'Yes. It was the right decision to come back, despite…'

'Your family?'

'Mmm. I miss Briony and Ava.'

Jamie was surprised she didn't mention her son, then remembered what Joe had told him, how her son resembled his father. Jamie felt a shiver run down his spine at the suspicion Erica might have been trapped in an unhappy marriage. At least he and Cindy had parted without too much hassle, and he had been able to get on with his life. He didn't want to imagine what Erica might have suffered.

'Tell me about them,' he said.

Jamie saw Erica smile. 'Briony's wonderful,' she said. 'She lost her own mother and has always called me Mum. I couldn't have wished for a better daughter-in-law. And little Ava's a delight, still a baby but so cute. I love them both to bits.' She was silent for a few moments, clearly remembering.

'But not enough to stay?' Jamie was curious about what had brought her to Pelican Crossing. She'd said the house had to be sold, and she had the option of moving in with her son and his wife, but he felt there must be more to it.

'I needed somewhere that was mine,' she said at last. 'It's why I moved into Livvy's place, didn't stay with Joe. My brother's too kind and said I could stay as long as I liked. But I know he intends to sell the house, and it was still *his* place. I hated the feeling of being obligated to someone, even my brother. I wanted to feel free. Is that too selfish of me?' Erica turned towards Jamie, her eyes widening.

'No, not at all.' He was gaining an insight into her marriage. If she wanted to feel free, it confirmed his suspicion that she'd felt trapped in her marriage. Bad though his marriage to Cindy had been towards the end, neither of them had felt trapped. His heart went out to Erica and he vowed he'd do whatever he could to ensure she never felt that way again.

'You deserve to be happy, and if being here in Pelican Crossing makes you happy, then it was the right decision to make,' he said.

'Thanks, Jamie. That means a lot to me.'

Her words encouraged Jamie to risk saying what had been on his mind since they stepped onto the sand. 'Being together on the beach like this… it brings back memories.' He wondered if he dared take Erica's hand again. It had felt so good when he grasped it as they left the wine bar, but he got the impression it wouldn't be welcome here on the beach.

'That was in a different lifetime, Jamie.' Erica's voice was cool. 'I don't believe in looking back. It can only cause heartache.'

Wow! What had happened to the happy-go-lucky girl he'd known to make her so cynical?

Not knowing how to respond, Jamie didn't immediately reply. They walked along in silence for a few minutes, then he said, 'How about we pretend we've just met? Now we're neighbours, can we become friends too?' He wasn't sure how he'd manage it, with the memories which filled his mind each time he thought about Erica… and which overflowed when he was with her. But perhaps she was right. They couldn't live in the past, nor could they change it.

Jamie held his breath waiting for Erica's reply.

*

Erica had been enjoying wandering along the beach, the gentle lapping of the waves, and the sand between her toes so different to the hard surfaces she was accustomed to walking on. Then Jamie had to go and spoil it by reminding her of the past, a past she wanted to forget. She saw his expression change, the look of disappointment he tried to hide, then his suggestion they pretend they had just met.

She thought for a moment. Could that work? Could she and Jamie put their past behind them and start over? Perhaps, though this time there would be nothing more than friendship between them. Erica knew she could never trust a man again, not even Jamie. And she couldn't trust herself to know a good man from a bad one. Geoff's influence had seen to that.

'I guess we could be friends,' she said warily, only to see his eyes brighten. 'But only friends,' she added quickly. 'I'm done with relationships.'

'Okay. I can handle that. We all need friends.'

'Right.' *Maybe she had read too much into his memories talk. Maybe they were on the same page. Why had she immediately jumped to the conclusion Jamie wanted to carry on where they'd left off? Was she the fool here?*

They continued to wander slowly along the beach, chatting about the changes Erica had noticed in Pelican Crossing till they came to the pathway which led up to her cottage.

'Looks like you're home,' Jamie said.

'Thanks for a lovely evening,' Erica said when they reached her gate.

'Thank you. I don't have the chance to get out very often, the odd meal with the boys, a drink with a mate, but they all have their own lives and don't have a lot of time for a single guy like me. Sorry, I don't mean to sound like a miserable old man.'

'You're not old,' Erica replied. 'You're the same age as Joe and he'd punch anyone who called him old.' *And you're still as handsome as you were at eighteen, perhaps even distinguished with the streaks of grey in your hair.*

'You're right,' Jamie sighed, 'but sometimes, when I look at Rory and Gary, I feel life has passed me by.'

'You and me both, then.' It was exactly how Erica had felt when she left Perth. But here in Pelican Crossing, it was as if she had a new lease of life.

'Well, friend, why don't we do something about it? When did you last go surfing?'

Erica laughed. 'Surfing? I can't remember, but I do join a group of wild swimmers each morning when my shifts permit. Does that count?'

'Wow, you're one of those crazy women? I've heard about them. You always did enjoy extreme sports. Sorry, as a new friend I'm not supposed to know that.' He chuckled.

Erica could see this might be more complicated than she'd thought. They couldn't completely expunge everything they knew about each other. 'How about kitesurfing? I see Gary organises "amazing kitesurfing adventures",' she said, quoting from Gary's publicity brochure, which she'd picked up soon after she arrived, meaning to do something about it one day.

Jamie seemed to think for a moment then, 'He hasn't managed to get me involved yet, but it could be a good idea. I'll check it out with him. Can I let you know?'

'Sure. Thanks again for tonight.' Erica smiled and slipped through the gate before Jamie could say anything more, and before he could make any move to… Her heart thumped at the memory of the kisses they used to share. Forgetting the past wasn't going to be easy.

Twenty

Erica desperately needed to talk to someone about Jamie. Joe was no use – he was Jamie's friend. And Gill would be sure to share anything Erica told her with him. That left Rhana, who had managed to make a life for herself without involving a man in it. Although Erica had always suspected there had been someone, a relationship that was doomed, one Rhana had chosen never to share, not even with her two closest friends.

As soon as she'd mentioned kitesurfing to Jamie, she'd wished she hadn't. But it was too late. He'd latched on to the idea, and now she'd agreed to join him on a kitesurfing adventure with Gary and a group of other people who would probably be half their age. *What had she been thinking?*

The truth was, she hadn't been thinking. All she had wanted was to change the topic of conversation which was veering too close to the past for comfort. Now she was stuck with spending more time with him. While the prospect of learning kitesurfing did appeal, it was the thought of doing it with Jamie and his son that worried her.

Now, after five days in the emergency department, during which she'd tried to switch off all thoughts of Jamie, she had a day off and was heading out to visit Rhana.

It was good to get out of town, to drive through the countryside, through the fields of tall cane. It reminded her of the early history of this part of the country and the slave labour which had once been brought here to harvest the crops, first burning it, then cutting it.

Thankfully, those days were long gone, and the farmers now used mechanical means to harvest the sugar cane while it was still green, using the roots to grow new crops.

By the time she reached the gate to Rhana's property with its now familiar sign featuring a cocker spaniel, Erica was feeling calmer than she had all week, and wondered if she had been worrying about nothing.

Rhana came to greet her, wearing her usual outfit of jeans and a tee-shirt, three dogs at her heels. 'How are you?' she greeted Erica. 'You sounded stressed on the phone. Not bad news from Perth, I hope?'

'No, nothing like that,' Erica said, though she did still harbour concern about Briony who seemed to be finding life challenging. She said it was with Kieren working all hours, but Erica couldn't help wondering if there was more to it, if Kieren was being as controlling as his father had been. She'd tried calling him and suggesting he needed to spend more time with Briony, to help her with Ava, but her words seemed to fall on deaf ears.

'Well, let's get you inside. I have coffee brewing and a batch of banana bread just out of the oven. You can tell me all while we eat. Everything seems better over coffee and cake.' Her tone was cheerful, but she shot Erica a piercing glance. It was difficult to hide anything from Rhana.

'Now, what's bothering you? You didn't come all this way for my company.'

'I might have. You're my only friend here, now Livvy's gone.'

'Rubbish. There are a few others from our year still around. There's…'

But Erica didn't want a list of former schoolmates, most of whom she hadn't related to when she was in her teens. She, Rhana and Livvy had formed such a closeknit group, there had been no room for others. She picked up her cup and took a sip of coffee. 'Mmm, this is good,' she said to stem her friend's talk.

'It's Gloria Jean's English Toffee. I buy the beans online. And stalling is pointless. Answer my question about what's bothering you.'

Erica sighed and put her cup down. 'It's Jamie.'

'You've seen him again? I thought you said you weren't interested.'

'I'm not! Oh, Rhana, it's complicated.'

'It usually is where a man is concerned,' Rhana said, making Erica wonder again what had happened in her friend's life, what she was hiding. 'Banana bread?' She held out the plate to Erica.

'Thanks.' Erica took a slice and put it down on her plate. 'Jamie came into Emergency. He had a fishing hook in his hand, and I had to help treat him, then…' she took a deep breath, '… I went to his cottage to remove the dressing.'

'So? That's it? Doesn't sound too complicated to me, though I don't expect you make a habit of treating patients in their home.'

'No, I don't.' Erica took a sip of coffee and a bite of banana bread before continuing. 'But it doesn't stop there. He wanted to thank me so invited me for a drink and…'

'You went on a date with him?'

Erica shifted uncomfortably in her seat. 'I suppose you could call it a date.' She decided to say nothing about their walk on the beach, or about the frisson she'd felt when Jamie took her hand in the wine bar. 'Anyway, I made it quite clear I didn't want any mention of the past and…'

'Jamie didn't get the message?'

'No, we came to an agreement to start over as friends and neighbours, nothing more. But we know so much about each other. He knows how much I enjoy the outdoors, like being adventurous – or did. There hasn't been much opportunity for that sort of thing for a long time. Now I've agreed to go kitesurfing with him. His son runs these adventure sessions.'

'Sounds like fun… your sort of fun. You wouldn't get me in one of these contraptions. So, what's the problem?'

'I don't know. It's just that… Oh, Rhana, what if he expects, if he thinks… if he wants more than friendship?'

'There's only one way to find out. And would it be such a bad thing? I know what you said about not getting involved with another man, but Jamie isn't a stranger. He's still the same person you dated for two years. Sure, you're both older and the years haven't been altogether kind to you – his life has been no picnic either – but deep down you haven't changed. He hasn't either. Jamie Whittaker is well-respected in Pelican Crossing. The way he coped with being left with two teenagers, set up a new business from scratch and made a success of it. There are a lot of women who'd jump at the chance of becoming the second Mrs

Whittaker, but he's remained single since Cindy left. I always thought he still held a candle for you.' Rhana put her head to one side and stared at Erica.

Erica felt herself redden. Surely not! Surely Jamie hadn't spent over thirty years yearning for her? No, it was too preposterous to contemplate. And it made their new friendship seem so false if he… She shook her head as if she could dismiss her friend's words. 'I doubt that,' she said.

'Don't be too quick to dismiss the possibility. Jamie's a good guy. He's not like your husband.'

Erica visibly shivered at the mention of her dead husband. But if what Rhana said was true, it put a whole new complexion on their friendship, one she wasn't sure she could cope with.

'I'm sorry, but you did start this conversation. Isn't it why you came?'

'Yes, I…' Erica floundered. Had she imagined Rhana would tell her she was mad seeing Jamie again, or hoped she would say exactly what she had, and encourage her to see his good points?

'You're not like me, Erica. You're not designed to be alone. You've always needed people around you. Look how you headed straight to Joe both times you left Perth.'

'But…' Where else would she have gone? Joe was family. Pelican Crossing was her hometown. Erica thought for a moment. Maybe Rhana was right, but… 'I'm on my own at Livvy's and I love it. I have no one to answer to. I feel free for the first time in my life'

'I'm happy for you, but is it what you really want… for the rest of your life?'

Rhana's words hit Erica like a splash of cold water. She was happy now. That was true. But what about in ten years' time, twenty? Did she really want to grow old alone? Almost everyone she knew – except Rhana and Livvy – was part of a couple, and while Rhana seemed to thrive on her isolated existence, Erica knew Livvy would love to have a partner, someone to come home to at night, cuddle up to in bed. There hadn't been much of that with Geoff in the latter years of their marriage. She had been too busy trying to avoid his anger to feel any sort of comfort. But what if…?

An image of Jamie appeared in her mind. Not the smart, clean-shaven, well-dressed Jamie she had drinks with, had walked on the beach with, but the Jamie wearing jeans and an old tee-shirt, his hair awry, his chin and cheeks peppered with stubble, the way he had been when she removed his dressing, the way she remembered him. What would it be like to come home to that Jamie every day, to know he was there to comfort her after a busy day at work, to be able to cuddle up to him and let all her cares fall away?

Twenty-one

It had taken Jamie two weeks to set up the kitesurfing with Gary, but the day was finally here, and he couldn't wait to see Erica again. Although they'd been in touch to make the arrangements, Erica's texts in reply had been brief and to the point. It was almost as if she regretted suggesting it.

Jamie was looking forward both to seeing Erica again and to the kitesurfing. He wasn't sure why he hadn't tried it before. Since Gary had added kitesurfing to his dive school and had gained his IKO (International Kitesurfing Organisation) certification, he'd been inundated with tourists wanting to learn and had even organised a kitesurfing carnival the previous year, drawing kitesurfers from all over Australia. Jamie was proud of what his younger son had achieved.

Initially, he'd been worried about learning the skill alongside a bunch of youngsters who might mock his and Erica's efforts, but Gary, clearly sensing his dad's concern, had assured him he'd teach them on their own. 'Don't want to have a group of teenagers show you up,' had been his son's words, but it had relieved Jamie, and he guessed Erica would feel the same.

It was a perfect morning, only a slight breeze rippling the water when he gazed out from his front veranda, sipping his morning coffee. His phone beeped.

All set, Dad?

Jamie grinned, as he texted his reply. *Did Gary think he was going to pike out?* But it reminded him to check with Erica.

Are we still on for kitesurfing?

Her reply came immediately, accompanied by a smiley emoji.

Sure. Looking forward to it.

Jamie gave a sigh of relief and went back inside to cook breakfast. It was almost like old times, preparing to spend the day with Erica. How he wished he could turn back the clock, go back to when they were a couple, to when everything seemed bathed in a rosy glow of happiness. But then, he reminded himself, there would be no Rory, no Gary, and no little Archie. There was no use harking back to the past, wishing for the future that had always been out of reach. He needed to concentrate on the present and the hope that fate had given him a second chance. And this time, he was determined not to blow it.

Erica was ready and waiting when he knocked on her door. She looked stunning, dressed in a pair of tight jeans and a long-sleeved skivvy in a shade of blue which matched her eyes – the one feature she didn't share with her brother.

'We can walk down to the harbour,' Jamie said, 'unless you'd rather drive.'

'No, walking's good. Isn't it a lovely day?'

Glad to hear Erica sounding more positive than he'd expected, Jamie agreed, and they set off at a brisk pace, only pausing when they encountered a pair of pelicans strutting across in front of them. Jamie was careful to keep the conversation general, choosing to recount an anecdote about one of his charter groups which made Erica laugh.

There was no time for further conversation when they reached the building next to his office which housed Gary's dive school and now his kitesurfing school too, as Gary immediately took over. The next hour was taken up by Gary instructing them on the basics of kitesurfing, where they learned the terminology and safety aspects before heading to the beach to discover how to launch, control and fly the kite.

By this time, they had donned wetsuits and were raring to go.

*

'Wow!' Erica landed the kite back on the beach and struggled out of the harness. She was filled with exhilaration at her achievement. The past few hours had been amazing. Gary had patiently shown her and Jamie how to launch, control, and land the kite, how to relaunch a kite from the water, and how to body drag through the water. Now she'd had her first experience of kitesurfing, she knew it wouldn't be her last. It hadn't been quite as difficult as she'd anticipated. Probably her history of sailing had helped there. She looked across at Jamie, seeing her own grin mirrored on his face.

'Let's go back and get out of these wetsuits,' he said, 'and grab a bite of lunch. All the exercise has made me hungry and given me a thirst.'

'You both did pretty well,' Gary said, adding, 'for beginners,' just as Erica was beginning to think he meant *for a couple of oldies*.

Jamie said it for her. 'Your dad's not so bad for an old bloke, eh?'

'You said it, Dad,' Gary chuckled. 'A few more lessons and the pair of you will be ready to go solo.'

Jamie grinned, but Erica flinched. She didn't want Gary or anyone else to view her and Jamie as a couple. Maybe this had been a mistake. After her initial regrets, she'd been looking forward to today, and she had enjoyed the sheer excitement of learning to control the kite, the adrenaline rush from sliding over the water, the thrill of weightlessness when her body left the water, the pure joy of the whole experience. She could understand why some people became addicted to it. But… and it was a big but… if it meant spending more time with Jamie and being perceived as a couple, she might have to give it a miss.

'Erica?'

She realised Jamie was still waiting for an answer to his invitation to lunch. 'I don't know,' she said. 'I should be getting back.' It was a weak excuse, and Jamie clearly thought so too.

'You have to eat,' he said. 'We can have a quick meal at *The Grand*.'

It was true. Erica realised it wouldn't be easy to wriggle out of this, and *The Grand* had always put on a good counter lunch, but again, she was beset with memories she'd been trying to stifle.

Back when she and Jamie had been dating, *The Grand*, the hotel opposite the harbour, had been where everyone had their first drink – often before they reached their eighteenth birthday. It had been where she had her first glass of wine, where Jamie had persuaded her to take a sip of his beer, and she'd almost choked at the bitter taste. She could still hear his laughter, feel the soft fabric of his tee-shirt against her bare shoulder, his knees touching hers under the table. It had been her seventeenth birthday and she'd felt so grown up, wearing a halter-necked dress she'd bought herself with money saved from her part-time job in a café.

'*The Grand*,' she said now, swallowing the temptation to decline. 'Sounds great.'

Once inside the old building which was dimmer than she remembered, Jamie led Erica to a corner table from where she was able to gaze around the room. Although the hotel had gone through several renovations over the years, not much had changed. The bar was still in the same spot, its dark wood surface covered by towelling cloths, presumably to soak up any spillages of beer, the array of bottles of spirits and liqueurs shelved behind, and the rows of glasses waiting to be filled. In these respects, it was no different from any other bar Erica had patronised, though those had been few and far between during her marriage, Geoff claiming they were no place for a respectable woman to frequent, and certainly not *his* wife.

The main difference from the bar she remembered was the presence of a large wide-screen television showing a footy game being played somewhere in the world, and the various blackboard menus scattered along the walls.

'What'll you have?' Jamie asked, once they were seated. 'I can recommend the pie and chips, and Ross stocks a few craft beers these days. I'm afraid I'm not much of a connoisseur of food or wine,' he said with a self-deprecating smile.

'A sparkling mineral water for me, thanks, and…' Erica twisted round to read the menu above their heads, '… I'll have the calamari and chips.' She decided it would be best to avoid alcohol so early in the day, and she wanted to keep all her wits about her. This place brought back too many memories.

But, as they waited for their meals, and Erica sipped her mineral water, any fears she might have had about Jamie trying to recapture the past were allayed, as they talked about their kitesurfing experience.

'I don't know why I've never tried it before now,' Jamie said, shaking his head. 'Gary has invited me often enough, but I always managed to find an excuse. I'm grateful to you for suggesting it, and I'm definitely going to have another go. How about you? You seemed to be enjoying it as much as I did.'

'I did enjoy it,' Erica said slowly, wondering how to tell him she hadn't been comfortable in his company. But it wouldn't have been true. She did enjoy his company, perhaps too much. It would be so easy to slip back into their old companionship, to be able to share her thoughts and feelings with him, knowing he'd understand. 'I liked the feeling of freedom,' she said at last, realising that was exactly what she'd liked best. It was similar to what she experienced swimming in the ocean at dawn.

Jamie frowned. It was clearly not the response he'd been expecting. 'Freedom? Sounds as if you've been feeling trapped.' He raised an eyebrow.

Erica winced, wishing she could take back her words. 'It was the sense of weightlessness,' she said, hoping to stem any further questions. There was no way she was going to reveal the secrets of her marriage to him.

'You're not wrong. I get it. I'm glad we did this together,' Jamie said, covering Erica's hand with his. 'And I'm glad you're back. I've waited a long time.'

Erica flinched. Jamie always had got her, and his meaning was clear. He was ready to pick up where they'd left off all those years ago when she left Pelican Crossing to study nursing in Sydney, just as if the last thirty-odd years had never happened. But they had, and while it would be all too easy to go along with him and give in to the flash of desire his touch triggered, too much had happened for her to trust her emotions, even when it came to an old friend like Jamie.

Twenty-two

Jamie stared at Erica's rigid back as she marched up the path to Livvy's cottage. He shook his head, trying to pinpoint what had gone wrong. Was it something he'd said? The kitesurfing had been marvellous, much better than he'd expected, and Erica had enjoyed it too. Her grin when they finished had mirrored his own delight at having mastered a new skill.

So, when had it started to go wrong? Jamie puzzled over it all the way to his own cottage, and while he poured himself a beer and took it out into the back yard. Then it struck him. It was in *The Grand*, when he made reference to the past. But those had been happy times, when they were young and carefree, and while he knew they could never go back and relive the past, surely it didn't do any harm to remember?

Deciding to do what he always did when things threatened to get him down, Jamie locked up and headed for the harbour. There was always plenty to do there, plenty to take his mind off Erica's changeable moods.

He was working on repairing a crack in one of the fibreglass boats he hired out, when he became aware of a panting sound close by, and a wet tongue licked his right foot.

'Coco!' a familiar voice called.

Jamie looked up to see Joe. It was his friend's chocolate labrador whose tongue was brushing his foot.

'Sorry, Jamie. She got away from me for a moment. Looks like you're busy.'

'Not too busy for you. It's about time I stopped, anyway. What are you doing here on the weekend? Thought you'd have other fish to fry, now you and Gill…' Jamie couldn't hide the envy in his voice.

'She's tied up today. Freya's home for the weekend and the pair of them are off somewhere. So, it's just me and Coco. I called in on Erica…'

'Oh!' Joe's presence now made more sense. *What had Erica said to have him come here?*

Joe rubbed his chin. 'She said you'd gone kitesurfing together.'

'Yeah, this morning. We had a lesson from Gary. It was pretty spectacular. You should try it… you and Gill.'

'We have. Had a few lessons, and you're right. It's a sensational experience. But that's not all. Erica seemed troubled, but when I asked, she changed the subject. You spent the morning with her. I wondered if you could shed any light on it.'

'Wish I could, mate. It's got me flummoxed too. I thought things were going well. The kitesurfing was amazing. Then we went to *The Grand* for a bite to eat.' Jamie drew a hand through his hair. 'And somewhere along the line, your sister changed, became distant. It was like she turned off a switch.' He shook his head. 'I've been trying to work out if it was something I said or did. It's why I came down here.' He gestured to the boat yard. 'Helps me take my mind off things, and there's always something to be done.'

'Know the feeling. Women, eh?' Joe chuckled.

'Mmm.' Jamie didn't want to get into this discussion. It didn't feel right to discuss Erica with her brother, though perhaps because he *was* her brother he could help. He thought for a moment then it came to him. It was when they'd been talking about the freedom of kitesurfing, and he'd said… 'I think it was when I said something about being trapped,' he said. 'No, wait. I may have said I was glad she was back, that I'd waited too long. It seemed to trigger something in her. But surely…?' Could it have been that simple, his reference to their past? Then it dawned on him. He remembered an earlier conversation when Erica had told him she didn't believe in looking back.

'That would do it, mate.' He peered at Jamie who was feeling all sorts of a fool. He should have realised, remembered… 'You look as if you could do with a drink.'

'You may be right. Let me finish up here and I'll join you.'

'I'll head over to *The Grand* and order the beers. Coco and I will be sitting outside.'

'Cheers, mate.'

When Jamie joined them a short time later, Joe was seated at a table with two glasses of beer beaded with condensation, and Coco was lying at Joe's feet, a bowl of water within reach. He picked up a glass and took a gulp.

'It may be time to fill you in on my sister,' Joe said. 'She'd wring my neck if she found out I was telling you this, but I think you deserve to know. It may explain her behaviour, why she shies away from any mention of the past and from any attempt you might make to get close to her.'

'I'm guessing her marriage was unhappy,' Jamie said. 'I thought as much when she turned up last year. You were at pains for me to keep my distance then. I couldn't understand why.'

'I know. It was difficult. Erica… Last year, she wasn't herself. I had no idea that she and Geoff… When she rang to say she'd left him, I was shocked. I'd never liked the guy, but he was her choice, and I thought they were happy.'

'What went wrong?' Jamie knew all about how an unhappy marriage could eat into you, but Erica had left the guy, and now he was dead.

'Abuse,' Joe said bitterly. 'At first, I thought it was just a case of coercive control, which was bad enough. Then I saw the bruises. I don't mind telling you, I wanted to punch the daylights out of him. When he came looking for her, I almost did.'

'He was here when he died, wasn't he?' Jamie had heard something about it at the time, but not the details.

'The bastard fronted up to Gill's office, threatened her then had a heart attack. He didn't survive.'

'Gill?' Jamie didn't know how she fitted in.

'Gill was Erica's solicitor, though it wasn't clear if Geoff knew that. I think the fact she was a divorce lawyer was enough.'

'Wow!' No wonder Erica was wary of Jamie, of any man. 'And now…?'

'I don't think Erica trusts men, or herself. Geoff managed to fool her at first. He could be very charming. But…' Joe shook his head. 'I suspect it's going to take her a long time to get over that mistake.'

Jamie felt numb. Was there no hope for him with Erica? While his mind went round and round in circles, he realised Joe was speaking again.

'I actually wanted to talk with you about a project I'm working on.'

'Oh, yeah?' Jamie pulled his attention back to his companion. Joe was always involved in one project or another. In the past couple of years, he had succeeded in saving the local newspaper, the dog beach, and had been active in identifying the culprit who was poisoning dogs on that very beach. Jamie had imagined that, now he was in a relationship with Gill, his old friend might have settled down. Obviously not.

'I'm not sure if you're aware, but many of our residents in Pelican Crossing are forced to go all the way to Brisbane for some healthcare, especially those suffering from cancer. It occurred to me that what we need is a facility right here where they can receive treatment close to home, maybe a palliative care centre too. It's a cause close to my heart.'

'Wow, that's a tall order, but a good idea.' Jamie could understand Joe's motivation. His wife had suffered from cancer. Barb had been able to die in her own home but not everyone had that choice. 'How do you propose to proceed?' Jamie was sure Joe already had a plan, but he wasn't sure where he could fit in.

'I already have Finn on board,' he said, referring to the editor of the local paper. 'He's writing a column to go in the next edition of *The Echo*, and Cam has promised to get behind it too. Gill and her women friends are aiming to run some fundraising events – a winter fair or some such thing and a coast walk. Liz Phillips' teenage granddaughter has come up with the idea of a video game tournament, but that might be a bit beyond our capabilities.' He laughed. 'All I'm asking for at this stage is your support and a commitment to getting your thinking cap on. We can't let the women do all the work. Oh, and to sit on the committee,' he added with a grin.

Jamie had been on board till Joe mentioned a committee. He wasn't good at committees where you were expected to have ideas to contribute. But Joe was a mate, and it was a good cause. 'Who else is on the committee?'

'All the usual suspects. Me, Cam, Finn and our womenfolk. Then there's Phil from the yacht club, Paul Clark, the CEO from the hospital, Kate, the town planner, and Erica, of course. We're hoping to persuade one of the medical staff to join us too.'

Jamie had been about to refuse until Joe mentioned his sister's name. If Erica was on the committee, at least it would provide him with the opportunity to see her, spend time in her company, maybe even break down some of her defences. 'I suppose,' he said with a sigh, 'though I'm not sure I'll be much help.'

'Good man.' Joe clapped him on the shoulder. 'Finn suggested inviting some of the younger guys in town, but I thought it best to stick with us oldies. We can always co-opt some others if we need them.'

'Right,' Jamie said, though he thought Rory and Gary might produce more ideas than he could when it came to fundraising. But he supposed they had busy lives, whereas he… He sighed again, aware of how lonely he often felt. At least this committee would fill in some of those empty hours, and maybe, just maybe, bring him closer to Erica.

Twenty-three

Erica turned on her back to float, her eyes on the dawn sky as its hues changed from pink to gold with the rising sun. She loved the peace of her early morning swims, her only regret that, with her changing shifts, she wasn't able to enjoy them every morning. But this morning, as she lay there, her thoughts went back to the previous day, to Jamie and to the feelings he'd engendered, feelings she'd thought gone for ever, feelings she had vowed never to allow herself to have again.

When she'd heard the knock at the door, soon after leaving Jamie, she'd thought it was him back, and had been about to ignore it, till she heard her brother's voice, and Coco's bark.

'Joe!' she'd said, throwing the door open and hugging him. 'And Coco,' she'd added, bending down to ruffle the dog's ears as the animal nudged her with her nose.

By the time they came in and were settled down in the kitchen with coffee for Joe, herbal tea for her, and water and a treat for Coco, she was able to tell her brother about her kitesurfing experience. But she recalled his concerned expression and presumed she hadn't been as successful as she'd hoped in hiding her worries.

Now she'd had time to reflect, she suspected Joe had only mentioned his new project to change the subject, but it would be good to have something to focus on besides herself and what might be happening in Perth. She swam back to the shore, intent on keeping that focus.

'You okay?'

Erica glanced up and paused in towelling herself dry to see Gill staring at her with a concerned expression. 'I'm fine. Why?'

Gill appeared embarrassed. 'No reason, but…' she hesitated then continued, 'Joe said you seemed a bit off yesterday.'

Blast her brother! He'd caught her at a weak moment. She hadn't expected him to tell Gill, but wasn't that what normal couples did? It hadn't been that way with her and Geoff, but what she was fast discovering was that their relationship had been anything but normal. The relationships she'd seen since returning to Pelican Crossing, especially this second time, were ones of mutual sharing and trust. Even Gill, who had been so violently opposed to forming a relationship, was now happily playing house with Joe, or would be as soon as they found somewhere to live.

'He caught me at a bad time,' she said, in the hope this might satisfy Gill.

'Hmm. Well, he suggested I make sure you join us for breakfast.'

'I don't…' Erica began, but Gill cut her off.

'I won't take no for an answer. *The Blue Dolphin Café* at eight. That gives you time to go home, shower and change. And if I know your brother, he'll want your ideas for his new project, so better start thinking about it.'

'Thanks.' Erica knew her brother too, and once he got his teeth into something, there was no stopping him. She'd be willing to bet he'd conned all his mates into being involved too. At this thought, her heart sank. Jamie was one of those mates.

'Joe said you went kitesurfing with Jamie Whittaker,' Gill said, as they walked up to the car park together. 'That must have been fun. Freya loves it, and Joe and I have had a few lessons with Gary too. What did you think?'

'It was amazing,' Erica replied, remembering the exhilaration, the adrenalin rush, the feeling of weightlessness, and the sensation of freedom. 'Gary's a great teacher.' As she spoke, Erica remembered too, how hot Jamie had looked, his wetsuit clinging to his body, and the flash of emotion she'd experienced. No, best not to remember that. 'Isn't Freya with you this morning?' she asked. 'Joe said she was home this weekend.'

'She had a late night.' Gill laughed. 'Oh, to be thirty again. She went out with Rory and some of their old mates from school, and I didn't expect her to be up this early. But I hope she'll be joining us for breakfast. I don't see nearly enough of her, but at least she's back in Australia,' she said. 'You must miss your son and daughter-in-law too. You seemed close.'

'To Briony, yes. Not so much, Kieren. He's too much like his dad.'

Gill raised an eyebrow.

'Maybe,' she said slowly, recognising the direction of Gill's thinking. She didn't want to go there. 'The jury's still out on that one.' She needed to call him again.

'So, see you at eight?' Gill said as they reached their cars.

'Will do.' Erica knew there was no getting out of breakfast, but at least if Freya was there, there would hopefully be no talk about her and Jamie.

*

By the time Erica arrived at the café, Joe and Gill were already there, accompanied by Freya, who looked as if she'd prefer to be still in bed. 'Late night?' she asked sympathetically, though it was a long time since she'd been out on the town. Looking back, her youth had been cut short by her marriage to Geoff. But it had been her choice, and there was no use wallowing in regret.

'Mmm,' Freya replied, taking a drink from the mug of coffee she was clasping in both hands. 'Oh, that's better.'

Both Gill and Joe laughed, though Erica felt some sympathy for the young woman. It would be nice to be Freya's age again, to have your whole life ahead of you, even if it meant being forced to come to breakfast with a hangover.

'How are you enjoying life in Sydney?' Erica asked Freya when they had all ordered breakfast.

'I'm loving it. It's very different to San Francisco, and the uni is different too. I'm sharing a neat townhouse in Glebe with one of the other lecturers, and we eat out a lot. A bit different to this too.' She waved a hand to encompass the ocean and the harbour.

During their meal, the conversation revolved around a recent article in *The Echo* which reported on the council's decision to remove the shark nets during the period of whale migration. Joe had been in favour of it, as had most of the councillors, but there were a few who worried about the risk of shark attacks.

'It was a good move, Joe,' Freya said, more alert after her breakfast of smashed avocado on rye. 'There have been so many cases of baby whales becoming caught in the nets. It's up to us to protect our wildlife.'

'Thanks for your support, Freya. But I'm afraid there will always be those who believe it's more important to protect our surfers and swimmers than the whales, despite the fact that, on this part of the coast at least, there are more incidents with whales than humans. And we will reinstate the nets in November before the main tourist season.'

'It's not easy for you,' Gill said, laying a hand on Joe's arm. 'As mayor, you have to listen to all points of view, and you can't please everyone.'

Erica listened to the exchange with interest. It had never occurred to her that her brother might often have to walk the line between different factions both in the community and the council. It couldn't be easy for him.

'At least most of the old guard are on my side,' Joe said with a sigh. 'Both Cam and Jamie are in favour. They've seen firsthand the damage the nets can do.'

Erica's stomach clenched at the sound of Jamie's name. She'd hoped to avoid any mention of him. Maybe… She glanced at her brother, but he appeared not to notice. It was Gill who picked up on it.

'Speaking of Jamie,' she said, looking at Erica, 'are you seeing him again? Erica and he went kitesurfing together,' she explained to Freya.

'With Gary?' Freya asked. 'He's the best. How did you like it?'

'Yes, with Gary. It was amazing.' Erica hoped that would be an end to it. She was wrong.

'So?' Gill asked. 'Joe says you and Jamie were together back when you were in your teens, before you left Pelican Crossing. It must have felt strange to meet him again after all this time. He's well-liked. Everyone has a good word to say for him, believes he's had a raw deal with his wife leaving him to bring up his two boys. Well, it's true,' she said to Freya who was rolling her eyes.

'Gill's right,' Joe said, joining in the conversation. 'Now you're on your own again, you could do worse than…' His voice trailed off as Erica glared at him. 'Sorry, sis, but it's true. I know how *my* life has changed since meeting Gill.' He smiled at her and took her hand. 'I didn't think I'd ever feel this way again, but here we are.'

'I'm not like you, Joe… or you, Gill,' Erica added, seeing Gill open her mouth to speak. 'My experience of marriage was not one I wish to repeat. Oh, I know what you're going to say. Jamie isn't anything like Geoff. And I know you're right, but I can't trust myself.'

'Are you talking about Gary and Rory's dad?' Freya asked, suddenly becoming aware of the conversation and looking up from her phone. 'I know they'd love it if he found someone. He's been on his own since their mum left when they were teenagers. What?' she asked when the other three laughed.

'We were saying exactly that,' Joe said.

'Oh!' Freya went back to her phone again. 'Rory has just sent me a message. He and his dad are going sailing today and he wants to know if I can join them. Is that okay with you, Mum?'

'Of course. It's lovely you've come to visit but there's no need to spend all your time with me.'

'Thanks. I'd better go home and change first. Have a great day, everyone.' She dashed off, leaving the others staring after her.

'Are she and Rory…?' Erica asked.

'No.' Gill shook her head. 'When she came home last year, I thought there was a chance, but they're just good friends. Rory isn't interested in a relationship. I suspect there may be someone in Sydney, but I'm not game to ask. I'll wait till Freya decides to tell me.'

'I remember what it was like when Kieren started dating Briony,' Erica laughed. 'It was ages before he plucked up the courage to tell us. He said he was afraid it wouldn't last.' She smiled at the memory, at how delighted she'd been when she and Briony finally met, how she had immediately warmed to the young woman who had stolen her son's heart. That had been before he'd become so close to his dad.

They continued to talk about Freya, and how grateful Gill was to have reconnected with her. Erica couldn't imagine how difficult it must have been for her when Freya took her dad's side in Gill's difficult divorce. It wasn't until his behaviour became too much for even his daughter to stomach that Freya became reconciled with her mother.

When breakfast was over, Erica farewelled Joe and Gill with promises to catch up again soon. She was glad there had been no more talk of her and Jamie, but as she made her way home, she couldn't help but remember what they had said, about what a good man Jamie was, how he was alone, just like her. And she began to think that, if he invited her out again, then maybe…

Twenty-four

Jamie was surprised when Rory turned up with Freya Dickson in tow. He knew the pair had been friends at school, and the girl had returned to Pelican Crossing the previous year, after spending time overseas. He thought he'd heard she was now working in Sydney. He supposed she must be home for the weekend and might be glad to get some time away from her mum and his friend, Joe. He didn't blame her. After being on their own for so long… and eschewing all thoughts of a relationship… the overt expressions of affection between Joe and Freya's mother, Gill, were sometimes difficult to handle.

'Welcome aboard, Freya,' he said, as she clambered onto the boat behind Rory. 'Not spending the day with your mum?'

'I was with her yesterday, and we had breakfast together with Joe and his sister. Thought I'd let them have some privacy.' She chuckled. 'I'm glad he and Mum have got together and I'm sure they don't want me around all weekend.'

Jamie barely heard her final remarks, her mention of Erica bringing back the memory of what Joe had told him about her and her husband. He felt his anger boil up again. If he'd known, he'd have been happy to have punched the guy himself when he turned up in Pelican Crossing. But he hadn't known, hadn't even been aware the guy was in town until he heard of his death. Then Erica had disappeared back to Perth again… until now.

'Okay, Dad?'

Jamie forced his mind back to the present. 'Okay, son. Ready to cast off?'

Rory nodded and they set off, sailing out of the harbour with the wind in their hair and the sun on their faces. It was a perfect day for it, and Jamie had come prepared with a picnic basket from the local deli and several bottles of Coke cooling in the esky below deck.

Jamie didn't say much as they made their way up the coast, steering the boat and letting the chatter of the two young people flow over him. He learnt that Freya was teaching at Sydney University and had met someone she thought might be *the one*, but was taking things slow after a bad experience in California and was reluctant to tell her mother about him. Rory was less forthcoming, but did share that he was keen to settle down, if only he could meet the right person. He alluded to someone he'd known in the past who had moved away. Jamie racked his brains but couldn't figure out who it could be. Rory had always kept his personal life to himself, unlike his brother who had seemed to date a new girl every week… until Mandy. He smiled to himself at how his younger son had settled down, and was now a married man, a proud dad and owned two businesses.

'This is amazing, Mr Whittaker,' Freya said, coming to stand beside Jamie. 'Thanks for allowing me to come along. While I love living in Sydney, I do miss all this.' She waved a hand to encompass the ocean. 'I missed it when I was in California too, but I was too pigheaded to admit it. I was a fool to believe my dad, but Mum and I are all good now.'

'Call me Jamie,' Jamie said. 'Mr Whittaker makes me sound like my dad. Your mum must be glad you're back in Australia.' He knew from what Joe had told him that Gill and Freya's dad had been involved in an acrimonious divorce, which had led to Freya and her mother being estranged for years. At least that hadn't happened to him and Cindy. Their divorce had been reasonably painless. She'd been eager to leave, and he'd been happy to see her go, though he hadn't bargained on being left with the boys. But it had worked out well. They'd always been closer to him than their mother and they did keep in touch with her from time to time.

'She is. I'm glad to be back, and I've even forgiven my dad. Rory says he still sees his mum?'

'She came to Gary's wedding.' Jamie wished he could forget that last meeting with Cindy, forget her not-so-veiled contempt that he was still involved with boats and fishing.

'Anyone hungry?' Rory called, making Jamie realise it was lunchtime.

They anchored in a narrow bay, the waves lapping gently on the side of the boat while Rory unpacked the picnic hamper and poured Coke for him and Freya. Jamie stuck to water, not being a great fan of the carbonated drink.

'Mum and Joe were talking about the article in *The Echo*,' Freya said, 'about the shark nets. I'm glad they've taken them up. What do you think, Mr... Jamie?'

'It's a good move, but not a popular one. There are those who are worried about shark attacks.'

'Surely not?'

'There hasn't been one on this part of the coast that I can remember,' Rory said. 'It's a lot of scaremongering, an attempt by the tourist operators to make everyone feel safe. They *are* safe... and now the whales are too.'

'But it would be horrible to be attacked by a shark.' Freya shivered, despite the heat from the sun.

'Not much chance in Pelican Crossing,' Rory said with a laugh.

'Mmm.' But Freya didn't look convinced.

'Another Coke?' Rory asked and handed her another can, just as the sun disappeared behind a cloud.

Jamie looked up. 'We'd better be getting back,' he said. 'I don't like the look of the sky. There wasn't a storm predicted, but it's best not to take the risk. If you two can pack up, I'll start heading for home.'

As they made their way back, the sky grew darker and darker. They had just tied up when the first large drops of rain fell, forcing them to run for cover in Jamie's office.

'Wow!' Freya said, shaking her dripping hair. 'That happened fast. I'd forgotten about the storms we get here.'

'It won't last,' Rory said. 'We can make a dash for my car, and I'll drive you back to your mum's. Will you be all right, Dad?'

'Sure thing, son.' Jamie chuckled. Rory was acting as if he was an old man. 'I'll sit it out here for a bit, then walk home.' He was glad to have some time to himself. Being out on the ocean with the young couple, plus Freya's mention of Erica, had brought back memories of his own youth, of days when Erica had been his sailing companion in the small eighteen-footer he'd been so proud of. He wondered if she remembered those days too.

Twenty-five

Erica had a restless night. In her dreams she was seventeen again, wandering along the beach hand-in-hand with Jamie. They stopped, kissed and he drew their initials in the wet sand at the edge of the water. Then his face morphed into Geoff's, his expression filled with anger and hate. She awakened, unrefreshed, to see rain streaming down the window and grimaced. Wet days were always busy in the Emergency department with the inevitable car accidents and falls as people lost their footing and slipped on wet surfaces.

As soon as she arrived at work, Erica was pulled into the aftermath of an accident between two cars on the road into town, giving her no time to think about anything other than the task at hand. The stream of patients continued unabated all day, interrupted only by a short break for lunch when she received a call from Joe.

Erica listened impatiently as her brother enthused about his latest project, wishing she'd told him she was too busy to be part of it. But she knew he'd immediately see through her lie. She flinched when she heard the names of the other members of the committee. If she'd known Jamie was going to be involved, she'd definitely have refused… and Malcolm Brown… Since her return to the hospital, she'd been plagued by invitations from the visiting medical officer who seemed to view himself as the answer to her prayers… and those of every other available female in his orbit. He was probably an okay guy, attractive even, but she wasn't in the market for a new partner. She was sure there were many of the nursing staff who'd be happy to be seen on his arm and wasn't sure why he'd picked her to be the focus of his attention.

'You will be there?' Joe asked, clearly worried by her lack of response. 'Thursday at six. You're not working, are you?'

'No, I mean yes, I'll be there. But are you sure you want me to be part of this, Joe? I'm not sure what I can contribute.'

'I do. You can provide the nursing perspective,' he paused, 'and you knew Barb. If we'd had this when she was…' His voice broke.

Erica immediately felt guilty. She should have realised Joe's motivation for this particular project. 'Barb would be proud of you,' she said.

'Thanks, sis.'

'Now, I'm sorry but I have to go. We're rushed off our feet here, and my break's up.' Erica entered the meeting into the calendar on her phone before hurrying back to Emergency where, as she expected, the waiting room was full again.

By the time her shift was over, Erica was exhausted. All she wanted to do was have a hot shower, something to eat and fall into bed. She was in her bathrobe, heating up a ready-cooked meal of cannelloni from the supermarket and sipping a glass of wine, when she heard a loud cry coming from the front yard. It sounded like a child or an animal in pain.

Placing her glass on the kitchen bench, she went to the door and peered out. At first, she couldn't see anything, then there was a loud howl, and two eyes glared at her out of the darkness. The creature, a large ginger cat, yowled again, as if in pain.

'Here, puss,' Erica said. But the cat evaded her outstretched hand, curling itself into a ball on the doorstep and baring its teeth. From the light streaming through the open door, Erica could see the animal was in pain, but every attempt she made to handle it failed, only resulting in her hand being scratched by the creature's claws.

'Who do you belong to?' she said. She hadn't seen the cat around before now, but that wasn't so surprising. From what she knew of cats, they were very territorial. This one must have strayed from home. It might be lost.

Erica was wondering what to do when a figure came rushing along the road calling, 'Tilly! Where are you?' Peering into the darkness, she recognised the woman from *Books and Coffee*.

'I think this may be your cat,' she called, pulling the collar of her bathrobe up to her neck. 'It seems to be hurt.'

'Oh, thank you.' The woman opened Erica's gate. 'I'm sorry if she's been bothering you. She doesn't usually take to strangers.'

'No, she's right,' Erica said, ignoring the scratches on her hand. 'I'm Erica.'

'I'm Lou,' the woman said, coming into the light from the doorway. 'I've seen you at *Books and Coffee*, haven't I? Is Livvy back? Are you staying with her?'

'I'm taking care of the place while she's overseas,' Erica said. 'We were at school together. I'm…'

'I know who you are.' Lou snapped her fingers. 'You're Joe Harris's sister. I should have recognised you straight away. I've seen you with him and Gill.'

By this time, the cat had moved to Lou's side, arching its back and meowing piteously. She picked her pet up, and it nestled into her.

'Why don't you come inside and see what's the matter?' Erica said, her tiredness suddenly vanishing. She was pleased to discover the woman from one of her favourite shops was a neighbour.

'If it's not too much trouble. You look as if you're getting ready for bed.'

'I'm not long home from work. I was just having a glass of wine. You sound as if you could do with one too.'

'Thanks.' Lou followed Erica into the house and through to the kitchen where she examined the cat carefully. 'I think she's been in a fight,' she said, indicating a bald patch behind the animal's ear. 'But I don't see any blood. No need to disturb the vet at this time of night. I think it's her pride that's been hurt. You're going to be all right, Tilly,' she said to the cat who was still meowing loudly.

'Would she like some milk or water?' Erica asked, after she'd poured Lou a glass of wine.

'Water would be good. Thanks for the wine. You work at the hospital, don't you?' she asked, taking a sip.

Erica grimaced. The Pelican Crossing gossip mill was alive and well. She wondered how much more Lou – and the rest of the Pelican Crossing community – knew about her.

'I don't mean to pry,' Lou said. 'A friend of mine had to take her granddaughter into Emergency with a minor injury the other week and she mentioned that our mayor's sister was working there. It's a small town,' she said apologetically.

'I know. I remember.'

'Of course. You grew up here.'

Erica hadn't known Lou back then. She must be at least ten years older than she was and would have left the high school long before Erica started there, before Joe too.

'Rachel is a friend of Gill's… your brother's new partner,' she said. 'Most of us who grew up here are connected one way or another. Take this row of cottages, for example. There's me, Troy Piper, who was in my year at school, your friend, Livvy, and Jamie Whittaker, who must be around your age too. I must apologise. I should have introduced myself sooner, when I became aware someone was living here. We all look out for each other, though we don't live in each other's pockets.'

'Right.' Erica gave a sigh of relief. She didn't want to become involved in any sort of neighbourhood event, the sort she remembered from when she and Joe were growing up. It was something their parents loved, and she and her brother always dreaded – the get-togethers with the neighbours whose children were much younger than they were and always pestered them to become involved in their games. Her relief was short-lived.

'But, as you're a newcomer, we should do something to welcome you, even if you're only going to be here for a short time. It's always good to know who your neighbours are. Leave it with me and I'll be in touch. Now I should leave you to get on with your meal,' she said, as the oven timer went off indicating Erica's dinner was ready for eating. 'Come on, Tilly. Time to get you home.' The cat jumped out of her arms and made for the door, with a mewl of what Erica took to be pleasure.

'Thanks for looking out for Tilly,' Lou said as she was leaving. 'She must have been really scared to come to your door. It's so unlike her.'

Erica wished the cat had chosen someone else's door. While it was good to have met Lou away from the shop, it seemed that fate was conspiring to push her into Jamie's company. First his injury, then the drinks and kitesurfing, for which she had to admit she was partially responsible, then this committee of Joe's, and now Lou's intention to arrange some sort of welcome to the neighbourhood event. She had agreed to being friends with Jamie, she remembered. Maybe this was life's way of sending her a message, maybe she should give in to the inevitable. She sighed. Although she knew her reaction to Jamie was the result of how Geoff had treated her, she felt powerless to change it and move on with her life.

Twenty-six

Jamie was humming to himself as he showered and changed, ready for the first meeting of Joe's new committee. He was looking forward to seeing Erica again. He'd hoped to catch sight of her earlier in the week, but she hadn't been around when he was coming home from work. He knew most of the other members of the committee, only the medico would be a stranger to him. It was typical of Joe to want to involve the people who'd have most to gain from his plan, and to take advantage of their specialised knowledge.

Joe and Cam were the only ones there when Jamie walked into the small meeting room in the council chambers. It was the first time he'd been there, and he felt like a fish out of water in this formal room, the long table surrounded by upright chairs, a credenza at one end on which there was an urn, a tray of cups and saucers, a plate of biscuits, a jug of water and an array of glasses.

'Help yourself,' Joe said, gesturing to the selection.

Jamie noticed he and Cam already had cups of tea or coffee. He would have liked something stronger but dropped a teabag into a cup and filled it from the urn. He heard voices behind him and when he turned back to the room, he saw Phil and an older man who he knew was Paul Clark from the hospital. He'd been on one of Jamie's fishing charters not long after he set up the business.

'Come and meet Paul,' Joe said, pulling him into the group. 'Paul, this is Jamie Whittaker.'

'Jamie, I remember the day you helped me catch a… what was it again?'

Jamie nodded. He couldn't remember either. He had led a lot of charters since then, not all of them as successful.

'The women aren't coming tonight, so perhaps we should make a start,' Joe said, pulling out a chair and indicating the others should do the same.

Just as Jamie was feeling a flash of disappointment at the news Erica wouldn't be there, she walked in with Finn, laughing at something he had said. His heart leapt. Joe was wrong. She was here. They were followed by a smooth-looking man whose black hair held tinges of grey. He was what Jamie supposed many would call distinguished. Joe introduced him as Malcolm Brown, a visiting medical officer at the hospital who would be able to offer his expertise in cancer care. To Jamie's annoyance, he took the seat next to Erica that Jamie had been eyeing for himself. Finn was seated on her other side.

Swallowing his irritation, Jamie sat down opposite Erica and next to Cam. Joe took his place at one end of the table and the meeting got underway.

It was more interesting than Jamie had anticipated. Joe started the meeting with a PowerPoint presentation showing examples of what had been built in other places, plus a projected costing of building the facility here in Pelican Crossing. It was clear he'd already spent some time on this, and Jamie had to admire his vision.

When the presentation was over, and Joe asked if there were any questions, Finn spoke up. 'After my article in *The Echo*, I had a call from someone who wanted to remain anonymous,' he said. 'He claims to have a plot of land he'd be willing to donate to the project, if we can raise enough to build it.'

There was a shocked silence.

'It reminded me of the anonymous donor who saved our newspaper,' Finn said.

Joe nodded, while the two medicos looked surprised. 'It was when we had almost given up,' Joe said. 'Someone donated a large amount which was instrumental in saving our paper.'

'Could it be the same person? Do we have a silent benefactor in Pelican Crossing?' Cam asked what everyone was thinking.

'Well, I guess now we have the incentive to raise the money,' Jamie said chuckling. He wondered who this person was, who was willing to make a sacrifice for the community but didn't want the recognition. He thought he knew most people in town but couldn't think of anyone who would fit this category. As he spoke, he glanced across at Erica and noticed how Malcolm Brown was leaning towards her and whispering in her ear. Damn the man! But he took comfort in the fact that she appeared uneasy with his closeness.

*

Erica shifted in her seat and tried to move away, irritated by the way Malcolm was whispering in her ear, treating her as if they were engaged in some sort of secret communication. She wished it was anyone else sitting beside her, even Jamie. He'd never behave like this. He had more sense than to embarrass her in public. She was interested in what Finn had said. She didn't know about the newspaper, though she was aware it had changed its name from when she was growing up here. She gazed at Joe and Finn. They had saved the town's newspaper? How many other things didn't she know about her brother?

'Erica?' Joe asked.

Erica blushed, suddenly aware that while she'd been wondering about Joe, he'd been going round the group asking for their opinion on his plan. 'It all sounds good to me,' she said, flustered.

He nodded and moved on to Malcolm, who had more to say… a lot more. But he did appear to know what he was talking about.

Erica had forgotten he worked with cancer patients, having only seen him when he passed through Emergency, or in the staff canteen. Perhaps she shouldn't dismiss him too readily, but there was something about him that reminded her of Geoff, that fake charm and a determination to get his own way. She glanced across at Jamie who seemed lost in the medical jargon Malcolm was spouting. She sympathised with him, aware Malcolm was probably only doing this to show his superiority to everyone else in the room. He had a habit of doing that, she'd discovered. It was one of the reasons she avoided him when she could. She sent Jamie a sympathetic smile, suddenly remembering – and appreciating – how down to earth he had always been and still was.

Everyone was right about Jamie. He was genuine and honest, nothing like Malcolm or Geoff. She'd been a fool to imagine anything else. He was the same Jamie she'd known when they were both teenagers, older, perhaps a little worn around the edges. Life had knocked him about – as it had her. He had married, divorced, brought up two teenagers, was now a grandfather – they were both grandparents – but he hadn't changed in ways that mattered.

After what seemed like an interminable time, Joe brought the meeting to a close. Sensing Malcolm was about to speak to her, Erica quickly pushed back her chair and headed over to where Joe was chatting to Jamie. 'Are you pleased with how it went?' she asked her brother.

'I think so. Difficult to judge, but at least everyone seemed to agree on the plan, and the offer of a plot of land is a huge bonus.' He turned away as the Hospital CEO captured his attention.

'How about you?' Jamie asked. 'I suppose you understood all that jargon from Brown.'

'Not all of it. He's a bit of a wanker,' Erica said quietly, not wanting the others to hear. Then, seeing Malcolm coming towards them, added, 'Can we get out of here?'

Jamie seemed surprised but, following her lead, walked with her to the door.

'What was that about?' he asked, when they were standing outside the council chambers.

'Thanks. It's Malcolm Brown. I can't stand the man. I thought he was…' Erica shook her head. Perhaps she had imagined it, but he always made her feel uncomfortable. 'Sorry, I was probably imagining it.'

'I don't think you were. He looks pretty sleazy to me… and you look in need of a drink. *The Grand*'s not far away. How about I drive us there?'

'No, I can drive myself, but a drink sounds good.' Erica couldn't believe how good a drink with Jamie sounded after the way Malcolm had acted in the meeting, as if they were more than passing acquaintances, as if… She shivered. Jamie was by far the preferable option.

Once settled at a corner table in *The Grand*, Erica was again flooded by memories of all the times she and Jamie had come here together in the past. But unlike the last time, tonight the memories didn't distress her. Instead, they produced a good feeling, one of familiarity.

She picked up her glass of wine, taking a sip as she gazed across the table at Jamie, at his smile as he raised his beer in a toast, her heart unexpectedly racing at what he might be about to say.

'To old friends,' he said.

'I'll drink to that,' Erica said, and they clinked glasses.

She took another sip of wine and found herself relaxing in her seat, not quite recognising the strange feeling at first. But for the first time in years, the tension that she carried around the whole time seemed to be lifting, buoyed by a comforting warmth.

'I do like it here,' she said without thinking.

'Me too,' Jamie said, glancing around the place. 'So many great memories.'

'You're right.' Erica raised her glass again. 'To old friends and great memories.'

Twenty-seven

There was a spring in Jamie's step as he made his way to the harbour next morning. Last night, for the first time since meeting up with Erica again, he sensed she was comfortable in his presence. As far as he was concerned, the meeting had been a disaster. He'd felt completely out of his depth, with no idea why Joe had invited him to attend, to be part of the committee. And that jerk, Malcolm Brown, hadn't helped by cosying up to Erica and spouting all that medical jargon which a non-professional like Jamie couldn't hope to understand.

He'd been stunned when Erica came up to him at the end of the meeting and suggested they leave together but had been happy to agree. Then there had been drinks at *The Grand* where it had felt almost as if they were back in the days when they were a couple. They had talked, laughed, shared memories. It was as if Erica was a different person from the one who had told him she didn't want to be reminded of the past. Whatever had happened to her, he wasn't going to question it. Maybe Malcolm Brown had done him a favour.

It was a pity they had travelled in separate cars to the meeting, but perhaps it was just as well. There was no opportunity for anything more than a "Thanks" and "Goodnight" when they parted. But Erica had agreed to go sailing with him on the weekend.

As the party which had booked today's charter straggled on board, Jamie could see they were already hungover from the previous evening. He knew from the booking that they were a group of guys up from Sydney on a bucks' getaway, and previous experience told him it would be a rough trip. He just hoped they hadn't managed to squirrel away more grog in their backpacks.

His worst suspicions were realised. They were barely out of the harbour when one of the group produced a bottle, said, 'The hair of the dog, guys,' and the scene was set for the day.

One plus was that they were happy drunks, and they didn't care that none of them managed to catch anything, seemingly satisfied that they were out on the water. By the time they returned to the harbour in the late afternoon, Jamie's ears were ringing from their raucous voices yelling out the lyrics of popular songs with little regard for the tunes. It was a relief to see them stumble across the wharf, leaving him to clean up the mess they had left.

Although he was desperate for a beer and a chance to unwind in *The Grand* with Cam or whoever else might be there, Jamie knew he didn't have time. He'd promised to take care of young Archie to enable Gary and Mandy to go out for the evening, so he headed home, hoping a shower and change of clothes would work their magic and re-energise him.

As the blast of hot water hit him, Jamie was reminded of the day he and Erica had spent in the rock pool. They hadn't known each other very long and were in the early stages of their relationship. It was when they emerged from the pool and stood together under the outside shower that they shared their first kiss. That was the moment when he knew Erica was the girl for him. Unlike this one, the shower that day had been cold, and they were both shivering when they left it to race to where they had left their towels, taking turns to rub each other dry before pulling their clothes on over their swimmers. Then they'd laughed, hugged and kissed again before heading back to their respective homes to pretend mothing earth-shattering had happened. But it had, and for Jamie, life would never be the same again.

The water was turning cold when he pulled his mind back to the present and the realisation he had to hurry, or he'd be late in arriving at Gary's.

*

It was Jamie's first experience of babysitting his grandson, and he was thrilled to have the opportunity of spending more time with little Archie, sure the boy was going to turn out to be a true Whittaker with the ocean in his blood. As soon as Gary had mentioned he wanted to do something special for Mandy's birthday, Jamie had suggested his son take her to *Crossings* and offered to babysit. But now he was here, although he'd assured a dubious Mandy he could cope, Jamie realised how much he'd forgotten about looking after a small baby. When Rory and Gary were Archie's age, it had been Cindy who did most of the work. He'd been too busy earning a living, leaving early morning on the fishing boat and returning in the evening, too exhausted to do more than have something to eat, take a hot bath and fall into bed. In retrospect, it was a miracle Cindy hadn't left before she did.

At first, everything went well. Jamie fed the little boy, changed his nappy and put him to bed, delighted when he fell asleep right away. He went downstairs, made himself a coffee and cut a slice of the fruit cake Mandy had left for him. As he settled down to watch the footy on Gary's widescreen television, he decided he'd offer to do this more often. It beat being alone in the cottage every night.

But that had been two hours ago. Archie hadn't slept for long. First, Jamie heard a small whimper, which had soon escalated into a cry, then a scream. Fearing the worst, he rushed to the little boy's bedroom to find him thrashing about in his cot, his face beetroot. First, he checked his nappy, then picked him up, trying to remember how Cindy had calmed their two when this happened. But his mind remained obstinately blank. Had he been such a bad father? Had he left it all to Cindy? Surely he had attempted to pacify Rory and Gary at least once?

Nothing worked, and Archie was becoming more and more distressed. Jamie knew he'd need to ask for help. Feeling foolish, he slid his phone out of his pocket and holding Archie in one arm, pressed the number of the one person he knew he could call on for help.

The phone rang and rang. Jamie had almost given up hope, wondering if he'd be forced to admit his failure to Mandy's mum, Liz, and call her instead, risking becoming the laughingstock of all his friends. Then, to his relief, a familiar voice said, 'Hello?'

Twenty-eight

It had been another busy day in Emergency. Erica was enjoying a mug of hot chocolate before going to bed, having decided that an early night was on the cards, and reliving her time with Jamie the previous evening.

Her reflections were interrupted by the ringing of her phone and at first, she chose to ignore it. Then it occurred to her it might be something important, a call in to work for an emergency, bad news from Perth. Had something happened to Briony, or Ava? Without looking at the number on the screen, she pressed to accept the call and, her heart beating rapidly, said, 'Hello?'

'Erica, it's Jamie. I need your help.'

Erica heard the cry of a child in the background. 'Where are you?'

'I'm at Gary's… babysitting, and…'

The crying became louder, turning into a scream. Erica heard Jamie give a groan of anguish, then emit an expletive. She chuckled. It was amazing how the cries of a baby could undo even the strongest man. Geoff would have been the same, though Geoff had never made any attempt to look after Kieren when he was a baby, considering it to be women's work. 'Give me time to get dressed and I'll be with you.'

'Oh, I'm sorry. Were you in bed? There's no need to…' Jamie's voice rose in an attempt to drown out the baby's cries.

'Don't be silly, and no, I wasn't in bed. Text me Gary's address… and in the meantime, try letting the baby suck on your finger.'

'Okay.'

A few seconds later, a text came through with the address for an apartment in an area of town Erica didn't recognise. She dressed in a pair of jeans and a long-sleeved tee-shirt, pulled a brush through her hair and applied a smidgeon of lipstick before heading out to enter the address into the satnav in her car. Then she set off.

Now wide awake and filled with a frisson of excitement at being the one Jamie had chosen to call on for help, Erica discovered she was enjoying driving through the night, the sky lit by myriad bright stars. Before long she arrived at a new apartment block close to the river where she remembered she and Jamie going swimming. She was surprised she hadn't recognised the address, but back then they hadn't been too concerned about street names, and this apartment block hadn't existed.

When she reached the ground floor apartment, the sound of the baby crying reverberated through the door, piercing Erica's ears. When she knocked, Jamie opened it immediately, the crying baby in his arms.

'Thank goodness you're here,' he said. 'I'm at my wit's end.'

Erica took one look at the little boy's red face, the tears running down his cheeks, his nose running too. 'Give him here,' she said, dropping her bag on the floor and reaching out her arms. 'So this is Archie?'

'My grandson,' Jamie said proudly. 'A chip off the old block.'

Erica stared at him, then grinned. 'And I bet you yelled just like this when you were his age. Hello, Archie,' she said to the little boy. 'What's your grandpa been doing to you?' Having a baby in her arms again, reminded Erica so much of her own grandchild, an ache of longing rising up to almost choke her. She missed Ava so much. Hiding her distress by focusing on the young child, Erica began to rock Archie, murmuring to him all the while, and following Jamie through to the little boy's bedroom. Gradually, the crying lessened, subsiding into sobs until his eyes closed and he fell asleep. Careful not to wake him, Erica placed the child in his cot and gently covered him with a blanket. When she looked up, she saw Jamie standing in the doorway, gazing at her with undisguised admiration.

Then she tiptoed out of the room, closing the door gently behind her, and followed Jamie into the kitchen where he took a bottle of wine from the fridge and poured two glasses.

'I think you deserve this, and I need it,' he said, handing one glass to her. 'I'm sure Gary can spare it. If not, I'll replace it. I don't know how you did it,' he said, shaking his head. 'It was magic.'

Erica took a welcome sip of wine and laughed. 'It comes naturally,' she said. 'I'm guessing you didn't have a lot to do with your two when they were babies.'

Jamie looked down into his glass. 'I was away on the boat a lot. Didn't often get to see them at bedtime… or any other time, come to think of it. I'm surprised Cindy put up with me as long as she did. But I did have a living to earn, and I was a fisherman. I know it's no excuse,' he said, clearly seeing Erica open her mouth to speak.

'I was only going to say that most men would say the same, fishermen or not. It usually falls to the woman to take care of the children when they're small. But you stepped up when you had to.'

'Mmm.'

Suddenly, the ache of longing for Ava that Erica had experienced when she had young Archie in her arms, returned like a sharp pain for which there was no relief. Her eyes moistened.

'Hey, what's the matter, Rici?'

At the sound of what had been Jamie's pet name for her all those years ago, a host of memories of those days resurfaced, and Erica began to sob uncontrollably. 'Sorry,' she said, 'it's…' She brushed back the tears with her hand.

'Hey, it's okay,' Jamie said, putting down his glass and moving closer. He took Erica's glass and placed it next to his on the benchtop.

Feeling as if time stood still, Erica didn't resist when he cupped her chin in his hands, then his lips met hers, gently at first, deepening into a passionate kiss, a kiss that felt so familiar, so all consuming.

So… *wonderful.*

Twenty-nine

When she awoke next morning, Erica was glad she didn't have to go to work. It had been late when she got back home, still trying to process that kiss. Although she'd harboured warmer feelings towards Jamie after Joe's meeting, even contemplated forming a closer friendship, kissing hadn't been part of her plan. He'd caught her at a weak moment, she decided, when she was missing Ava. But that didn't excuse her response and the way her heart raced, the surge of excitement she felt as their lips met. It had been like coming home.

Now, in the cold light of day, she wondered how she could have allowed her emotions to take over. But she couldn't suppress the memory of Jamie's lips on hers, his arms around her, the familiar scent of his cologne. It was as if they'd never been apart, as if all those years with Geoff had never happened, and she and Jamie were teenagers again. Erica blinked to dismiss the image of Jamie which filled her mind, and leapt out of bed. An early morning swim was what she needed to bring her back to her senses.

When Erica arrived at the beach, she was glad Gill wasn't there. She didn't want to face her while she was still trying to work out why she had responded to Jamie's kiss. She ran into the ocean, flinching as the cold water hit her skin, and swam out through the waves, the need to keep moving sending everything else from her mind. But when she turned to float on her back, as she always did, and looked up at the changing colours of the sky, it all came back to her – Jamie, the kiss, the way she'd felt. She didn't know how long she lay there, trying to forget his strength, his warmth, the dizzying current of emotion which had raced through her, reminding her… It was time to go back to the shore.

Gill was already there, standing next to Erica's towel, waiting for her.

'You were out there a long time,' she said. 'A lot on your mind?'

Erica gave her a puzzled look. How did she know?

'I used to do that when I felt confused,' Gill said. 'There's something about the ocean and the morning sky that helps you get things in perspective.'

'Hmm.' It hadn't done Erica much good this morning, and she hoped Gill wouldn't pursue her line of thought.

She didn't. 'I hear you were at Joe's meeting on Thursday,' Gill said instead. 'I don't know why he invited you to join that one. The women are meeting separately. Unless…' She raised one eyebrow. 'Was Jamie Whittaker there?'

Erica stared at her in amazement. She couldn't mean…? Joe wouldn't be so devious, would he? *Of course he would*, she thought. Once her big brother got an idea in his head, he'd do whatever it took to make it happen. 'Yes,' she said abruptly, vowing to take Joe to task next time she saw him, to tell him to butt out of her love life. She was so incensed, it was a few minutes before she realised the words she had used in her head. She wasn't in love with Jamie Whittaker. She didn't intend to fall in love with anyone ever again.

'We're meeting today for lunch. Why don't you join us?' Gill asked.

'You and Joe?' Erica didn't know if she could face her brother just yet, if he had knowingly pushed her into Jamie's company, hoping… and she'd fallen right into his plan. Though not last night, she reminded herself. Helping Jamie out with little Archie… and that kiss… had nothing to do with her brother.

'No,' Gill laughed, as she rubbed her hair with a towel, 'the group of women who are working on Joe's project. We've decided to meet separately as we don't want to be bothered by all the building issues the others will be discussing. I think you know evryone. Besides me, there's Poppy, Liz, who's practice manager at the medical centre, and Rachel. They were all at the barbecue. The four of us have known each other since our eldest were babies and we've continued to meet for lunch every month. Now we've decided to become involved in Joe's latest project, we've added some extra meetings. We've invited Kate too, though she will probably also be involved with the other group, given her role as town planner. We're meeting at Poppy's today at twelve.'

*

Still fuming at the way Joe had managed to manipulate her into meeting up with Jamie again, even though everything that had happened after the meeting was all her own doing, Erica prepared to attend this other meeting. She pulled on a pair of grey tailored pants and a pale blue cashmere sweater which always made her feel good and applied a touch of makeup.

Erica knew the way to Poppy's home on the clifftop, having been there with Joe on her previous visit. Growing up in Pelican Crossing, Erica had always admired Poppy, wishing to emulate the older girl's elegance and style. She remembered hearing how Poppy and her husband had built this house and brought up their three daughters there before he drowned in a freak accident. It happened just as they were about to open their restaurant, which was now *Crossings*. It had been Poppy who recommended Gill to Erica as her solicitor, the woman who had become her close friend and Joe's partner.

She was looking forward to seeing the other women too. She'd met Liz and liked the outspoken woman, but the thought that she was now Jamie's son's mother-in-law did give her pause for thought. It seemed that, wherever she went in this town there was some link to, or reminder of Jamie. At least she didn't believe there were any connections between him and the other two woman who'd be at the lunch meeting, though Rachel and Kate had both been at the barbecue at Joe's where she'd met Jamie and… Her stomach churned at the memory of how he'd appeared behind her in the kitchen and sent her emotions swirling.

Taking a deep breath, she got out of the car and made her way to the house. As soon as she knocked on the door, there was the sound of barking. Erica had forgotten about Poppy's dog, a cute little West Highland Terrier.

'Angus!' Poppy said, when she opened the door, and the little ball of white jumped up on Erica.

'He's fine,' Erica said, ruffling the dog's ears. 'I'm used to Joe's Coco, and she's more than twice Angus's size. I love dogs.'

'Maybe you should get one of your own. Angus proved to be wonderful company for me after Jack died. I'm sorry, I didn't mean to…' Poppy reddened.

'There's no need.' Erica brushed away Poppy's apology. She wasn't sorry about Geoff's death. 'You may be right about a dog.' It occurred to her that a dog would be good company, and Rhana would be sure to have a litter available sometime soon. Maybe she should ask Livvy if she'd be okay with Erica having a dog in the cottage.

'We're on the deck.' Poppy led the way through the house and out onto the wide deck overlooking the ocean, where three women were seated with glasses of wine at a table on which were several platters of cold meats, cheeses and breads. It looked more like a party than a business meeting.

'Kate wasn't able to make it,' Poppy said. 'I think you know everyone here.'

'I saw you at your brother's barbecue, but we haven't been introduced. I'm Rachel,' said one of the women. She looked older than the others and was wearing a loose shirt. Erica wondered if she was self-conscious about her size. The others were all slim. Having often felt self-conscious herself, due to Geoff's treatment of her, Erica immediately felt a connection with her.

'I saw you at the barbecue. It's lovely to meet you properly,' Erica said.

'Now we're all here, why don't we get started,' Poppy said, handing Erica a glass of wine. 'Erica was fortunate – or unfortunate – enough to be at the meeting the men held on Thursday. Maybe you can fill us in on what was discussed, Erica? Meanwhile, everyone, feel free to help yourselves to food.'

Stunned to be placed in the spotlight, Erica hesitated for a few moments. Then, seeing the interested expressions on the faces around the table, she began to speak, outlining what she could remember of the meeting and ending with, 'and there was a lot of medical jargon spouted by Malcolm Brown who was the token doctor.' It suddenly occurred to her she had perhaps been the token nurse, as she was in this group.

'Thanks, Erica.' It was Rachel who spoke first. 'What a wonderful gesture from this benefactor who wishes to remain anonymous. I wonder who it can be.' She gazed around the group, but everyone shook their heads. 'You've given us a clearer picture of what Joe plans. What we need to do, ladies, is make sure we raise sufficient funds to make it happen.'

There was a murmur of agreement, then Poppy took charge. 'Well, so far, we've agreed on a winter fair. Any other ideas?'

'How about we make it a Christmas in July fair?' Liz suggested, evoking a burst of laughter from the others.

Erica was puzzled.

'Liz always insists we have a Secret Santa at our July lunch,' Poppy explained, 'but it's a good idea. Thanks, Liz.'

Liz beamed.

'Anything else?'

'There was mention of a walk,' Liz said. 'I'm sure Mandy would be prepared to organise that, and it would be good to get the younger generation involved.'

'Good plan,' Poppy said, making notes on a notepad. *She was the leader of the group*, Erica thought. It wasn't a surprise. She'd always been a leader at school.

While hesitant to make a suggestion, Erica said, 'What about a ball? When I was a student nurse in Sydney, before I married, the hospital held a ball to raise funds for a new wing. I believe it was very successful.'

'Sounds like something you could organise, Poppy,' Gill said. 'Thanks, Erica.'

Erica sat back, pleased to have contributed, happy now to listen as the others bandied about some other suggestions.

Finally, the meeting came to an end, with Erica feeling more a part of the group than she'd expected when she arrived. She was preparing to leave, and the others were saying their farewells, when Poppy pulled her aside.

'I'm glad to hear you and Jamie are seeing each other,' she said. 'He's been lonely for a long time and needs someone to care for him.'

'I'm not...' Erica began, while wondering how Poppy knew, but she was interrupted by Gill saying, 'Why don't you come back with me? Joe has something he wants to show you.'

Erica hesitated, wondering if this was a ploy of her brother's to quiz her about Jamie. She couldn't bear to spend an evening being interrogated about their friendship, because that was all it was, for now anyway. But this was Joe who had been so good to her, who had provided her with refuge – twice – when she had nowhere else to go. 'Okay,' she said, hoping she wasn't making a huge mistake.

Thirty

Jamie had just returned from a day out with a group of Rotarians from down the coast. They had been a pleasant bunch to spend time with and to his delight they had all managed to make a catch. He was tying up and looking forward to a beer and a hot shower, not necessarily in that order when his phone rang.

'Hey,' he said, seeing Joe's number. 'What can I do for you?'

'You free for dinner? I won the raffle in the club last night and have a huge tray of steak Gill and I need help eating. Also, I have something I want to show you.'

'Yeah?' Jamie was curious, not so much about the steak which he guessed was a ruse, but what could Joe possibly have to show him?

'Yeah,' Joe said, clearly unwilling to give anything away. 'So, are you free?'

'Never let it be said I turned down a free feed, but you've sparked my interest. Any clues?'

'Wait till you get here. Come when you're ready.' He ended the call.

Jamie stared at his phone for a moment, then shrugged. It wasn't like Joe to be so secretive, but there was no sense in wondering what he was up to. He'd find out soon enough. He finished with the boat, went to the office to update the data on his computer, then walked home, enjoying the sight of a trio of pelicans crossing his path. These big birds were such a common sight here, and one he never tired of.

Once home, he headed for the shower, enjoying the jet of hot water cascading over his body as it washed away the detritus of the day, his mind going to the previous evening, to Erica and their kiss. He hadn't planned it, but it was something he'd wanted to do ever since he saw her again. She'd been so upset, he couldn't help himself, and she hadn't resisted. After they'd pulled apart, she'd explained how being with Archie had made her miss her granddaughter even more. He'd hugged her then, and for a brief moment she'd leant into him for comfort, before pulling away and apologising. He'd never understand women.

Deciding there was no need to dress up for Joe, while wondering why his friend had chosen him to share his meat tray rather than one of his other friends, Jamie pulled on a pair of jeans and teamed them with one of his better tee-shirts before adding a checked overshirt. Then, pulling a six-pack out of the fridge, he set off. He glanced at Erica's cottage as he passed, but there was no sign of her.

Jamie was whistling as he walked up to Joe's open door to be greeted by Coco, who sniffed at his feet before heading back inside. He knocked and called, 'Anyone home?' then followed the dog into the house.

'We're out here,' Joe called, and following the sound, Jamie went through the house and out into the yard where Joe and Gill were seated with… Erica.

Erica was laughing at something Gill had said. She looked up when Jamie walked in, her expression changing. It seemed she hadn't been expecting to see him either. Jamie was immediately transported back to the previous evening, to the moment their lips met. He reddened and rubbed the back of his neck with his free hand. 'Hey,' he said, including all three in his greeting, and dropped the beer on the bench by the barbecue.

'Thanks, mate,' Joe said with a grin, clearly enjoying his embarrassment. Had Erica said something about…? 'Erica was telling us how you called on her to help you out with the grandson.'

'Oh! Yeah, she was a big help.' He glanced at Erica who was blushing too. Maybe she hadn't mentioned the kiss. *Was she regretting it? Was that why she'd pulled away and left soon afterwards?* 'It's a long time since my two were little… and Cindy was there to carry most of the load.'

'Typical man!' Gill said, but her smile belied her words.

'How is the little fellow?' Joe asked, handing Jamie a beer.

'Thanks. He's good, thriving, has a fine voice which he proved last night.' He grimaced.

'They'll do that,' Gill said with a grin. 'It's a long time since Freya was that age, but I remember. You were spared that joy, Joe.'

'Sadly.' It was Joe's turn to grimace, and Jamie remembered how sad Joe and Barb had been that they never had children.

'Sorry, honey.' Gill patted Joe's arm.

Joe sighed. 'I didn't have much to do with Kieren either,' he said to Erica.

'No, not my doing, it was Geoff who…' She bit her lip. 'But if I have anything to do with it, you'll see more of Ava. Last night made me realise how much I'm missing her. Briony promised to visit me here. I need to get her to set a date.'

Jamie glanced across at Erica sympathetically, but she didn't meet his eyes. He wondered why he was really here. Had Joe brought him here on false pretences? The meat tray was real enough. It was sitting by the barbecue – more meat than the four of them could possibly eat, but was there really anything Joe wanted to show him?

Jamie took a swallow of beer, then said, 'What's this all about, Joe? You said you had something to show me?'

'Me too,' Erica said, sounding annoyed. 'Was it just a ploy to get us both here?'

'Now, why would you think that?' Joe asked. 'I do have something, but all in good time. Let's eat first.'

Gill rolled her eyes as Joe rose and went across to the barbecue, Coco following at the prospect of something to eat.

'Need a hand?' Jamie joined Joe at the barbecue. He had the distinct impression that Erica wasn't pleased about his presence and he wanted to put as much distance between him and her as possible in this small backyard.

*

Erica couldn't believe Joe had done it again. When Jamie walked in, her heartbeat throbbed in her ears and a surge of desire flared through her, followed by a spurt of annoyance at her brother. He'd got her here under false pretences. And it looked as if he'd pulled the same trick on Jamie. She wondered if Gill had been part of the plot, but she seemed as surprised to see Jamie as Erica was. She was tempted to finish her wine and go home, to leave Joe to explain to Jamie why he was here. But something stopped her.

'Did you know?' she murmured to Gill, gesturing to where Joe and Jamie were loading steaks onto the hot plate, a salivating Coco at their feet.

'Not a whisper,' Gill replied, 'but it's not a big deal, is it? You two are friends. He's a good guy, and you're both single. Joe's just doing what a good brother does. He's looking out for you. He wants you to be happy, especially now he and I…'

'That's the point,' Erica broke in, not allowing Gill to finish. 'They talk about women matchmaking, but they've got nothing on my big brother.'

'Don't you like Jamie? I think he's rather hot.'

'I…' Erica felt her face warm. 'I agree he's a good guy… and attractive. But, Gill, you know what I've been through. How can I let another man into my life and how can I ever trust my own judgement again?' She took a gulp of wine.

'I understand. I see women like you every day, and my own history with men is nothing to boast about. But if you let your experiences with Geoff colour your view of every other man you meet, you're allowing him to continue to control you. Do you really want to do that?'

'Of course not! But…'

'What are you two looking so serious about?' Joe asked, when he and Jamie returned with a platter of enormous steaks.

'Women-talk,' Gill said with a smile, much to Erica's relief. 'I'll just fetch a couple of salads from the fridge.' She rose.

'Need any help?' Erica asked, reluctant to be left with the two men. Her mind was still reeling from what Gill had said. *Was she still allowing Geoff to dominate her?*

'No, thanks. I won't be a minute.'

Left alone with the two men and Coco, who was chewing on a piece of steak Joe had dropped into a bowl for him, Erica forced a smile to her face and took a sip of wine.

'Let me top you up,' Jamie said, picking up the bottle of wine.

Erica held out her glass, her eyes meeting Jamie's which were filled with such affection, she felt a warm glow envelop her. 'Thanks,' she muttered trying to deny the pulsing knot that had formed in her stomach. She was glad when Gill returned with two bowls of salad. She took one from her and placed it on the table as her breathing returned to normal.

The steak was delicious, cooked to perfection, and Erica made a mental note to ask Gill for the recipe for one of the salads. To her relief, the conversation revolved around Joe's latest project, and the fundraising activities the women proposed. Joe liked the idea of a ball, but it seemed to make Jamie uncomfortable.

'I'm not one for dressing up in a fancy suit,' he said with a frown.

Erica could remember him wearing one for the school formal. She could still picture him in the black tuxedo with satin lapels, a pale blue frilled shirt and black bow tie, his hair almost brushing his shoulders. She'd thought he looked so grownup and dashing.

'What?' he said, staring at her.

'Nothing.'

'Erica can probably remember we all got dressed up in dinner suits for our formal,' Joe said with a grin. 'We got together at our place for a few bevvies beforehand to give us Dutch courage. Those were the days.'

'I think I might be glad I didn't know you then,' Gill laughed.

When the meal was finally over, and Gill had gone into the kitchen to make coffee, Coco following in the hope of more food, Joe said, 'Let's go inside.'

Erica and Jamie followed him into the living room. Erica was curious as to what was coming next and assumed Jamie was too. Knowing her brother's old propensity for playing pranks and given his current tendency to push her and Jamie together, she was wary of what he wanted to show them.

Joe waited till Gill appeared with coffee and a tray of biscotti before launching into his explanation.

'Now I've decided to put this place on the market, I've been doing a bit of clearing out,' he said, 'and in the process, I've come across some old school magazines I thought you might be interested in. I invited Cam and Poppy over too, but they had something else on. We'll catch up another time.'

Erica felt more comfortable at the news Cam and Poppy had also been invited. Perhaps she had maligned Joe unfairly, but she still didn't trust his motives. She had never been part of his peer group at school, so why was *she* here?

'There are some of you too, Erica,' Joe said, when he and Jamie were laughing over photos of them playing footy and dressed in weird outfits for Halloween and the school play. 'Look!' He opened one to show Erica a photo of her with Livvy and Rhana. The three girls were standing behind a stall, above which was a sign which read *Help our Animals.*

'Oh, I remember that day,' Erica said, laughing now too. 'It was all Rhana's doing. She was besotted with animals back then too. We made cakes and biscuits and brought them to school, sold them in aid of the RSPCA. As I recall, we did very well.'

'I remember it too,' Jamie said with a grin. He seemed about to say more but stopped.

Erica was glad. She remembered that day all too well. She and Jamie had only just started dating and after school, he had taken her out on his boat. He had received the Princess 18 monohull sailboat as an eighteenth birthday gift, and it was his pride and joy. It had been the first of many such trips, trips she'd always remember. She swallowed hard when Joe opened the next magazine because there, on the third page, was a photo of Jamie with his sailboat, along with Joe, Cam and Jack, who'd been Cam's best friend and was Poppy's late husband.

'That was a cracker,' Joe said, pointing to the boat. 'You were always going to spend your life on the water, weren't you?'

'Couldn't imagine doing anything else. Interestingly, I recently managed to locate a Princess 18, built in 1990, one of the last.'

'You bought it?'

'Of course.' Jamie glanced across at Erica as he spoke.

She blushed.

'Excuse my ignorance. Are we talking about a yacht or a motorboat, and what's so special about it?' Gill asked.

Jamie was quick to reply. 'The Princess 18 is an eighteen-foot sailboat with a fibreglass hull. It's beautifully designed, an award-winning yacht. There's nothing quite like it… in my opinion anyway. I was lucky to find this one. And it brings back so many memories for me.' He glanced across at Erica again.

'Right.' Gill appeared satisfied. 'Any more coffee, anyone?'

Erica checked her watch. The time had flown. 'I should be going,' she said. 'Thanks for dinner… and for this, Joe. What do you intend to do with them?' she gestured to the pile of magazines.

'I'm not sure. It seems a pity to toss them, but they're not much use to anyone, unless…?'

'I'd like the one with the photo of me with Livvy and Rhana. I'd love to show it to them.'

'Sure, it's all yours.' He handed it to her. 'Jamie?'

'I'll take the one with the Princess, thanks,' Jamie said, reddening. Do what you like with the rest of them, after Cam and Poppy have a look.'

'Will do.'

'I should be going too,' Jamie said. 'Are you walking or driving, Erica?'

'I'm driving. I came here straight from Poppy's. You?' she asked, without thinking.

'I walked.'

There was a pause while his words sunk in. Joe was busy gathering the magazines together, and Gill was collecting the empty cups.

'Would you like a ride?' Erica wasn't sure what prompted her to make the offer, perhaps the memories the photos had stirred up, perhaps Gill's words about Geoff.

'Thanks, that would be great.' Jamie grinned, making Erica's stomach churn. Now she was going to be stuck in her car with him. At least it would be a short trip.

No sooner were they in the car than Jamie said, 'You remember the Princess, don't you?'

'Of course.' How could she forget those summer days out on the water, the wind in her hair, the sun beating down on her and Jamie, his tanned arms, the way his muscles rippled as he trimmed the sails.

'She was a beauty, but this new one is pretty good too. Want to come out on her sometime?'

Did she? Did she want to revive those memories she'd consigned to the back of her mind, the ones which kept re-emerging each time she saw Jamie? She remembered her decision, how she couldn't trust men, couldn't trust her own judgment. Then she remembered Gill's words again. *Was she going to allow Geoff to control her for the rest of her life?* And this wasn't just any man. This was Jamie. 'I'd love to,' she said.

Thirty-one

Jamie was humming to himself as he made his way to the marina where the sailboat he called Princess Two was berthed. His Princess was too elegant to be moored among the fishing boats and his charter vessel in the harbour. He could scarcely believe Erica had agreed to come sailing with him. It seemed only yesterday that he had been out sailing with Rory and Freya remembering when it had been Erica sailing with him.

He wasn't sure what had happened at Joe's last night to bring this about. He'd been positive Erica hadn't expected him to be there; her expression when he walked in had been far from welcoming. But somehow, over the course of the evening, she'd thawed, and when their eyes met over the old school magazines, he'd known she was remembering, just as he was.

It was all down to Joe and his new lady. Gill didn't say much, but Jamie had the impression she might have had a quiet word with Erica when he and Joe were busy with the barbecue. Whatever she'd said, it seemed to have helped change Erica's mind which Jamie was sure had been firmly set against seeing more of him, even after he kissed her. He would be eternally grateful to Joe for arranging last night, even though it could have gone horribly wrong.

Hearing footsteps, Jamie looked up to see Erica walking towards him. This morning, she was wearing a pair of tight pants topped with a hooded jacket in the same shade of blue as her eyes. She looked good enough to eat. Thinking of eating reminded him that he had arranged to pick up a picnic basket from *The Blue Dolphin Café*. He'd already stashed a couple of bottles of water and a flask of coffee in the cabin.

'Good morning.' Erica's smile sent Jamie's heart racing. It was as if time had stood still, the past thirty-odd years had disappeared, and they were teenagers again.

'Morning.'

'You were right. She's a beauty,' Erica said. 'Can I come on board?'

'Sure. But I need to head over to *The Blue Dolphin* to pick up our lunch. Do you want to…?'

'I can come with you.' She smiled.

Jamie swallowed. This was a very different Erica from the one who had cold-shouldered him, who had pulled away from his kiss. He wondered how long it would be before she became distant again but decided to enjoy this version of her while it lasted.

The picnic hamper picked up and safely stowed in the cabin, Jamie cast off, the slight breeze helping their journey out of the harbour. Once in the open sea, he headed up the coast aiming for the small bay where they used to anchor, where they'd swim into shore and lie together on the sand. It was too cold for swimming today, though he guessed Erica might have already plunged into the ocean at the crack of dawn with the other wild swimmers.

'This is lovely,' Erica said, coming to stand by Jamie's side.

'Bring back memories?' Jamie risked saying, mindful of her earlier comment that she didn't want to be reminded of the past. But how could they not? The past was all around them. It was what made them the people they were today. It was impossible to ignore.

'Mmm.' Erica was silent for a few moments, then added, 'I know what I said earlier. I did want to put the past behind me, start afresh. But I've discovered it's not so easy. Being here, meeting you, it's brought it all back. The good times, and the bad.'

'There were bad times?'

Erica gazed into the distance. 'Not here. My memories of Pelican Crossing are all good. I loved growing up here. It was after I left…' She stopped, and it was as if she'd gone back to that place where Jamie couldn't follow.

'Do you want to talk about it?' Jamie kept his eyes on the horizon to allow Erica the space he felt she needed, hoping she'd feel she could confide in him.

For what seemed like for ever there was silence, then Erica said, 'As you may have gathered, my marriage wasn't happy. That was why I came to stay with Joe last year. I intended to divorce Geoff. Gill helped me set up an AVO, an apprehended violence order. Then he followed me here. The rest you know.'

It was much of what Joe had told him, though he suspected Erica had left a lot out. She'd stayed in the marriage for a long time, longer than he and Cindy had been married. Had she been too afraid to leave him? Jamie risked a glance at her face. It was wet with tears. He wanted to pull her into his arms and comfort her, but wasn't sure any expression of affection from him would be welcome right now. 'I'm sorry,' he said. 'You deserved better.'

'Thanks, Jamie. You always knew how to make me feel good.'

Jamie smiled. At least he'd got something right.

*

Erica wasn't sure why she'd confided in Jamie, told him things about her marriage she'd vowed to keep to herself. But there was something about being out here with him on the ocean, in this boat which was a replica of the one they used to sail in, that made her feel safe, safe enough to tell him about her unhappiness, to reveal why she'd left Geoff.

It was a glorious day. Out here on the water, skimming along with the light breeze in her hair, the sun on her face, the sea sparkling like diamonds in the sunlight, it was easy to forget the more recent past, to forget Geoff, even to forget her worry about Kieren. She made a deliberate attempt to put it all behind her and live for the moment, just as she had done when she and Jamie were together all those years ago.

Erica was glad Jamie hadn't asked any more questions. There were still things she wasn't prepared to share with him. It was enough they were here together.

They sailed on in silence, Erica's thoughts on the man beside her, how he hadn't changed from the boy she'd fallen in love with. Although she had no intention of reigniting those feelings, it was tempting to imagine what her life could be like if…

'Recognise where we are?' Jamie's voice broke into her musing, and Erica realised they were entering the small bay where he used to anchor, where they had spent so many hours swimming, lying on the sand and planning their future, a future which had never come to pass.

What would her life have been like, Erica wondered, if she had never met Geoff, if she had returned to Pelican Crossing after she graduated, if she had married Jamie. 'I do,' she said, horrified by her choice of words. *Could Jamie tell what she was thinking?* 'But it looks a lot different to what I remember,' she added hurriedly.

'Time has taken its toll here, like it has everywhere else. Nothing stays the same. The bushes have grown and taken over what was just rough grass last time you saw it. I often come here, and I've watched it change over the years. It's changed, just as we have. But change isn't always a bad thing.'

'I suppose not.'

By this time, they had sailed into the bay, and Jamie had dropped anchor.

'Hungry?' he asked.

Erica realised she was. It was a long time since breakfast which had only been a slice of toast and vegemite. After her early morning swim, she'd been too wired to eat any more, excited at the prospect of going sailing with Jamie. After a quick breakfast, she'd called Briony, knowing she'd catch her before Kieren was up and about. The car yard opened late on Sundays, and like his dad, he enjoyed sleeping late on what was for most people a day of rest. 'Starving,' she said.

'Good.' Jamie's face crinkled into the lopsided smile that hadn't changed from the one which had stolen her heart at the tender age of sixteen, though now it was surrounded by wrinkles and the skin of his face was tanned by years of being out in all weathers. It was still a handsome face, she decided, perhaps more so due to the passage of years and the struggles he'd endured.

He disappeared, to reappear carrying a basket which he placed on the deck. 'Be right back,' he said, going into the cabin again. When he came out, he was carrying a bag from which he pulled out a flask, two bottles of water and two plastic mugs.

'No wine?' Erica said with a laugh.

'Not while we're sailing. Passengers who bring alcohol on board are the bane of my life.'

'Sorry, only joking.' Erica remembered how careful Jamie had always been about safety. He had never allowed alcohol on his boat.

When opened, the basket proved to contain a collection of delicacies including individual quiches, slices of ham, crusty bread, cheeses and pieces of fruit. It was a veritable feast and far removed from the corned beef and tomato sandwiches and cans of Coke she used to pack for their sailing trips.

When they had finished eating, Erica leant back against the side of the yacht and closed her eyes, letting the sun beat down on her face, the only sound the lapping of the waves on the side of the vessel and the cry of the seabirds circling overhead. 'This is perfect,' she said, her lips turning up into a smile.

'Perfect,' Jamie agreed.

Opening her eyes, Erica saw he was looking straight at her.

'You're perfect too, more beautiful than ever.'

Erica blushed, suddenly feeling awkward, and wishing they were anywhere but in the middle of the ocean. There was no escape. *But did she want one?*

'It's okay,' Jamie laughed. 'I'm not going to rush you into anything. I just want you to know that when you're ready, I'm here. I always will be.'

'Thanks.' Erica swallowed hard. She'd known she could trust Jamie. He seemed to understand. It was just that out here, if anything did happen, there was nowhere to run. She had always been in the habit of ensuring she had an escape route when Geoff's anger built up. Sometimes, it had only been the bedroom, at others the backyard. Once, she'd even taken Kieren, who was a toddler at the time, and spent an hour in the park, till she judged Geoff would have calmed down. Sometimes, she didn't manage it. Those were the times she ended up with bruises which she explained away as her having been clumsy.

Jamie didn't respond. He merely smiled.

It was late afternoon by the time they reached the harbour again. It would soon be dark. Erica helped Jamie tie up and secure the boat. 'Thanks for a wonderful day,' she said, as they stood together on the dock. 'I'll…'

'We're going the same way,' Jamie said. 'Why don't we walk together?'

'Okay.' Erica wasn't sure what she'd expected, perhaps that he'd have work to do in his office before returning home. She wondered how he normally spent his Sunday evenings, the weekday evenings too. Like her, he lived alone and… hadn't he said something about not getting out much? Should she invite him in for a drink when they reached Livvy's cottage? She glanced at him out of the side of her eye, noting his cheerful expression. What was he thinking?

When they came to a halt at her front gate, Erica, having made the decision to move out of her comfort zone, asked, 'Would you like to come in for a drink?' and held her breath waiting for his reply.

'Thanks,' Jamie said. 'I'd love to some other time, but I promised to catch up with Rory this evening. He has something he wants to discuss with me.'

'Right. Another time, then. Bye, and thanks again.' Without waiting for Jamie to make any other sign of farewell, Erica pushed open the gate.

Her heart was thumping as she fitted the key into the door, forcing herself not to look back to see if Jamie was watching. She wasn't sure if what she was feeling was disappointment or relief. She knew it should have been the latter – she didn't want the complication of a relationship with Jamie Whittaker again – but suspected it wasn't. It had been so good to go sailing with him again, so good that she'd forgotten herself sufficiently to invite him into her home for a drink. Then what, she wondered. She trusted Jamie, but did she trust herself? It had been so long since she'd found a man attractive, since anyone had told her she was beautiful. That was it, she told herself. She had only responded to the first compliment anyone other than her brother had paid her. It was nothing to do with Jamie's undoubted attraction, how he had matured over the years to become *hot*, just as Gill had said.

Having decided that to her satisfaction, Erica dropped her bag on the hall table and went through to the kitchen to pour herself a much-needed glass of wine. She needed one, even if Jamie didn't.

Taking the wine through to the living room, Erica retrieved her phone to check her messages, pleased to see one from Briony. When they'd spoken earlier, Erica had broached the subject of her daughter-in-law's promised visit, telling her how much she missed both her and little Ava, singing the praises of Pelican Crossing, and offering to pay their airfare if Kieren objected. She didn't want to cause trouble between her son and his wife but wanted Briony to know she was there for her in the event she needed an escape route. Erica wished she'd known of one herself when Kieren was a baby, though perhaps she wouldn't have been sensible enough to take it, always hoping things would get better.

Erica opened her phone, took a sip of wine and read Briony's message.

Good to talk this morning, Mum. Would love to visit you. Pelican Crossing sounds perfect. Didn't get a chance to see it properly last year with Dad dying like that. Spoke to Kieren and he's okay for me and Ava to visit for a few days – maybe a week? No need for you to pay our fare. Will let you know dates as soon as. She finished with a smiley emoji.

Erica smiled too. She quickly replied.

Fantastic. Look forward to hearing from you. Give Ava a hug for me. Mum x

She'd concentrate on Briony's visit, Erica decided. Anything else was the sure route to disappointment or worse. And while she wasn't quite sure what worse might look like where Jamie was concerned, she didn't want to find out.

Thirty-two

It was almost two weeks since she'd gone sailing with Jamie. Erica hadn't heard from him and was wondering if she'd said something to offend him. Although her days were busy at the hospital, she still had the evenings to remember what it had been like to be with him on the ocean and how he had made her feel. She knew she was being foolish when she was the one who didn't want a relationship, but he had said he was there for her. Did he mean she had to be the one to make the first move? While she wasn't sure she was ready for that, she did miss the easy companionship they'd fallen into on his boat.

It was Friday night, and she had arranged to meet Joe and Gill at the yacht club along with a group of their friends. She already counted Cam and Poppy, and Liz and Finn as *her* friends too, and tonight Kate was joining them. It would be good to get to know her better. There had been no mention of Jamie, but Erica suspected he might be included, though if so, why had no one said?

To Erica's annoyance, she felt a stab of disappointment when there was no sign of Jamie at the table Joe had booked. *What was wrong with her?* She smiled and greeted the other members of the group and was soon involved in a discussion about Joe's pet project, while Gill rolled her eyes.

'It's all he can talk about these days,' she murmured to Erica during a break in the conversation, 'but there's something attractive about his single-mindedness, and it's such a good cause.'

Erica agreed. She knew what her brother was like when he got the bit between his teeth. She remembered Barb despairing of him too but like Gill, she'd loved him for it.

The discussion wound up when their meals arrived, the group having chosen to share several seafood platters which they washed down with a Margaret River sauvignon blanc and followed by decadent chocolate mousse.

During the meal, Erica had noticed Jamie's sons at a distant table with a group of friends, but there was no sign of their father. She hoped all was well with Jamie. Perhaps she should make an effort to contact him, but she didn't want to give him the wrong impression.

'Something the matter?' Gill asked.

'No.' Erica realised she'd been frowning as she tried to decide what to do. 'Well, yes,' she added, taking a sip of wine. She was glad the others were engaged in a debate about the upcoming election, something which didn't interest her. 'It's Jamie.'

'Ah!'

'No, not what you think.' Though how did she know what Gill was thinking? 'We went sailing the Sunday before last and… when we parted, I thought… it seemed… I expected to hear from him.'

'And you haven't?'

'Not a word. Do you think…? What if there's something wrong, or if I offended him in some way? It's not as if I…' Erica bit her lip. She'd said too much. Now Gill would really think she was interested in him.

'I wouldn't worry. I'm sure it's only that he's been busy… or he's giving you space. You probably gave off mixed signals, and he's trying to figure out how to approach you. How was the sailing?'

'It was brilliant. I loved it. It was a perfect day. We put into a little bay for lunch. It was one where we used to go when…' Erica bit her lip. *Had she given away too much?*

'Sounds as if you took a trip down memory lane.'

'Mmm.'

'You have a problem with that?'

'Yes and no. When I came back to Pelican Crossing, I fully intended to start afresh, put the past behind me… then I met Jamie again and…'

'It hasn't been as easy as you thought?'

Erica gave a sigh of relief. Gill understood. 'No, everywhere we go, everywhere I look, the memories resurface no matter how much I try to suppress them.'

'These memories, are they happy ones?'

'Yes, but it was a long time ago. I'm a different person now. We're both different people.'

'Has Jamie changed very much?'

'He's older, shows signs of having been hurt, but apart from that he's still the boy I dated when I was a teenager.' As she spoke, the image of Jamie rose so forcibly behind her eyes, she had to blink to make sure it wasn't real, that he wasn't standing there in the yacht club.

'Hey, you two, we're about to leave.' Joe's voice interrupted their conversation.

'Sorry,' Gill said to him, before whispering to Erica, 'Why don't you call him? You've nothing to lose.'

Nothing except my pride, Erica thought, as she joined the others, and they made their way out of the club. Once outside, she found herself alone with Kate as the three couples disappeared to their cars.

'I'm glad to have this chance to talk,' Kate said. 'I haven't made many friends here yet and we seemed to have a lot in common when we first spoke. I'd love it if we could meet for coffee some time.'

'So would I. How about tomorrow in *Books and Coffee*? Ten o'clock suit you?'

'Perfect. I look forward to it.'

When Kate had left, Erica turned to walk home. She was becoming so accustomed to living close to the harbour, the yacht club and the town, she'd be sad to leave Livvy's cottage when her friend returned. Fortunately, there was no sign of that happening anytime soon, so there was no immediate cause for concern. But Erica knew she couldn't rely on Livvy remaining in England indefinitely. She would eventually return, and Erica would have to find alternative accommodation. Hopefully, by that time she'd have added enough to her savings to put down a deposit on a small place of her own.

When she walked into the cottage and turned on the light, Erica noticed a light blinking on the phone. Puzzled, as she had always used her mobile since moving here, she picked it up to listen to the message, her heart thumping when she heard Jamie's voice.

'Is everything okay? I've been leaving messages for you, but you haven't replied. Did I do something to upset you? I wondered if you'd like to go sailing again on Sunday. Looks like it's going to be another lovely day. I'll understand if you don't want to spend more time with me, but can you call me?'

He'd called her, left messages? Erica took her phone out of her bag and stared at the blank screen, trying to remember when she'd last used it. She normally turned it off at work, so as not to be disturbed. *Had she forgotten to turn it back on? If so, when?* She turned it on now, to see a list of messages pop up on the screen, most from Jamie, but one from Briony and one from Lou, the owner of the cat who had come to her door. She felt a flutter of excitement as she scrolled through those from Jamie.

Had a great time last Sunday. Want to do it again?

Did you get my message? It's going to be fine on the weekend. Are you up for another trip on Princess Two?

Is everything okay? Are we good?

Please call me.

Erica almost wept. While she'd been wondering if she'd done anything to offend Jamie, he'd been wondering the same about her. They were a pair of idiots. She pressed his number, her heart racing when she heard it ring.

*

Jamie had almost given up hope of hearing back from Erica. She hadn't replied to any of his messages, and his mind had been going around in circles wondering if he'd come on too strong and she had chosen to ignore him, or if something had happened to her. If he didn't hear by tomorrow, he decided, he'd knock on her door as any concerned neighbour would do. There had also been the message from Lou about a welcome to the neighbourhood for Erica planned for the following weekend. Erica would have received one too. Had she replied to it?

He was sitting in his favourite chair nursing a glass of whisky and wishing he'd agreed to Rory's suggestion he join him, Gary and Mandy for dinner at the yacht club. Instead, he'd heated up one of the frozen meals he seemed to live on these days and spent another lonely night at home, switching channels on the television trying to find something to watch that would hold his attention. He'd given up and his eyes were beginning to close when his phone rang. Expecting it to be Rory calling to make sure all was well – he and Gary did fuss over him these days – his heart did a flip at the sight of Erica's number.

'Erica, is everything all right?'

'Oh, Jamie, I'm sorry. I only just saw your messages. I turn off my phone at work and I must have forgotten to turn it on again. I was about to call you when I heard your message. I thought something had happened to you, or you'd decided you didn't want to see me again.'

'Never! When I told you I'd always be here for you, I meant it.' Jamie was so relieved to hear her voice. If she had been there, he'd have found it difficult not to pick her up and swing her around. As it was, he had to be satisfied by gripping the phone tightly.

'I know,' she said, 'and I'd love to come sailing on Sunday, but this time, I'll bring lunch. It's only fair.'

'Okay,' he said, relieved she was sounding more like the old Erica, the one who'd always insisted on bringing sandwiches along when they used to go sailing together. 'It'll be like old times,' he risked saying, pleased to hear her laugh.

'I saw your sons at the yacht club tonight. I was there with Joe and Gill and some friends.'

'Right.' Jamie could have kicked himself. If only he had accepted when Rory made the suggestion he join them. But what difference would it have made? They were talking now. 'So, Sunday. How about we make an early start, and we can sail further up the coast. Is seven too early for you?'

'Sounds good. I can help you set up.'

'Okay,' Jamie said, surprised. 'I'll pick you up on my way.'

When the call ended, Jamie drained his glass then headed to bed feeling more positive than he had for some time. Maybe things were going to work out with Erica after all.

Thirty-three

Erica was feeling cheerful as she prepared to meet Kate next day. It had been too late to call Briony last night, but she'd done so this morning before breakfast and confirmed that her daughter-in-law and granddaughter would be arriving the following Saturday to spend a week with her. She had already arranged to have the week off work and was looking forward to spending time with them. The message from Lou had been a surprise, inviting her to the neighbourhood welcome drinks she'd mentioned when she picked her cat up. It was to be next Saturday too, the same day Briony was arriving. Erica was yet to reply. She'd work out what to do later.

Arriving early for her meeting with Kate, Erica wandered through the bookshop part of *Books and Coffee*, browsing the table of new releases. She had picked up a book by one of her favourite authors and was reading the blurb before deciding whether to buy it, when a voice asked, 'Did you receive my message about drinks next Saturday?'

Damn! She should have realised she'd bump into Lou here. She hadn't forgotten it was her bookstore but had been too busy thinking of other things. 'Hi, Lou,' she said, stalling. 'I did, but I got home late and…' She really had no excuse and didn't want to appear rude. It was kind of the older woman to arrange for her to meet her neighbours. 'Thanks for going to the trouble of arranging it. My daughter-in-law is arriving with my granddaughter that day so…'

'Bring them along. The more the merrier. And we oldies could do with some livening up. How old is your granddaughter?'

'Only a few months. She'll probably sleep through it.'

'Well, then. No problem.'

'No.' Erica knew there was no way of avoiding the event. 'I guess I'll see you there.'

'We'll be in my place if it rains,' Lou said, 'and no need to bring anything. I'll pick up some food from here and the guys will provide the grog.'

'Right.' Now she'd agreed to attend, Erica hoped it would be a fine evening. The plan was to meet at four on the beach across from the row of cottages. Her heart lightened. Perhaps she'd enjoy it. At least Briony would be there to help her overcome any of the awkwardness she might feel at meeting a group of strangers.

'Do you want that one?'

Erica realised she was still holding the book. She glanced down at it. 'Yes, please.'

She took it to the counter where Lou dropped it into a paper bag with the name of the store emblazoned on the side, paid for it and promising to see Lou the following week, made her way through to the café.

Kate was already there, seated at a table by the window.

'Sorry I'm late,' Erica said. 'I got caught up in the bookshop.' She held up the bag containing the book.

'No problem. What did you buy?'

Erica pulled out the latest Di Morrissey. 'I've always loved her books,' she said.

'Me too. We should read this one at the book club. It's my turn to select the book next month and I've been trying to decide what to choose. I didn't see you at this month's meeting.'

'No, I had a late shift at work and was too exhausted to make it. I was sorry to miss the discussion as I really enjoyed the book. How did it go?'

Erica listened with interest as Kate gave her a rundown of what the members of the book club had said about the Nicci French book, until they were interrupted by Denny asking them if they wanted to order.

'Sorry,' she said, 'I'll have a skinny cappuccino thanks.'

'The same for me,' Kate said, 'and can we have two of today's muffins specials, please? You don't mind me ordering a muffin for you, do you?'

Kate asked Erica when Denny had left. 'They do such amazing ones here. I always have the daily special.'

'You come here a lot?'

'As often as I can. I love this place. The danger is that I usually end up buying a book too.' She laughed.

Erica laughed too. She was sorry she hadn't made time to meet with Kate before now. It was so good to talk about books with someone who shared the same taste, and to do it over coffee in these delightful surroundings was a bonus. 'We should do this more often,' she said.

'Absolutely!'

Their coffee and muffins arrived, the strawberry and white chocolate muffins warm from the oven and smelling delicious.

'Tell me about yourself,' Kate said, when they had devoured the muffins and ordered a second cup of coffee. 'What brings you to Pelican Crossing? I know you're Joe's sister but not much else.'

Erica winced. She didn't want to recount her sorry story to her new friend, but she had to say something. She took a deep breath. 'My husband died recently. I grew up here, and it made sense to come back to be close to Joe.'

'Oh, I'm sorry. I do recall hearing something… How does it feel to be back? I'm not sure I could go back to my hometown.'

Erica thought for a moment, a variety of emotions flooding her. 'Good, on the whole, though the memories can be difficult to handle,' she said, trying to be as honest as she could, while also trying not to think of Jamie and the memories he invoked. 'What about you? You're a relative newcomer too.' She took a sip of coffee and waited.

'Oh, a chance to do something different, you know, the opportunity to get out of the city, to have a sea change. Isn't it supposed to be what everyone is looking for these days?' She picked up her cup as if to signal that was all she was prepared to say.

Erica wanted to ask more, but didn't want to pry. No doubt Kate would reveal more in her own good time, if their friendship progressed. She was aware of all the things she had chosen not to reveal too.

'Joe tells me you have a dog,' she said instead, deciding to change the subject.

'Bear,' Kate clasped her cup in both hands, a warm smile on her lips, 'my German Shepherd. He's a dear. I don't know what I would have done without him.' For a fleeting moment, her eyes clouded over before lightening again. But that moment told Erica that her new friend had suffered too, and she felt a strong sense of affinity with her.

'I'd love to meet him,' Erica said, remembering what Poppy had said about her getting a dog herself. She'd forgotten that conversation in the excitement of going sailing with Jamie. She'd speak with Rhana soon, she vowed, find out when her next litter was due and check with Livvy about having a dog in the cottage.

'You must come to dinner. I live in one of those old houses behind Main Street, a couple of blocks from here. You?'

'I'm renting a cottage from a friend. It's on the other side of the harbour.'

'Oh, one of those cute little cottages? Isn't that where that friend of Joe's lives, the one with the fishing charter business?'

'Jamie Whittaker? Yes.' Erica didn't want to talk about Jamie, especially not with Kate. She remembered the interest she'd shown in him at Joe's barbecue.

'You and he… you're friends, aren't you?' she asked.

'We know each other, yes. We both grew up here.'

'Is that all or…?' Kate raised one eyebrow.

Erica blushed. 'We have started seeing each other recently,' she admitted.

'I knew it! I saw the way he looked at you that night at Joe's. He's quite a hunk. I'm not in the market for a man, but if I was…' She grinned.

Erica blushed again. She hated this sort of conversation. Perhaps she and Kate weren't so alike after all.

Kate dispelled that thought by adding, 'I'm sorry if I sound crass, but I had a bad experience before I came here, one I don't want to repeat, and sometimes I say things that…'

'You're forgiven. Now, I should go. It's been lovely meeting you again.'

'I meant it about dinner… if I haven't put you off. Call you?'

'Please do.' Despite her comments about Jamie, Kate had been good company, and Erica was willing to give their friendship a chance.

As she made her way home, however, it was Kate's comments about Jamie which she remembered… and agreed with. Jamie Whittaker might be in his fifties, but he was quite a hunk, and he seemed interested in her. If only she could trust her own judgement.

Thirty-four

Sunday had been good, better than good, Jamie thought as he headed out of the harbour with yet another group of Sydney businessmen, all raring for a fun-filled day of fishing.

He had collected Erica at seven as arranged, pleased to see she appeared relaxed and was smiling. As promised, she had packed an esky for their lunch. He picked it up, and they made their way to the wharf where Princess Two was waiting for them. He'd risen at the crack of dawn to prepare her, before going home to shower and change.

Once aboard, Erica seemed different. It was as if she'd cast off the doubts which had been plaguing her and decided to enjoy his company. The day had been perfect. There had been none of the distancing which had prevailed in some of their previous outings. He had felt an invisible web of attraction building between them, and when he pulled her in for a kiss at the end of the day, instead of drawing away, she had responded with the fervour he remembered, leading him to believe there was a chance for him.

Now, he couldn't wait to see her again, but she was on night shift this week, and her daughter-in-law was due to arrive on Saturday, so he would have to wait. His one consolation was that he'd see her on Saturday at this welcome to the neighbourhood event Lou was arranging to introduce Erica to the other residents of the row of cottages along the shore. It would be good to catch up with everyone again. They used to hold these events on a regular basis, but it had been some time since the last one. Livvy had been the instigator, he realised, and with her gone, they had let them lapse. Maybe after this one, Lou would take over until Livvy returned.

A yell from one of his passengers forced Jamie to concentrate on the task at hand – ensuring he provided the best possible fishing experience for his clients, and for the remainder of the trip he focussed on them.

But as he walked home at the end of the day, and glanced at the darkened windows of Erica's cottage, he wished she was there, that he could knock on her door, see her smiling face, and pull her into his warm embrace.

*

Erica hated working nights, and it meant she was on another twelve-hour shift of seven pm till seven am. Although it was usually a busy time, giving her little time for thinking about herself and her growing feelings for Jamie, it sent her internal time clock into disarray. At least it was only for one week this time she consoled herself, and she had the next week off to spend with Briony and little Ava. The thought of their reunion would help her get through the week.

She was also determined to make good her vow to talk with Rhana, and the opportunity came in the middle of the week when, on Wednesday, she wakened much earlier than usual. After a shower, she made a quick call to her friend to make sure she was home, then, gulping down a coffee she headed off.

'Hello, stranger,' Rhana greeted her, the inevitable swarm of dogs at her heels.

They hugged, the dogs managing to wind their way around Erica's ankles.

'Sorry. I've been meaning to get here, but…'

'I know, I know, too many other things to do.'

Erica felt guilty. She really had no excuse. She must make the effort to visit Rhana more often. She was her old friend, the only one around, with Livvy still overseas.

'Come in, anyway, and tell me what's been happening to you.'

Erica followed Rhana inside. It was a good feeling to be with her old friend again, someone to whom she could talk without fear of being censured. As soon as Rhana had poured coffee and slid a plate of freshly baked date and walnut loaf across the table, she found herself confiding in her about her outings with Jamie, her growing feelings and her doubts.

'Wow! That's a lot,' Rhana said when Erica had finished. 'But I don't see the problem. It sounds as if Jamie still has feelings for you… and you for him. You're neither of you getting any younger so why not go for it?'

Erica bit her lip, took a sip of coffee and a bite of Rhana's delicious loaf. It was so close to what Gill had said to her, but… 'What if I'm wrong again?' she said. 'What if Jamie's another mistake, just like Geoff was?'

'Erica, this is Jamie we're talking about. You've known him since you were sixteen. Okay,' she put her hands up defensively as Erica opened her mouth to reply, 'I know that was a long time ago, but Joe has known him since they were in kindergarten, and all through those years. Do you really think your brother would encourage you to form a relationship with him if he didn't believe he was one of the good guys?'

'Joe could be biased… for that very reason.'

'Erica, listen to yourself. This is your brother you're talking about. Mr integrity, Pelican Crossing's mayor. He's as honest as the day is long and has only ever wanted what is best for you.'

Erica knew Rhana was right. Joe had always looked out for her, even when she was making a nuisance of herself and trailing around after him and his mates. He'd never suggest anything that would cause her grief, or encourage her involvement with anyone he didn't trust. She sighed. 'You're right, Rhana. I should have thought of that. I've been all sorts of a fool. It's just…' She sighed again.

'It's understandable after what you've been through, but you deserve some happiness, and if Jamie will make you happy…' She peered at Erica as if she could read her mind. 'Can he?'

'Maybe.' Erica felt the stirrings of hope. Maybe she could finally find peace in a relationship that worked, one in which she wasn't always on edge wondering when things would go wrong. She knew Jamie would never treat her the way Geoff had, the way Kieren had tried to, so why did she feel the need to pull away each time she felt herself becoming closer to him? 'Thanks, Rhana. Now, I didn't come here to bare my soul about Jamie Whittaker. A couple of people have suggested I should get a dog, and I do like the idea of a furry companion – I love Joe's Coco and missed her when I went back to Perth. So… I wanted to ask when your next litter's due.'

'Wow! I certainly didn't expect that. But you're right. There's no better companion, and Betsy is due to give birth any day. These were Bonnie's pups you saw in April.' She laughed at Erica's puzzled expression. 'I have a regular nursery here.'

'You'll keep me one then, if Livvy agrees I can have a dog in the cottage?'

'You can have the pick of the litter.'

'Thanks. Now I should be going. I need to get ready for work. Thanks for the advice too. I'll take it on board.'

'I hope you'll do more than that. Seriously, Jamie's a catch, always was. I always thought you were a fool to let him get away.'

Erica gave her friend a piercing look. But no, she knew Rhana had never been interested in Jamie. Her interests had lain elsewhere, but she and Livvy had never been able to discover where that was.

As if to confirm Rhana's view – or by a weird quirk of fate, Erica's phone rang as soon as she stepped inside the cottage. Seeing Jamie's number she pressed to accept his call, her heartbeat throbbing in her ears.

Thirty-five

Jamie was holding his breath as he listened to Erica's phone ring, wondering what her reaction would be this time. There had been no sign of her at the cottage when he walked by on his way to or from work on the past three days and he wondered if she had been inside, asleep, the thought of her lying in her bed flooding him with yearning. Perhaps she hadn't even been home. He had no idea what her day looked like when she was on night shift. But he intended to find out.

He'd decided he couldn't wait till Saturday to see her again, when she'd be accompanied by her daughter-in-law and granddaughter, and there would be lots of others around. So, after a glass of beer to give him Dutch courage – much like he had when he was younger – he'd picked up the phone.

Erica answered on the third ring.

'Jamie? I thought I wasn't going to hear from you this week.'

Was she pleased? Annoyed? Jamie couldn't tell from her tone. What the hell! He'd just say what was on his mind, but he'd start off casually. 'Hi Erica. How has your week been?'

'Busy, but good. You?'

It was the opening he'd been waiting for. 'Mine's been busy too.' He took a deep breath. 'I had such a good time on Sunday. I haven't been able to stop thinking of you. I know you're going to be busy preparing for your visitors, but I can't wait till Saturday to see you again.'

Did he imagine her gurgle of laughter? He ploughed on. 'Is there any chance we could meet tomorrow? I only have a short morning charter. I don't know what your days look like when you're on night shift, but if there's any chance…' He let his voice trail off, wondering if he sounded too needy. He was out of practice at this stuff, but it was Erica…

This time he didn't imagine her laugh.

'I'm always so exhausted when I get home that I go straight to bed, so mornings don't exist for me. But I do usually emerge in the early afternoon, and my shift doesn't start till seven so…' There was a pregnant silence.

Jamie couldn't believe his luck. 'Could we meet around two, two-thirty, three?'

Erica laughed again. 'Three might be best.'

Jamie thought quickly. 'We could have coffee at *The Blue Dolphin* or take a walk along the beach or…' He tried to think of something else they might do at that time of day.

'A walk along the beach sounds good. I'll be feeling in need of some fresh air by then. It's been a pretty hectic week.'

'That's great. I'll pick you up at three.'

Jamie gave a whoop of delight when he finished the call. Erica had sounded good, pleased to hear from him and most importantly, had agreed to meet him again next day. He couldn't wait.

*

Next day, Jamie couldn't wait for his charter to finish. Luckily, it was a small, well-behaved group, who were happy to be there, regardless of their success in catching anything. Afterwards, he went straight home to shower, change and have a bite to eat, then had to figure out a way to keep himself occupied till it was time to meet Erica.

He wasn't used to doing nothing. Normally, when he was home, he'd get stuck into gardening, or turn on the telly to watch the cricket, but it was the wrong time of year for cricket and he didn't want to get himself dirty gardening, now he had changed. Searching around for something to occupy himself with, he caught sight of the shelf containing some old photo albums. They mostly contained photos of the boys in various stages, though some predated his marriage to

Cindy – shots of the old days when he, Cam, Jack and Joe had gone around together. He'd been meaning to throw them out, but looking at them now brought back memories. He was about to close the one he was looking at when a loose photo fell out. He picked it up, stunned to see it was one of his old sailboat, his first Princess 18, and there, sitting cross-legged on the deck, grinning up at the camera, her long dark hair curling around her face and tumbling over her bare tanned shoulders, was Erica.

Jamie remembered that day. It was a week before she left for Sydney. On that day, he'd been on top of the world. Erica had promised to come back as soon as she could. She had intended to find a nursing position in the local hospital, and he had planned to ask her to marry him as soon as she graduated. What a fool he had been. He should have asked her there and then. But they had both been so young. They had thought they had all the time in the world. It had never occurred to him she'd meet someone else, marry him and move all the way across Australia to Perth.

He slipped the photo into the top pocket of his shirt, closed the album and put it back on the shelf, amazed the photo had lain there for all that time, only to fall out now when he and Erica had started seeing each other again. It was an omen.

*

Erica was filled with a strange inner excitement at the prospect of seeing Jamie again. As a result of her conversation with Rhana, and those she'd had with herself since, she had managed to stifle her qualms, decided to accept what fate had to offer, and enjoy their time together.

Jamie's kiss when they parted on Sunday had unlocked something in her, a tumult of emotions she'd forgotten existed, and although she'd tried to deny the shaft of desire that shot through her, she'd known she wanted to investigate where it might lead.

She was glad Jamie had called, glad he'd suggested the option of a walk on the beach. She didn't want them to meet in a café where there would be other people, where there was the risk of being recognised. She wasn't ready to become fodder for the Pelican Crossing gossip mill just yet, and the beach opposite the cottages was normally deserted, unlike the other beaches in Pelican Crossing.

Erica felt like a girl on her first date as she waited for Jamie's arrival. She knew it was silly, as they'd already had dinner together and gone kitesurfing and sailing. But that had been before… when she was still unsure about him… unable – or unwilling – to trust her own judgement. Now, although nervous, she felt confident she was making the right choice.

Although she'd been expecting it, Erica was startled when she heard the knock on the door. Grabbing her hat from the hook just inside the door, she opened it to see Jamie standing there with a smile on his face. 'Hi,' she said, suddenly feeling shy with her old friend.

'Hi, yourself. Ready?' He was wearing a pair of well-pressed jeans and an unzipped, lightweight, beige jacket over a white shirt, unbuttoned at the neck, and looked as if he might have walked out of an advert for men's cologne. Erica swallowed.

'Yes.' She felt in her pocket to ensure she had her phone, though didn't expect to need it, then went out, closing and locking the door behind her.

When Jamie tentatively reached for her hand as they crossed to the beach, Erica didn't reject his touch as she might have done a week earlier. Today she relished the warmth of his fingers holding hers, the warm glow which filled her as they made their way across the soft sand to the firmer surface close to the edge of the water.

Once there, they stopped. It was peaceful here, the only sounds the lapping of the waves, the cries of the seagulls, and the whirr of a helicopter overhead. They looked up. 'It's one of those joy flights.' Jamie said, shading his eyes. 'The American fellow who runs the hot air balloon rides has started offering flights along the coastline. Seems to be a bit of an entrepreneur, though no one knows much about him. He arrived in Pelican Crossing out of the blue a few years ago. Lives outside town and keeps himself to himself, though I've heard he sometimes drops into the yacht club for dinner.'

'Mmm. Difficult to keep a low profile in this town.'

'You're not wrong. I'm glad you agreed to see me today,' Jamie said, as the helicopter disappeared into the distance. 'It's been a long week.'

'For me too,' Erica admitted. 'Tell me about yours.'

They began to meander along as Jamie described the various groups which had engaged his services in the past few days, making Erica laugh at some of their antics.

'How about you?' he asked, when they had almost reached the end of the beach.

'Oh, you know, the usual collection of broken bones, car accidents, a couple of elderly people who suffered falls, a suspected heart attack…'

'Wow! I had no idea.'

Erica laughed. 'There's never any downtime.'

'But you enjoy it?'

'I do.' She smiled, remembering all the years when she wished she could get back to her chosen profession.

'And your daughter-in-law, who's coming to visit. Tell me about her.'

'Briony? She's lovely. I worry about her.'

'How so?'

'It's Kieren, my son.' She bit her lip, wondering how much to reveal, then, seeing the tenderness and concern in Jamie's eyes, continued, 'I worry he's becoming like his dad.'

'And that would be bad?'

Erica stopped in her tracks and turned to face Jamie. She took a deep breath. 'I haven't told you everything about Geoff. He…' her voice broke then strengthened, '… he was a control freak. They call it coercive control. Then he became violent. It's why I left him, came to stay with Joe last year… then, when he died, I felt I could go back home. I see so much of him in our son that I fear for Briony.'

'Oh, Erica!' Jamie pulled her into his arms and hugged her tightly.

Erica allowed her head to drop onto Jamie's chest, the warmth of his body seeping into her and filling her with a sense of calm and release. She felt safe here in his embrace.

They stood like that for a few moments, lost to the world, then Jamie gently drew away, keeping his hands on Erica's arms. He gazed into her eyes. 'I wish I'd known.'

'There was nothing you could do, even if you had.'

'No, but… The bastard!'

'He was, and I was too afraid to leave. I thought it was my fault that he…' Erica's voice broke again.

'I know it's a terrible thing to say but I'm glad he's dead, that he can't hurt you anymore. Is that why he was here in Pelican Crossing?'

Erica nodded. She didn't want to talk about it anymore. Geoff was her past. Maybe, just maybe, Jamie was her future.

Thirty-six

Erica couldn't contain her excitement as she waited for Briony and Ava's flight to touch down. She'd spent the morning rushing around, making sure the bed in the spare room was ready, checking out the cot she'd managed to borrow from a work colleague whose daughter had outgrown it, and buying more food to fill her fridge and pantry than the three of them could possibly eat.

She clutched the takeaway coffee she'd purchased and watched as the plane came to a halt on the tarmac, then taxied to the gate. Then she threw the empty cup into the bin and headed to the spot where she would be able to catch sight of Briony as soon as she stepped through the gate.

Briony was one of the first to appear, a smiling Ava in her arms. Erica rushed forward to greet her with a hug and a kiss. 'Let me take her,' she said, taking the young child into her arms and giving her a hug. 'Do you remember me, sweetheart?' she said, her eyes filled with happy tears, then turning to Briony, 'Welcome back to Pelican Crossing. I'm so pleased to see you.'

'And I you,' Briony said. 'I was afraid we weren't going to make it.'

Erica's eyes widened. 'What happened?'

'Oh, it was Kieren. He thought Ava was too young to fly, then he… Anyway, we're here now.' Her face broke into a smile. 'I'm really looking forward to seeing everything. Last year there wasn't time to look around.'

The two women were silent, remembering the dark days before and after Geoff's death.

'Let's collect your luggage,' Erica said to break the mood, and they headed to the luggage carousel.

Once there, it wasn't long before they'd collected Briony's case and a stroller for Ava, one designed with a capsule which could convert into a car seat. Erica was glad Briony had told her about it. It had saved her worrying about a baby seat for her car.

Soon, a delighted Ava was strapped into the capsule and they set off for home.

'I'd forgotten how pretty it is here,' Briony said, as they drove up the coast, the ocean on one side, paddocks on the other, some with cattle, some with horses. As they entered Pelican Crossing, a couple of pelicans strutted across the road in front of them as if welcoming the visitors. Ava pointed at them and gurgled happily.

'Oh, this is lovely!' Carrying Ava in her arms, Briony followed Erica into the cottage. 'And you're so close to the beach. You said it belongs to a friend?'

'Yes, Livvy. I've been lucky. She's in England right now, visiting her daughter and granddaughters. One of them is around the same age as Ava.'

On hearing her name, Ava let out a little cry. It sounded strange to Erica to hear a baby's cry in her cottage. She smiled. She wished they were staying for longer than a week but intended to make the most of it.

'What are your neighbours like?' Briony asked, walking across to the window and gazing out.

Erica was glad her daughter-in-law had her back to her and didn't see her blush. 'I haven't met all of them,' she said, 'only Lou, who owns a combined bookshop and café, and Jamie, who's an old mate of my brother's. Lou has arranged a neighbourhood get together today in the late afternoon… if you feel up to it, we could go.' She didn't add that it was by way of an introduction to the neighbourhood for her.

'I'd love to,' Briony said, turning back to face her, her face wreathed in smiles. 'I haven't been out much since you left.'

Erica gave her an odd look. Surely Kieren wasn't preventing Briony from seeing her friends, the way Geoff had with her? She determined to use Briony's time here to find out exactly what was going on in her marriage. She didn't want her to fall into the same trap she had.

There was still time for her to extricate herself if Erica's suspicions were correct.

After a lunch of the quiche Erica had prepared earlier, Briony fed Ava and settled her down for a sleep before taking a nap herself, while Erica relaxed with the book for next month's book club. Gill had dropped off a copy for her after the meeting she'd missed, and Erica was enjoying becoming lost in the small Scottish village of Crovie as she turned the pages of *The Cottage on the Cliff* by Sharon Golding. She'd become so interested in the setting, she'd checked out the village online, surprised to discover the line of cottages set between the sea and the cliff actually existed.

Erica was so engrossed in her book, she didn't move until Briony appeared with Ava in her arms. 'What time does this thing start, and will it be all right if we take Ava along? She'll probably fall asleep.'

'Of course we can. Lou said to go down to the beach around four. I expect it'll only last an hour or so. Evidently the guys are providing the drinks, and Lou said she'll bring food from the café, though I did make a dip. It's one I used to make years ago, before… Well, anyway, a long time ago.' She remembered the first time she'd made it for Geoff as a treat. He took one look at the creamy spinach dip served in a cob loaf and turned his nose up, refusing to even try it. This was the first time she'd made it since then. 'It's three now. How about a cup of tea before we leave?'

'Sounds good.' Briony settled herself in one of the armchairs by the large window. 'Is that where we're meeting your neighbours?' she asked, pointing across the road to where they could see the ocean and a long stretch of sand. 'I don't think I've ever been to a gathering on a beach.'

'We did a lot of things on the beach when I was growing up here.' Images of all the times she and Jamie had spent on the beach flitted through her mind. She was surprised to discover they no longer bothered her, quite the opposite.

'You were lucky,' Briony sighed. 'We only went there for one week each year when I was young, and now… Kieren says he doesn't like the beach.'

Erica's lips tightened remembering the few times they'd gone to the beach as a family when Kieren was little, before Geoff decided it was a waste of time and money. The little boy had loved paddling in the ocean, building sandcastles and digging holes in the sand. He'd clearly forgotten those halcyon days and chosen to accept his dad's view about that too. *She had to talk to Briony.*

When four o'clock came around, Briony settled a wide-awake Ava into the stroller, and the two women made their way across the road and down to the sand where a small group had already gathered around a table and a few canvas chairs. Erica's heart raced as she caught sight of Jamie. He was wearing the same outfit as he had on their beach walk, making her remember the warmth of his embrace, the firm grip of his hands on her arms, his mouth on hers.

'Are you okay, Mum?'

Briony's voice brought Erica back to the present and to the realisation she had stopped in her tracks.

'Yes, sorry. Can you manage the stroller on the sand, or shall I help you carry it?'

'No, we're fine. It has wide wheels.'

Erica nodded, seeing Ava seemed to be enjoying the bumpy ride, giggling away in her capsule.

'Here you are!' Lou came forward to greet them. 'And this is?'

'My daughter-in-law, Briony and my granddaughter, Ava. Briony, this is Lou,' Erica said.

'Come and meet everyone.' Lou steered them towards the rest of the group, most of whom were men. 'This is Erica, everyone,' she called. 'She's taking care of Livvy's cottage while Livvy is overseas. She grew up here in Pelican Crossing and is our mayor's sister.'

There was a general murmur of greetings before most of the group resumed the conversations which Lou had interrupted, the exception being Jamie who came over to greet Erica with a kiss on the cheek. 'Hello, you must be Briony,' he said to Briony. 'Erica has told me about you. And this is your granddaughter,' he said to Erica. 'She must be about the same age as my grandson,' he said, turning to Briony again. 'Erica came to my rescue when I got into trouble babysitting him.'

Erica was conscious of Briony's eyes on her. 'This is Jamie. He's a friend of mine.' She wasn't sure why she felt awkward introducing Jamie to Briony. There was no reason for her to feel embarrassed, but she couldn't help wondering what Kieren's reaction would be when he learned about him. 'He and Joe are mates from way back,' she added hurriedly.

'Hi, Jamie. You live along here too? It's a beautiful spot.'

'I do, and it is. I've lived here since my two sons moved out. It's perfect, within walking distance to the harbour and the town.'

As Jamie and Briony continued to talk, Erica slipped away to place the platter containing her dip and corn chips on the table, and Lou took the opportunity to introduce her to the others in the group. Erica remembered some of them from when she was growing up here, though of course, they were all older now, and all were very welcoming. Lou had been right. It was good to meet her neighbours.

The next two hours passed in a flash. The sun had set and Jamie and Troy, one of the other men, had lit several camping lanterns they'd sourced from somewhere or other, and the party had continued. But it was turning cool, and Ava was making small cries of protest. 'I think we should go,' Erica said to Jamie, to whom she had been chatting, along with Lou.

'We'll all be leaving pretty soon,' he said. 'Need any help with the stroller?'

'That would be good.' It would be harder to handle in the dark.

Jamie picked up the stroller, earning a happy sound from Ava, and Erica and Briony followed him up to the roadway.

'We'll be fine now. Thanks for your help,' Erica said, as Jamie set the stroller down on the path.

'Right.' Jamie seemed reluctant to leave, and Erica wished he didn't have to. But she had Briony and Ava to look after. 'I'll see you soon?' he asked.

'I hope so,' she whispered. 'But I'm going to be pretty tied up with…' she gestured to where Briony was already wheeling Ava across to the cottage.

'You said you have the week off. Maybe we could organise something with Mandy and Archie. It might be good for Briony to meet someone her own age. Not that I'm suggesting anything…' He chuckled.

'You're right. I'll mention it to her.'

'And I'll talk to Mandy. I'll call you.'

'Right. Now I need to go.' Erica could see Briony was already at the door of the cottage and was looking back for her.

'Not before…' Regardless of Briony, of the fact they were still in sight of the group on the beach, Jamie pulled Erica into his arms, his lips gently brushing hers, before he headed back down to the beach.

Erica watched him go for a moment, a now familiar warmth surging through her, then she turned and joined Briony.

Briony didn't say anything when they went inside, then became busy with bathing and feeding Ava and putting her down to sleep. It wasn't till later, when they were snacking on cheese and biscuits which was all they felt like eating after what they'd consumed on the beach, that she said, 'Who's Jamie, Mum? You seem pretty friendly.'

'I told you, he's a friend, a mate of Joe's. We all grew up together.' It wasn't entirely a lie.

'I saw him kiss you. It looked like… I'm glad if you've found someone, Mum. I know it wasn't always easy for you with Dad, but…' she frowned, 'he hasn't been gone a year yet. Don't you think it's too soon?'

Thirty-seven

Erica couldn't sleep. She tossed and turned, Briony's words going around and around in her head, guilt consuming her. Was her daughter-in-law right? Was it too soon for her to form a new relationship? Had she been too busy wondering if she was making a mistake, if she could trust Jamie, trust her own feelings, to remember that it had only been months since Geoff died? She knew she didn't owe her late husband anything. She hadn't mourned him. His death had been a welcome release. But what if…?

By the time morning came, she was a wreck. She knew there was only one thing that would revive her. Slipping out of bed, she pulled on her swimmers, covering them with a pair of loose pants and a hoodie, and tiptoeing through the house so as not to waken Briony and Ava, she set off to meet the other wild swimmers on the beach.

Erica felt better as soon as she was out in the fresh air and, by the time she reached the beach, she had almost persuaded herself she had nothing to be ashamed of. She and Jamie had done nothing wrong. Surely a few kisses didn't amount to a betrayal of her deceased husband? But even as that thought crossed her mind, she remembered how her body had leapt to life at these kisses, how they struck a vibrant chord in her, a chord that had been silent for too long.

The others were already there, so putting aside all thoughts of Geoff, Briony and Jamie, Erica stripped down to her swimmers and ran into the ocean to join them, swimming swiftly out to sea, before turning to float on her back to watch the sunrise, as she always did.

This morning, the sight of the changing colours of the sky had none of the usual effect on Erica, and she was glad to return to shore where the other members of the group were already getting dressed and chatting about the fundraising coast walk which had been publicised in the latest edition of *The Echo*. It seemed that almost everyone in the group knew someone who had been struck down with the dreaded disease, and even those who didn't were keen to support Joe's project.

'Will you be taking part, Erica?' Kate asked, as Erica was slipping her arms into her hoodie.

'I certainly will. Joe would never forgive me if I didn't. It would have made such a difference to him and Barb if we'd had something like that back then.'

'It sounds as if she was quite a woman,' Kate said, referring to the article Finn had written in which he'd described Joe's reason for embarking on the project and outlined Barb's contribution to the town.

'She was.' Erica was silent for a moment, remembering her late sister-in-law. It had taken Joe years to recover from her death, to be willing to find love again. Was she so uncaring that she had renewed her friendship with Jamie so quickly, so soon after Geoff's death? And it was more than friendship, she admitted to herself, or at least it had the potential to be more.

'Want to meet up again this week sometime?' Kate asked, towelling her hair.

'I'd love to, but I have my daughter-in-law visiting with my granddaughter. Perhaps the week after?'

'That's the week of the walk… on the Saturday.'

'Of course.' Erica had forgotten the actual date they had set, and they had agreed to meet again before then to finalise their plans. 'Why don't we catch up for a drink earlier in the week?'

'We never did get together for that dinner I promised you, so why don't we make it dinner, if it suits you. I'll call or text you. Okay?'

'That would be lovely thanks.' Erica had enjoyed Kate's company, but was already regretting having let slip her involvement with Jamie. She'd have to ensure they kept the conversation away from anything personal, though she was curious to find out more about Kate. It seemed she had a past she wanted to keep secret too.

Briony was already up when Erica arrived home. She was sitting in the kitchen feeding Ava. 'Where were you?' she asked. 'I got a shock when I realised you had gone out.'

'Sorry, I should have left a note. I thought I'd be back before you were up. I went swimming.'

'At this time?' Briony stared at Erica, then out the window, to where the sky was still changing colour.

'I belong to a group of wild swimmers. We meet on the beach before daylight each morning. I didn't intend to go while you were here, but I didn't sleep well and…' She spread her hands.

'I'm sorry you had trouble sleeping, Mum. I hope it wasn't anything I said.'

'Of course not,' Erica lied. 'I have a few things on my mind, that's all. Out in the ocean… it helps me think.'

Briony didn't look convinced, but said, 'I made tea. Would you like some?'

'That would be lovely. I'll just shower and change first, then I thought we might go out for breakfast. There's a nice café just a short walk away, and it's a lovely morning.'

'Oh, I'd like that. I can't remember when Kieren and I last went out for breakfast… or any other meal. It's difficult with Ava…' She dropped her eyes.

Erica felt her stomach give a familiar lurch at Briony's words. It all sounded too familiar. But now wasn't the time to confront her about Kieren's behaviour. 'I understand,' she said, aware she might understand all too well what Briony was going through.

When Erica returned to the kitchen, dressed in a pair of smart jeans topped with a bright red sweater, Briony had poured two cups of lemon and ginger tea, and Ava was lying in her stroller, gurgling happily. 'Thanks, Briony,' she said with a smile, taking a seat beside her daughter-in-law.

'You look very nice, Mum. That colour suits you. I don't think I've ever seen you wearing red before.'

'No, I…' Erica decided not to tell her how Geoff had hated to see her in bright colours, how over the years, he'd bent her to his will till she became a mere shadow of her former self, wearing the dowdy clothes he preferred. One of the first things she'd done after his death was to refresh her wardrobe. 'I bought it recently.'

When they had finished their tea, Erica and Briony set off for the café. Erica pushed the stroller, enjoying the unfamiliar pleasure of watching her granddaughter's enjoyment as she was wheeled along. It was something she'd done regularly in Perth and one of the things she'd missed.

'Look, Ava!' Erica said, as they passed a group of pelicans waddling towards the edge of the harbour in the hope of a feed. The little girl's eyes lit up and she reached out as if trying to grab them.

'They look like little old men,' Briony said. laughing as a couple more flew in to join them, their large wings flapping as they came in to land. 'I hadn't realised. I suppose that's where the town got its name.'

'There are a few different stories,' Erica said, 'but I'd say you're right. Here we are,' she added as they approached the café. There were a few empty tables outside, and Erica parked the stroller at one. 'You get a good view of the harbour and the marina from here, if it's not too cold for you,' she said.

'Not at all.' Briony gazed around her. 'This is perfect. I can see why you wanted to come back.'

They had just ordered, each choosing flat white coffees and eggs benedict with smoked salmon, when Erica saw Jamie approaching. Her stomach churning, she bit her lip, mindful of her sleepless night and what had caused it. It was a paradox that while she had planned to interrogate Briony about Kieren, it was Briony who had raised questions about *her* life and her friendship with Jamie. He was the last person she wanted to see this morning.

Thirty-eight

Jamie blinked, unable to believe his eyes. He was on his way to *The Blue Dolphin Café* to meet his boys with Mandy and little Archie for breakfast, when he caught sight of Erica with her daughter and granddaughter seated outside the café. Quickening his step, he approached them. 'Good morning. This is a piece of luck,' he said, surprised when instead of the smile he expected, he was greeted by a frown.

'I didn't expect to see you here,' Erica said, her voice far from welcoming.

'I didn't expect to see you here, either. Rory called me last night to say he and Gary were having breakfast here, along with Mandy and Archie, of course, and invited me to join them. I never refuse the opportunity to spend time with my grandson. You'd understand that.' He gestured to where Ava was watching him intently. 'Here they are now,' he added, as they came into sight, Mandy wheeling a stroller not unlike the one Erica's granddaughter was lying in. It would provide a chance to introduce the two younger women and perhaps arrange a get-together.

To his surprise, Erica's expression changed to one of relief. 'Oh, you're meeting your family,' she said. 'How nice.'

Jamie was perplexed. Where was the woman who had welcomed his embrace, who had kissed him passionately only a few days earlier?

His family arrived before he could respond, and there was the usual kerfuffle as he introduced them to Briony and her to them, then as the two young women admired each other's babies. Then they went inside the café and the opportunity for any further conversation with Erica was lost… for the moment. But he determined to talk to her later. He needed to find out what was wrong, what had happened to change her.

They ordered breakfast, Jamie and his sons choosing the Big Breakfast, while Mandy opted for smashed avocado on toast and berated Gary for his unhealthy choice, to which Gary only laughed and said it was Sunday.

While they continued to bicker amicably, and Rory teased Gary about being henpecked, Jamie checked on Erica through the window. She seemed happier now, laughing and chatting with her daughter-in-law and cooing at the baby. So, it was him she was displeased with. Puzzled, he tried to figure out what could have happened between them saying goodbye the previous evening and now, but couldn't come up with anything.

'What's with you and Erica, Dad?' Gary asked. 'You haven't been kitesurfing again. I thought you both enjoyed it.'

'We did.' Jamie pulled on one ear. 'It's complicated.'

'Isn't it always,' Mandy said, 'but I'll tell you what I told my mum.'

Jamie gave an amused smile. He didn't need Mandy's help. But he forced himself to listen.

'I suspect, like her, you get lonely at times, now both Gary and Rory are gone.' She nodded as if to confirm her words. 'You need more fun in your life. Why don't you try…'

'Steady on, Mandy,' Gary interrupted. 'You can't tell my dad what to do… though maybe…' he added with a grin. 'Mandy signed her mum up to one of those online dating sites.'

Jamie didn't know whether to laugh or flare up. A dating site? Him? That was for people desperate to connect. He wasn't desperate for a woman. There was only one woman he wanted in his life, and she seemed to blow hot and cold. With Erica, it was a case of one step forward, two back. 'I don't think so,' he said, as he watched Erica and her little family leave without a backward glance. He sighed.

'You okay, Dad?' Rory asked. He was always more sensitive than his brother. 'Gary didn't mean anything. It was a joke.'

Jamie sent him a grateful look.

But Gary hadn't finished. 'You didn't answer, Dad. You and Erica. Is it a thing? Maybe Dad doesn't need the help of a dating site,' he said to Mandy.

'I'm not sure what you mean by a thing, what that entails in today's parlance. We are friends. We go back a long way. I've always been good mates with her brother. We grew up together,' he said, unconsciously parroting Erica's explanation of their relationship to Briony.

'Okay,' Gary said. 'Mandy was just trying to be helpful.'

'I know. It's okay.' Jamie had a vague recollection of hearing how she had tried to set her mother up before she and Finn got together.

No more was said on the topic as the conversation turned to the coast walk the group of women were organising and in which all three of the young people intended to participate. 'What about you, Dad?' Rory asked. 'Going to join us? You're not too old,' he laughed.

'And you're not too old for me to cuff your ear,' Jamie responded. 'For your information I do intend to go, along with Cam and Poppy, Finn and Liz, Joe and Gill, and Rachel and Luke.' As he spoke, he remembered that Erica would no doubt be part of that group too. He needed to find out what was bothering her. He'd call as soon as he got home. Maybe he was imagining things.

*

Erica hadn't enjoyed her breakfast. She had been too aware of Jamie sitting inside the café, conscious she had acted cool towards him. It had been a shock to see him, for him to behave as if nothing had happened, which of course it hadn't for him. He hadn't been privy to Briony's comment, been aware of Erica's sleepless night, of the guilt which had flooded her at her daughter-in-law's words.

He deserved an explanation. The poor man must be wondering what had happened to change her from the woman who had accepted, even encouraged his embraces, to one who could barely speak to him. Erica bit her lip as she tried to fashion the words which would describe her predicament in a way he would understand. She was no further forward in her thinking when her phone rang, and she saw Jamie's number on the screen. Glad Briony was busy with Ava, she walked out to the back yard and pressed to accept the call.

Without waiting for him to speak, Erica said, 'Jamie, I'm sorry. I owe you an apology. What must you think of me?'

There was a moment's silence then Jamie said, 'Is everything all right, Erica?'

The sound of his voice, his concerned tone, sent Erica's heart plummeting. 'It is and it isn't. Briony saw us kissing and she said something that concerned me. We need to talk. I'm not sure…' Her voice trailed off as she tried to work out how they could meet without Briony knowing. There was no way.

Seeming to understand her dilemma, Jamie said, 'Could you slip out when she's asleep? Why don't you text me? We could meet at your gate and go for a walk along the beach… in the moonlight.'

'O…kay.' A few days ago, she'd have been excited about the prospect of a romantic walk with Jamie in the moonlight. Now, the only emotion coursing through her was the worry of how she was going to tell him they needed to pause their relationship until… until when? Erica was at a loss. There were no guidelines for this sort of thing, no accepted pattern of behaviour. She guessed most people in her situation would undergo a period of grieving, but she felt no grief at Geoff's death, only a profound sense of relief. She supposed there had been an initial period of grief, but that had more to do with her shock than anything else. It had quickly been overtaken by the realisation that he couldn't hurt her anymore.

The rest of the day passed pleasantly. Erica showed Briony and Ava around Pelican Crossing, they called in to see Joe and Gill, who welcomed them, and where Coco took a liking to Ava and stood guard over her stroller. Then they came back to the cottage for a quiet dinner. To Erica, it seemed ages before Briony stretched her arms above her head and said, 'I'm off to bed now, Mum. It's been a lovely day, thanks. I'll see you in the morning. Will you be going for an early morning swim again?'

'Not tomorrow,' Erica replied, though she had a feeling she might well feel like one, depending how the conversation with Jamie went. 'Goodnight, sweetheart.' The women hugged, and Briony went off to bed.

Erica picked up her book but was unable to concentrate. When she was sure Briony would be asleep, she texted Jamie then, pulling on a jacket, opened the door and went out. It was a cool, clear evening. Erica wrapped her arms around her and looked up at the sky where the stars seemed to be shining even more brightly than usual.

Despite her decision to put their relationship on hold, Erica couldn't prevent the way her heart leapt at the sight of Jamie hurrying towards her.

'Hey,' he said, taking hold of her shoulders and kissing her gently on the cheek.

Erica didn't resist, as she breathed in his familiar scent, a mixture of his cologne and soap. It felt so good. *He* felt so good. How could she give this up? But Briony and Ava were important to her. They were family, while Jamie was… What was he? An old flame? A promise for the future, a future which she might now have to give up – or at least put on hold – until sometime in the distant future when people might think a suitable period of mourning had passed? She couldn't ask Jamie to wait that long.

'Good to see you. You got away okay?'

'As you see.' Erica felt like the teenager who had slipped out without her parents' knowledge, as she had done many other times. It had been to meet Jamie then too. She smiled at the memory.

'Just like old times,' he said, reading her mind. He'd always been good at that, but he could have no idea what she was about to say. He took her hand, and Erica didn't resist as they made their way down to the beach.

It was only when they reached the sand, that she noticed he was carrying a blanket and she was transported back to her teens, to the nights they'd gone to the beach to lie on a blanket on the sand, gaze up at the stars and make plans for the future. Tonight, when he laid the blanket on the sand, they sat on it instead of lying.

'Now, are you going to tell me what's up,' Jamie asked, throwing an arm around her shoulders, 'why you acted so oddly at *The Blue Dolphin* this morning?'

The firm grip of Jamie's hand on her shoulder gave Erica the courage to speak. 'It's Briony,' she said.

'Is she sick? Or has she said something about your son? You did say you were worried he might be like his dad.'

'No.' Erica shook her head. 'I haven't had a chance to talk to her about Kieren yet.'Though she must. Briony had said a few things that confirmed her suspicions. 'It's you... you and me. She saw us... last night, and... she says she's pleased for me, that I deserve to be happy, but...' Erica picked at a loose piece of thread on the blanket, '... she thinks it's too soon.'

'Too soon for what?'

'Too soon after Geoff's death for me to form a relationship.' Erica glanced at Jamie to see his lips tighten.

'That's rubbish. From what you've told me about him, your husband was a violent, controlling bastard... and she expects you to observe what she considers to be a suitable period of mourning?' His voice was shaking with anger. 'Surely you're not going to agree?'

Erica pulled on the loose thread again before replying. 'She's my daughter-in-law, Jamie. It's hard to explain, but I've been like a mother to her, and I have to respect her wishes. You'd do the same if Mandy...' her voice trailed off as not only did she realise Mandy would never suggest such a thing but that, even if she did, he'd tell her it was none of her business. Jamie's next words confirmed it.

'What you choose to do or not to do is none of her damned business. You mean to say you're going to let her dictate to you who you can see, who you can...'

Erica was glad Jamie stopped there, and didn't continue that line of thought... or didn't voice it, anyway. He wasn't making this any easier for her. But had she thought he would? 'I'm sorry, Jamie, but...'

He didn't allow her to finish, rising and saying, 'If that's the way you feel, we're done here,' and leaving her sitting on his blanket, he stormed off.

Thirty-nine

It wasn't the way Erica had expected their meeting to end, though she couldn't really blame Jamie. But she'd hoped they could at least remain friends. Now, it seemed even that was to be denied her. She picked up the blanket, folded it and hugged it to her, a reminder of what could have been. Then she returned home, slipping in as quietly as she'd slipped out, knowing she'd have another sleepless night.

Next morning, Erica tried to put on a cheerful expression to face Briony at breakfast. She'd promised to take her and Ava to the river for a picnic in the expectation of seeing more of the pelicans which Briony was so fond of.

Unaware of Erica's mood, Briony made cheerful conversation over breakfast before going outside to call Kieren. 'I promised to call him every morning,' she said with a slight grimace which contributed to Erica's suspicion all was not well in her son's marriage. The cloud in Briony's eyes when she returned did nothing to dispel that impression.

'Everything okay?' Erica asked, when Briony came back into the kitchen where Ava was happily playing with a soft toy.

'I guess,' Briony said with a frown. 'Kieren misses us. He's worried about the yard, and he thinks you're planning to turn me against him. As if...'

Erica felt a stab of anger. Maybe now was the time... 'Take a seat, Briony. I want to talk to you,' she said.

'Why do you think Kieren said that?' she asked, when Briony had taken a seat.

'I don't know, Mum. Maybe because you didn't agree to come to live with us. He was angry about that and…'

'Did he try to blame you?'

Briony shifted uncomfortably in her chair. 'No, not really. Things are difficult for him at the moment. Dad left a bit of a mess which he's trying to sort out. Sometimes he… he doesn't always mean what he says.' She looked down to where she was twisting her hands in her lap.

Erica took a deep breath. 'That can be how it starts, Briony. I think Kieren is more like his father than you realise. I wish I'd known sooner, left sooner, but…'

'Kieren's Ava's dad!' Briony said, her voice echoing in the small room. 'He doesn't mean anything by it. He loves us.'

'I'm sure he does… in his own way. But is this how you want your life to be?' she asked, making one more attempt to get through to her daughter-in-law. 'Have you heard of coercive control?'

'That's not Kieren. You should know. He's your son.'

'Yes,' Erica said sadly. She realised she wasn't going to get anywhere with Briony, not today anyway. 'Why don't you take Ava outside while I make up some sandwiches? It won't take me long, then we can set off.'

'Okay, Mum,' Briony said seemingly satisfied. She picked up Ava and telling her, 'We're going for a picnic to see pelicans,' carried her outside.

Left alone, Erica shook her head. She'd tried, and she'd try again before Briony left. But she felt she was beating her head against a brick wall. Briony couldn't see Kieren's behaviour for what it was – and Erica was now convinced he was following in his father's footsteps. But, she wondered, would she have been any different from Briony when Kieren was a baby. She'd been just as blind to Geoff's faults, believing his behaviour was normal, that she needed to try harder. Then it had been too late. She didn't want Briony to endure the same future as she had.

*

They had been sitting by the river for some time and had enjoyed their picnic lunch, Briony delighted at the arrival of a group of pelicans who seemed unafraid to come close, when a dog ran up to them, followed by its owner.

Erica recognised the woman… and the dog. It was old Agnes, and Erica remembered, the last time they'd met, how she had the strange impression Agnes could read her mind. The dog ran up to the stroller and sniffed at Ava who gurgled with pleasure.

Briony jumped up to ward the dog off, but Agnes called out, 'Lady's an old dog. She won't harm the baby.'

When the old woman reached them, she stood looking at Erica. 'Your granddaughter, I suppose. It's always lovely to see a new generation. She doesn't live here?'

'No, my daughter-in-law and she are visiting from Perth.'

'Hmm.' Agnes turned to Briony. 'Pelican Crossing is a good place to live… a safe place. You would do well to listen to your mother-in-law. Come, Lady,' she said to the dog, and the pair sauntered off.

'What was that about?' Briony said. 'Who is she and what did she mean?'

'That was old Agnes. She's lived in Pelican Crossing for what seems like for ever, and she's always seemed old.' Erica chuckled. 'She lives close to here and takes care of sick and injured pelicans. She often seems to talk in riddles, but she's known for her wisdom. It pays to listen to her.'

Briony stared at Erica for a few moments then shrugged and said dismissively, 'She's just an old woman.'

But Erica was remembering some of the stories she'd heard about old Agnes, about how people had benefitted from following her advice, and wished she could acquire some for herself.

*

Jamie cursed, as the spanner he was wielding fell to the ground. Nothing had gone right today. First, his fishing charter had been cancelled. The whole group had come down with a stomach upset, suspected food poisoning, so there was nothing he could do about it, but it threw out his plans.

He'd decided to spend the day on repairs instead, but that wasn't going well either. Then Gary had called to leave a message about them getting together with Erica and Briony so the two young women could talk babies. He ought not to have been annoyed as it had been his idea in the first place, but that had been before Erica dropped her bombshell.

Everything had been going so well. He and Erica had almost been back on their old footing. He'd had such plans. Now, thanks to Briony, they had been thrown into the bin. He shook his head, not for the first time. How could Erica allow a throw-away comment from her daughter-in-law to destroy what they had together? Had she already been having second thoughts?

Picking up the spanner, Jamie made another half-hearted attempt to finish the task he'd started, but his heart wasn't in it. He needed to reply to Gary, and he wasn't sure what he was going to say. He tidied away his tools and headed over to *The Grand* in the hope a cold beer might help.

When he walked in, blinking at the change from the bright sunlight to the dimness inside the hotel, Jamie was surprised to see Joe standing at the bar with a beer. 'Don't normally see you here at this time on a weekday,' he said, before ordering a glass of the craft beer he'd lately developed a taste for.

'A meeting finished early, and Gill's tied up,' he explained.

'Coco?'

'With Erica. She's found a fan in her granddaughter. I thought you'd have known that.' He gave Jamie a puzzled glance.

Jamie winced.

'Something the matter? Let's get a seat.'

The pair moved over to a small booth at one end of the bar.

Joe was the last person Jamie wanted to talk to about Erica, but it seemed there was no way of avoiding it. 'We're not seeing each other anymore.' He took a long draught of beer, hoping Joe wouldn't pursue it.

'What happened? I thought you two…' He looked pensive for a moment. 'I know she'll be pretty tied up with Briony and Ava, but…' He peered at Jamie, who flinched.

'It's Briony,' he said after a pause. 'She has suggested to Erica that it's too soon after her husband's death for her to be getting involved with me.' He sighed.

'And Erica agrees with her? I can't believe it, after the way that bastard treated her.'

'Yeah.' Jamie stared down into his beer, then looked up to meet Joe's eyes. 'I found it hard to believe too, but there it is. Your sister is a strange one, blows hot and cold. I thought… well, it seems I was wrong. I take it that she doesn't want to upset her daughter-in-law, but…' He sighed again.

'Hell! I'm sorry, mate. If there was anything I could do… But Erica's always been her own person, apart from when her bastard of a husband had her under his thumb. I guess in a way I can understand her going along with Briony. She's been through a lot and apart from me, Kieren and Briony are the only family she has left, but…' he shook his head, '… this is going too far, even for Erica. I wonder…'

Jamie raised an eyebrow.

'I wonder if it's all down to Kieren,' Joe said. 'I know Erica's been worried that he was turning into his dad, exercising control over Briony just as Geoff did over her. Has she mentioned her son to you?'

'She's told me a bit about him, about her worries, but surely…? He's in Perth.'

'I don't think that matters. If she thinks Briony is under Kieren's thumb, Erica would probably agree to anything Briony suggested if she thought it would keep her daughter-in-law safe.'

Jamie stared at him in amazement. Would Erica really stop seeing him because of some cockeyed idea that her son might somehow punish his wife? It seemed ridiculous but what did he know about what went on in some men's minds. He'd seen a lot of the news recently about domestic violence and knew the perpetrators thought differently from guys like him.

'Briony's only here for a week,' Joe said. 'Maybe, when she goes…' He picked up his beer and took a drink. 'Anyway, it's worth a try. Gill and I both think the pair of you are well suited.'

'Thanks.' Joe's opinion meant a lot to him. He hoped he was right.

Forty

The week with Briony and Ava passed quickly, too quickly for Erica who loved having them with her. Briony was good company, and little Ava was a delight. Erica was sad when Saturday rolled around, and it was time for them to leave. At various times over the week, she'd tried to raise the topic of Kieren's controlling behaviour with Briony again, but each time had been met with a refusal from her daughter-in-law to accept that Erica's suspicions might be true.

Erica hadn't given up. When they were at the airport, she made one last attempt. 'You don't have to go back, Briony. Why don't you stay, at least for a few more weeks? I'm sure Kieren can do without you for a bit longer.' It might give Erica time to work on her, to show her she wasn't dependent on Kieren, that she could make a life here in Pelican Crossing.

'I need to go home to Kieren. He misses us, misses me. He's my husband. My place is there with him. I know you mean well, Mum, but you don't understand.'

Erica bit her tongue, knowing nothing she could say would change Briony's mind. 'Promise me one thing, Briony,' she said at last. 'Promise me, that if Kieren hits you, just once, you'll leave him straight away. You'll always have a home with me.' Erica wished someone had given her that advice when Kieren was a baby, but she wondered if she'd have taken it, or if, like Briony she'd have believed she knew better.

Briony didn't reply. Her flight was called, and she picked up her bag.

With a heavy heart, Erica hugged the younger woman and kissed Ava, hoping she'd see them again soon. She didn't intend to let her granddaughter grow up without knowing her grandmother, neither did she relish returning to Perth to watch Briony being treated by Kieren the way Geoff had treated her.

Erica watched her daughter-in-law walk through the departure gate carrying Ava, on her way back to Perth and to Kieren. She hoped she was wrong, but feared she wasn't and could only comfort herself that she'd tried her best.

She worried all the way back to Pelican Crossing, where, feeling the need for company, she parked outside Joe's house, the *For Sale* sign in the front yard an indication of how things were about to change.

'You've found a house?' she asked, when she had hugged Joe and Gill and been affectionately greeted by Coco.

'Just a few days ago,' Gill said with a big smile. 'We finally found somewhere we both agree on.' She gave Joe a loving glance.

'Where is it? Tell me all about it.'

'Let me make us coffee first,' Joe said, 'or would you prefer one of Gill's teas?'

'Tea, thanks.' Erica took a seat at the kitchen table. Leaving this place with all its memories would be a wrench for Joe, but she could understand Gill's desire to start afresh. She would hate to move into the house Jamie had shared with Cindy. *Where had that thought come from?* Erica shifted in her chair as if her companions could read her mind. Not only was there no likelihood of her and Jamie sharing a home, Erica was pretty sure Cindy had never lived in Jamie's cottage.

When Joe had brewed coffee, Gill had made ginger and lemon tea for her and Erica, and Coco had been provided with one of the bone-shaped dog biscuits she loved, they took their drinks and a plate of ginger biscuits out to the yard, Gill carrying her iPad.

'You'll never guess,' Gill said, her voice brimming with excitement. She opened her iPad and turned it to face Erica.

Erica peered at the screen, at an image which looked very like Livvy's cottage. She looked back at Gill and Joe who were both smiling widely.

It was Joe who spoke first. 'We couldn't believe it when we saw it advertised, and we didn't want to say anything till our offer was accepted. It's at the far end of the row of cottages, a deceased estate. It had only just come on the market, and after seeing Livvy's place and what she had done to it, we snapped it up. We're going to be neighbours!'

'That's… good.' But Erica wouldn't be staying there permanently. Once Livvy returned home, she'd have to find somewhere else to live. But she was glad Joe and Gill had found somewhere they liked, and she remembered how Gill had been so taken with the cottage when they visited her. 'I'm so pleased for you,' she said somewhat belatedly.

The other two didn't appear to have noticed her hesitation as Joe described their purchase. 'It'll need a lot of work,' he said. 'The place has had the same owner for decades, but that's what makes it so perfect for us. Gill can't wait to have the kitchen rebuilt, and I must admit to having plans to redecorate the other rooms.'

'Including the bathroom,' Gill put in. 'You should see it, Erica.' She rolled her eyes.

'I'm looking forward to doing just that. When do you expect to settle?'

'That's the beauty of it,' Joe said. 'Given it's a deceased estate, we are able to get the keys in the next few days and can start to get quotes, though of course we can't actually do anything till the sale goes through.'

'Wow!'

The morning passed quickly with Joe and Gill sharing their plans, and making Erica wish she was in a position to purchase a home of her own too. But her time would come. She had been lulled into a sense of false security, assuming they weren't going to ask her about Jamie, when Gill said, 'Joe says you and Jamie have broken up. He met Jamie in the hotel earlier this week, said he was devastated, didn't you, Joe?'

Joe rubbed the back of his neck, something Erica knew he did when he was embarrassed. 'Devastated might be too strong a word. But he was upset.'

And broken up might be too strong too, Erica thought. There hadn't really been anything to break up – a few meetings, a couple of kisses. She felt a shudder run down her spine at the memory of those kisses. 'It wasn't a good idea,' she said.

But Gill didn't intend to let it go. 'Why not? You're perfectly suited to each other. If you have some dumb idea in your head that you owe your late husband anything, you can disabuse yourself of that right away. As you know, I see women like you all the time. If I could have five dollars for every one of them who'd jump at the chance to meet someone as genuine and honest as Jamie Whittaker, not to mention he's a hunk, I'd be a rich woman.'

'I…' Erica began, but Joe interrupted her.

'Gill's right,' he said. 'You'd go far before you'd meet a better man than Jamie, and I'm not just saying that because he's a good mate.'

'It's not that simple,' Erica said. 'It's… Briony. She thinks it's too soon for me to be in another relationship, and I think she may be right.'

Joe and Gill looked at each other, communicating silently. It was Gill who spoke first, her voice gentle. 'I know you've made your decision for the best of reasons, but don't you think you've gone overboard trying to please your daughter-in-law who…' She stopped there and looked at Joe again.

'What Gill's trying to say, sis, is that Briony isn't you, and you're the only person who can decide whether or not it's too soon. I'd understand your thinking if you'd had a happy marriage like Barb and I had. As you know, I grieved for years, and if I hadn't met Gill…' he reached over to take her hand and squeeze it, '… I might have stayed single for the rest of my life. But I did meet her and I'm glad I did. It's a rare thing to meet your special someone, and I've been lucky enough to find mine twice. If you think Jamie might be that someone for you, then I'd say go for it and to hell with anyone who tells you otherwise.'

Erica stared at her brother in surprise. This was such a departure from his usual way of talking. He must feel strongly for him to speak so bluntly. But she did get the impression the pair of them had planned this and were ganging up on her. For a few moments she didn't say anything, too astounded to speak. Then she rose, surprising Coco who had been lying at her feet. 'I can't do this,' she said. 'I need to leave.'

Forty-one

Erica was so upset when she left Joe's that she didn't go home immediately. Instead, she drove to the bluff on the outskirts of town. There was a car park there which was often used by surfers. It overlooked a long stretch of white sand and today it was deserted. She sat, staring out at the ocean, her eyes filled with tears.

Time passed, a few surfers arrived, their cars breaking the silence of this isolated spot, then peace descended again as they made their way down to the beach. Erica watched as they entered the ocean and paddled out through the waves to surf back in, only to do it all again. Life seemed so simple for them. She remembered when it had been like that for her too. Why did it suddenly seem so hard, so difficult to know what was the right thing to do? She felt she was being pulled in two directions. She could do what Briony wanted or follow Joe's advice. Both were family and she loved them both.

'Are you all right?' Having closed her eyes while she tried to gather her thoughts, Erica opened them with a start to see Rachel standing there peering at her through the open window. She was accompanied by a small white dog which looked exactly like Poppy's.

Erica opened her mouth to say, 'I'm fine,' every woman's stock answer to that question, but instead she found herself saying, 'No, not really.'

'Molly and I have been having a walk. I live just over there.' She pointed to a large house some distance away. 'Why don't you come back with me for coffee or a bite to eat?'

Erica hesitated, then, seeing the concern in Rachel's eyes, and hearing the little dog give a bark of encouragement, she agreed.

The two women walked along in silence, Molly prancing along beside them, until they reached the house. It was a large family home perched on the top of the bluff, its windows facing the ocean. The thought that it must have amazing views flittered through Erica's mind as she followed Rachel inside and through to the large family kitchen.

'I'll just fill Molly's bowl, then I planned to have some bread and cheese for a late lunch. Have you eaten?'

'No, but there's no need,' Erica said. But she realised she was hungry. She hadn't eaten since breakfast, had barely touched the biscuits Gill had served, and it must now be well past her normal lunchtime.

'Well, I have to fix something for myself anyway, so you may as well join me. Do you prefer tea or coffee?'

'Tea please.' It was pleasant to have someone else take charge, without making demands on her or asking questions.

Without any more ado, Rachel took several cheeses out of the fridge, cut slices from a loaf of sourdough bread and set them on a platter along with some grapes and slices of apple. Then she made a pot of peppermint tea, and settled down at the table beside Erica, the little dog positioning herself under Rachel's chair.

'Help yourself,' Rachel said. 'I'm not going to ask you what brought you all the way up here to sit in your car with your eyes closed, but if you want to talk, I'm happy to listen. I've always been told I'm a good listener, I'm not easily shocked and I can keep a secret.'

Erica laughed. She'd only met Rachel briefly before now, but she'd been impressed by the way Gill and her other friends seemed to defer to her. She was a few years older than Erica, than Gill too. Maybe that was why. She wasn't ready to confide in Rachel but was curious about her. 'Have you always lived here?' she asked. 'It's a lovely spot, though quite isolated.'

'That's what we loved about it.' Rachel relaxed back in her chair. 'My husband and I bought it when I was pregnant with Jess, my oldest. Our three children grew up here and it was a wonderful place to bring them up. When they all left, Kirk and I rattled around in it, but we loved it too much to sell. Then...' her eyes misted over. '...

Kirk got sick.' She paused for a moment, gazing into space. 'When he passed away, I couldn't leave. There were too many memories. I turned the place into a bed and breakfast. I'm winding that down as I'm now taking care of my granddaughter. She's having a playdate today with a little friend in town. That's why she's not here.'

While Rachel had been talking, Erica had helped herself to a slice of bread topped with cheese and taken a sip of the peppermint tea. Now she said, 'I'm sorry about your husband.' It sounded as if, unlike Erica, Rachel had enjoyed a happy marriage, only to have it cut short. 'How old is your granddaughter?'

'She's four. You may think it strange that I'm taking care of a four-year-old. It's a long story. It wasn't by choice, but her mother's dead, my son is currently working overseas, and his lifestyle isn't compatible with looking after a young child. However, he is planning to come back here to live as soon as he can arrange it.' She smiled, a secret smile, and Erica wondered if there was another story Rachel wasn't going to reveal.

'More tea?'

'Thanks,' Erica said, her mind filled with Rachel's story and the realisation that her companion had had her own cross to bear, yet seemed to have managed to survive and to remain optimistic about life. 'Don't you get lonely out here?' she asked, glancing out the window where all she could see was the distant ocean.

Rachel blushed, as she refilled Erica's cup. 'I was for a time after Kirk passed, then I started my B&B, and looked after my twin granddaughters several days a week. They started school at the beginning of this year. Now I have Verity and…' she blushed again, '… when I thought I was finished with love, I met someone I knew when I was in my teens. Luke came back to Pelican Crossing to do a locum for our vet who lives just across there.' She pointed to the other end of the bluff where Erica could see a roofline. 'He'll be moving in with me when Bob, the regular vet, gets back.'

Erica stared at Rachel again, stunned by her revelation, the reference to reuniting with someone Rachel had known in her teens resonating with her. Their stories were completely different. Rachel's husband had been gone for years before she met this man. But… she felt an affinity with this woman who was practically a stranger to her, so much so she was emboldened to confide in her.

'So that's it,' she finished, when she described meeting Jamie again, the reawakening of their feelings for each other, then Briony's suggestion it was too soon after Geoff's death, the knowledge her son wouldn't approve either, followed by Joe and Gill's advice. 'I don't know what to do.'

'Oh, my dear. Family can be a blessing and a curse. I've been lucky with mine, but a couple of my friends have had challenges with theirs. What do *you* want to do?'

'But it's not just up to me, is it?' Erica said. 'Briony and Kieren are important to me, even if I do suspect Kieren's controlling her… maybe because of that. I'd hate to think anything I do causes problems for her. But I value Joe's opinion too. He knows me, and he knows Jamie.'

'What if it *was* up to you? If Briony had never suggested it was too soon? A ridiculous statement, anyway. How can anyone judge how soon is appropriate for another person? I suspect that if Luke had appeared on the scene shortly after Kirk's death, I'd have done exactly what I did last year. We have no control over when fate puts someone in our path… or when we fall in love.'

Erica's stomach churned. She felt shaken by Rachel's mention of love. *Was she falling in love with Jamie?* If Briony had never made the suggestion it was too soon, she'd still be seeing Jamie, they'd have got together with Mandy and his grandson as he suggested and… 'I'd never have stopped seeing him,' she said.

'Then you have your answer.'

Molly whined at that point and Rachel rose to let her out, leaving Erica to ponder over her conclusion. *Was it that simple?*

Erica was still considering Rachel's words when she returned, leaving Molly outside. 'I'm sorry but I need to go to fetch Verity. You're welcome to stay till I get back if you want.'

'No,' Erica rose, 'thanks for the tea and the bread and cheese, and thanks for listening. I'll consider what you said. It seems you agree with Joe and Gill. I just have to work out what's best for me.'

'Of course you do. But I suggest you don't leave it too long. Men like Jamie don't grow on trees, and life can get lonely as we grow older.'

Rachel's words gave Erica an insight into Rachel's life. Despite her positive outlook, her attempt to paint her life after her husband's death as full and happy, Erica suspected she'd been lonely too.

Driving home, she remembered she still had Jamie's blanket, the one he'd taken to the beach. Perhaps she should return it.

Forty-two

It was a week since Erica dropped her bombshell, and Jamie had walked off and left her on the beach, knowing anything he said might ruin any chance of their getting back together. After his meltdown on Monday when he'd unloaded on an unsuspecting Joe, he'd been lucky to have full charters, leaving only the evenings to fall into a blue funk wondering if there was any way he could retrieve the situation. Now he'd found Erica again, he didn't want to lose her. But it looked as if he might, if he couldn't persuade her to ignore her daughter-in-law's wishes. They seemed completely unreasonable to him, but he could see Joe's point. Briony was family, and he could appreciate the importance of family. His was important to him too. But her daughter-in-law should be going back to Perth soon, if she hadn't left already. Perhaps Erica would have a rethink. After all, Perth was a long way away. How would her son and daughter-in-law know if she and Jamie were seeing each other?

Jamie had only eaten a few slices of the pizza he'd picked up on the way home, before throwing the rest into the bin. He was pouring himself a glass of whisky, in the hope it would help him get a better night's sleep than he'd had in the past week, when he heard a rustling at the front door. He rose with a sigh, expecting it to be Lou's cat. The large ginger cat had developed the habit of wandering at night and had often found her way into Jamie's garden. On a few occasions he'd weakened and fed her. He guessed that was why she kept coming back.

He opened the door prepared to shoo her off, but instead of Tilly, it was Erica who stood there, holding an orange checked bundle.

*

As soon as she walked into the cottage, Erica saw the blanket. It was still lying in the hall where she'd dropped it when she got back from the beach, a reminder of Jamie and everything she'd lost. She picked it up and buried her nose in it as if she could detect his scent. But all she smelled was damp wool mixed with a faint whiff of the ocean. Folding it carefully again, she took it into the kitchen with her and laid it on a chair, before pouring herself a glass of wine.

It was too early for wine, but after the day she'd had, she was in need of something stronger than coffee or tea. Taking her drink out to the back garden, she replayed the day in her mind, her farewell to Briony and Ava, the visit with Joe and Gill, their advice, then Rachel.

Rachel was right. She had to do what *she* wanted, not what other people told her to do, and that included Joe, Gill *and* Rachel. The trouble was that she was torn. Deep down, she wanted Jamie, but not if it meant losing contact with Briony and Ava. One thing she was sure of, she needed to return the blanket. Having it here would be a constant reminder of Jamie.

She waited till she thought he'd have gone to bed, then picked up the blanket and slipped out. She walked down the road, the only light coming from a particularly bright moon, until she came to Jamie's cottage. Taking a deep breath, she pushed open the gate and walked up the path.

At the door, she hesitated, tempted to knock. Then, as she was about to drop her bundle on the doorstep and flee, the door opened, and a shaft of light streamed across the spot where she was standing. Erica blinked at the sight of Jamie standing there looking even more attractive than ever in a pair of old grey track pants and a black tee-shirt, his hair dishevelled.

'Erica!'

Erica's heart thudded in her chest. She cleared her throat, pretending not to be affected. 'Jamie, I…' She hesitated, torn between turning to flee as she'd planned and throwing herself into his arms. 'I brought back your blanket.'

'So I see. Why don't you come in?'

'Oh, I…' Erica didn't seem able to finish a sentence. This wasn't what she'd planned.

Jamie opened the door wider.

As if propelled by some unseen source, Erica found herself walking through the door, into the hallway, then into the living room. She placed the blanket on one of the two armchairs and looked around. She was reminded of the last time she'd been in Jamie's cottage, when she'd come to dress the wound on his hand. So much had happened since then.

'Won't you take a seat? And you look as if you need a drink.'

Erica saw a bottle of whisky sitting on the coffee table alongside a half-empty glass. She hadn't known Jamie was a whisky drinker. 'I've had a glass of wine,' she said.

'Sorry, I'm clean out of wine, but you're not intending to drive anywhere tonight, are you?'

'No.' Erica sat down tentatively, perching on the edge of the sofa.

Jamie poured a glass of whisky and handed it to her.

Erica was glad when he took a seat on the other armchair and didn't join her on the sofa. She took a sip, flinching as the fiery liquid burnt her throat. But it did remove some of the tension she was feeling.

'You didn't intend to knock, did you?' Jamie asked with the lopsided grin she remembered so well. 'You were going to dump the blanket on the doorstep and run.'

Erica blushed. He knew her so well, how she hated confrontation.

'I thought it was Lou's cat at the door and was planning to chase her away. You were a surprise… a good surprise.'

Erica gave a small smile. She'd never been mistaken for a cat before.

'I'm glad you're here. We need to talk,' Jamie said. 'I'm sorry I rushed off like that… and left you on the beach. I shouldn't have done that. I should have stayed and talked, but…' he picked up his glass and took a sip, '… I was so upset, so mad. I couldn't trust myself to stay. So, I left. I've regretted it ever since.'

'I'm sorry too,' Erica said, clutching her glass in both hands. 'I shouldn't have been so… I should have explained more. It wasn't so much that I agreed with Briony, but… things are difficult for her. I knew what Kieren's reaction would be if she told him I was seeing you so soon after Geoff's death. He thought the world of his dad and expects me to be grieving as much as he is. He doesn't understand… doesn't want to understand.' For the first time, Erica wondered if

Kieren was as blind to his dad's treatment of her as he pretended to be, or if he just considered it to be normal. *Where had she gone wrong with her son? Or had Geoff's influence been too great for anything she might have done to ameliorate it?* She thought about the last time she'd spoken to him, when she called to check in with Briony and he answered the phone. She'd made a tentative approach, tried to discover his thoughts, suggested he needed to pay more attention to Briony, help her around the house, with Ava. His curt response that he didn't need her to tell him how to behave had stung her into silence, and done nothing to reassure her.

'I spoke with Joe.'

Erica stared at him. He and Joe had been talking about her? She should have known. They were mates. Gill had said they'd met. It was how she knew she and Jamie were no longer seeing each other, but… what else had been said?

'He reminded me that Briony was family and said he thought you might be worried about Kieren, about how he might react…'

Erica swallowed. That was exactly what she had been worried about, but as Rachel said, Kieren and Briony were in Perth.

'Has she gone back now… your daughter-in-law?'

Erica nodded, all the advice she'd been given swirling around in her head.

'So…' Jamie began.

Erica knew what he was going to say. It was what had been going through her mind too. But nothing had changed… or had it. She needed time to think. 'Thanks for the drink,' she said. 'I should go now. I've had a busy day and…' She rose, intending to put her empty glass down on the table. But as she reached down, somehow Jamie was there, so close she could smell his cologne, the whisky on his breath. She froze as her senses leapt to life, her pulse quickening. Suddenly, she was in his arms.

'I've missed you,' Jamie murmured as his lips claimed hers.

Forty-three

When Erica opened her eyes, it took her a few moments to realise where she was, then she remembered. She gazed around the unfamiliar bedroom… at the television perched on top of a chest of drawers, the old-fashioned curtains open to reveal a tidy garden, then her eyes fell on the heap of discarded clothes – hers and Jamie's. She'd only come to return the blanket, to leave it on Jamie's doorstep. She couldn't believe she'd ended up in his bed. But there was no denying she was here. She glanced down at the face on the pillow and smiled. She guessed Rachel had her answer. This was what she wanted.

She also guessed Joe would be pleased, Gill too. But what about Kieren and Briony? Her heart sank as she imagined their reaction. But they weren't here. She smiled again at the memory of the previous night, at the consummation of what had started so long ago. It had been worth the wait. Nothing had prepared her for the tumult of passion unleashed by that kiss, for Jamie's gentle lovemaking. It was as if she had been waiting all her life for this moment.

The man lying beside her in the bed stirred. Jamie's eyes opened. He gave a lazy smile. 'I didn't dream it. You're really here,' he said, pulling her into his arms.

Erica gave a sigh of pleasure as her head fitted perfectly in the hollow between his shoulder and neck. It was warm here. She felt safe. She wished she could stay here for ever. Then with one finger he tipped up her chin and their lips met in a searing kiss.

'Good morning, beautiful,' Jamie said when they finally drew apart. 'No regrets?'

'No regrets,' Erica said with a smile. 'Last night…' Her smile grew wider.

Jamie pulled her into a hug, this one lacking the passion of his earlier embrace. 'I've waited a long time for this.'

'Me too.' Erica hadn't realised how much she'd missed Jamie. It was as if all the years between had fallen away, and she and Jamie were back together where they belonged.

They finally rose and with much laughter and more kissing, showered together before pulling on the clothes they'd discarded so hurriedly the night before.

'Hungry?' Jamie asked.

'Mmm.' She hadn't eaten since the bread and cheese at Rachel's the day before. 'But I should get home.' She looked down at her wrinkled clothes.

'Why don't I cook breakfast first? I do a mean omelette. Then you can go home and get changed into something suitable for a day's sailing. I'm assuming you're not averse to spending the day on Princess Two again?'

'That sounds wonderful.' Erica was glad it was Sunday, and she didn't need to go into work. Work was the last thing on her mind right now. The prospect of spending the whole day with Jamie on his yacht sent a wave of anticipation through her. 'I can pack some food for us,' she added.

'Great. Now, you'd better let me get to the kitchen, wench.' He gave her a gentle tap on the bottom which was both affectionate and intimate.

It was almost two hours later when Erica and Jamie made their way to the marina where Princess Two was berthed. They were welcomed by a pod of pelicans who waddled over to greet them, and Erica and Jamie laughed at the large birds. The sun was shining, everything smelt fresh. It was as if they had awakened to a whole new world.

*

The day passed quickly, too quickly for Erica who was revelling in this new feeling of being with Jamie, of being on top of the world. They had sailed and talked, anchored, eaten lunch and spent the afternoon in each other's arms. It was as if the rest of the world ceased to exist.

But now they were back in the harbour, making their way between rows of other boats in the marina, to tie up at Jamie's mooring. At this time on a Sunday, the marina was a hive of activity as the local boat owners and visitors to Pelican Crossing returned from their day on the ocean, many preparing to spend the evening on their decks, and calling to each other across the water. It was so different from the peace she and Jamie had enjoyed.

Tired but happy, Erica helped Jamie tie up and secure the yacht, then hand-in- hand, they walked back to the row of cottages, stopping at Erica's gate. 'Do you want to come in?' she asked shyly. Although they had spent the whole day together, their new closeness was so novel she was reluctant to leave him.

It seemed Jamie felt the same. 'How about dinner at the yacht club?' he asked. 'I can pop home to shower and change, give you time to do the same. Pick you up in an hour?'

'Oh, yes please!' Erica said, then in case she sounded too eager added, 'I'd like that.'

Jamie chuckled, gave her a brief peck on the cheek and left.

Erica stared after him, marvelling at how her life had changed in less than twenty-four hours, and headed inside to shower and change as he'd suggested. Standing under the shower, Erica looked down at her body which showed the ravages of time and motherhood. It was no longer the slim taut figure she had when she and Jamie first dated. Last night they had been in too much of a rush, too hungry for each other for her to worry about it, but now… Then she remembered how Jamie had told her she was beautiful, how he had caressed her, kissed her skin, and realised he didn't care about the way time had ravaged her body. To him, she was still the teenager he'd fallen in love with, just as to her, he was still the tall godlike creature who all the girls yearned after but who had chosen her to spend time with.

This was what love was like, an acceptance of each other just the way they were. It was so unlike what she'd had with Geoff who'd always demeaned her, making her feel inferior, unlovely and insecure. She shook her head, scattering water drops everywhere. Why was she thinking of Geoff? The two men were so different, like chalk and cheese. It was Jamie who was in her life now.

Erica had just stepped out of the shower and was trying to decide what to wear to dinner, whether to choose pants with a shirt or a light wool dress, when her phone rang. Seeing Briony's number, she flinched as if her daughter-in-law could see her, could know how she'd spent the previous night and the day, could read what was in her heart and know… She gave herself a shake for her overactive imagination and pressed to answer the call.

'Hi Briony,' she said, hoping her voice didn't give away the fact she and Jamie had made love.

'Mum. I wanted to let you know we're home safe and sound. I tried to ring you last night and again this morning. I was worried about you.'

Erica bit her lip remembering how she had left her phone at home last night, expecting only to be gone a few minutes, then put it on mute today not wanting to be disturbed. 'Sorry. It ran out of charge, and I didn't notice,' she lied. 'I'm glad you caught me now. How was the trip?'

She listened as Briony described her plane trip in great detail, finishing with, 'I'm glad to be home, but I wish you were here too. Ava misses you.'

While Erica doubted her five-month-old grandchild was really missing her, she was flooded with guilt at the knowledge she'd been with Jamie, first in his bed, then on his yacht, while Briony was trying to contact her. What if there had been an emergency? Then reason prevailed. She'd been out of contact for less than twenty-four hours, twenty-four hours that had changed her life, she reminded herself.

'I miss her too,' she said, remembering the feel of her granddaughter's soft skin against her cheek, how she reached out her little fingers to grasp Erica's. 'And how's Kieren?' she asked.

'He's good,' Briony said, her tone indicating he was there, listening to the conversation.

'He must be pleased to have you back home.'

'Of course. I've never been away without him before.' There was a long pause, during which Erica could hear Kieren's voice in the background. Then Briony said, 'Kieren wants to know when you plan to come home.'

Erica took a deep breath. 'This is my home now, Briony. You must know that. It's where I grew up. My brother lives here. I have a job and friends. I told you and Kieren that before I left. I promised to visit… and I will, and you can come to visit me again. Kieren too,' she added, though doubting her son would set foot in Pelican Crossing again, and not sure if she wanted him to.

When the call ended, Erica was unsettled, the bubble of happiness in which she had been floating suddenly burst. Making a decision, she pulled on the dress, brushed her hair and applied her makeup, determined to put Briony's call out of her mind, to refocus on Jamie. But she found it impossible to dismiss the guilt which had resurfaced at Briony's words. Was she being unfair putting her own happiness first?

Erica was still feeling shaken when Jamie knocked on the door. Her expression must have given her away.

'What's up?' he asked, taking her into his arms and giving her the warm hug she was in desperate need of.

Erica hid her face in his chest, feeling her eyes moisten at his nearness, at the comfort of his strong body close to hers. 'I had a call from Briony,' she murmured, her voice almost inaudible. What must Jamie think of her? One minute she was bursting with happiness, the next she was acting as if her world had ended.

'Sorry,' she said, pulling away. 'I'll be right in a minute.'

'It's okay. I understand. I know what families can be like. What did Briony say to upset you?'

'Only that Ava was missing me,' Erica sniffed, 'which I know is an impossibility… and that Kieren wanted to know when I was coming home.' With the recounting of Kieren's demand, it was as if Erica found the strength to regain her earlier mood. 'It sounds ridiculous now I'm repeating it. I know it's only another attempt to control me… just like his dad did. I won't let it upset me any longer.' She smiled and standing on tiptoe, touched her lips to his, the shivers of delight that resulted doing more to restore her earlier mood than anything else could.

'Better?' Jamie asked as their lips parted.

'Much. You have a magic touch, Jamie Whittaker.'

He chuckled. 'You still okay to go to the yacht club? We don't have to if you'd rather not.'

'No, I'm okay now.' Jamie's presence had managed to banish the guilt she'd been feeling. 'Let's go.'

As soon as they walked into the yacht club, Erica saw her brother. Joe and Gill were seated at the far side of the restaurant with a group of others who Erica recognised as Gill's three friends and their partners.

'Want to join them?' Jamie asked, gesturing to the group.

'No.' Erica shook her head. She wasn't ready for Joe or Gill to tell her, 'I told you so', though she knew Rachel would be more compassionate. 'I'd prefer it to be just us. Do you mind?'

'Mind? It's what I'd prefer too. I only thought you might want to be with your brother.'

'Not tonight. I think I may have had enough of my family for today.'

'I'm sorry.' Jamie took her by the arm and steered her to a table well away from the others. It was by the window and looked out over the marina.

Once there, Erica gave a sigh of relief. Although family was everything to her, the call from Briony had shaken her more than she wanted to admit, even to Jamie. She looked across the table at his kindly face, the wrinkles of age only increasing his attractiveness, and thanked her lucky stars she'd ignored Briony and taken Joe and Gill's advice.

'I think a celebration is called for. Champagne?' Jamie asked.

Erica smiled and nodded, her heart racing at the memory of exactly what they were celebrating. When the wine came, they toasted each other, the touch of Jamie's knees under the table sending shivers of delight through Erica with the promise of what was to come when they returned home. Would it be to her cottage or Jamie's, she wondered, the reminder that she did have to work tomorrow intruding on her thoughts and threatening to ruin the promise of a night of lovemaking.

'Penny for them?'

Erica shook her head and picked up the menu to hide her blushes.

After a delicious meal of crabcakes followed by seafood gamberetti – Atlantic salmon, cuttlefish and prawns tossed in a creamy tomato, garlic, fresh basil and chilli sauce and finished with bocconcini, smashed avocado and lemon – with a vanilla pannacotta dessert, Erica was ready for home. They were rising to leave when Joe caught sight of them and, a huge grin on his face, came over to greet them.

After hugging Erica and slapping Jamie on the shoulder, Joe said, 'Glad to see you two have come to your senses. We'll see you both at the walk next weekend?'

Erica and Jamie looked at each other and nodded. Erica had forgotten about the fundraising coastal walk in which she'd planned to walk with Joe and Gill.

'Good,' Joe said. 'I'll be in touch before then, Erica. I'll let you go now.'

When they were outside the club, Jamie said, 'What was that about?'

'Just some brotherly advice Joe gave me… about you. He was right.'

'He usually is.'

They laughed and set off arm-in-arm for the row of cottages, stopping only for a moment at Erica's gate before heading inside.

Forty-four

The next three weeks passed in a blaze of happiness for Erica. After their dinner at the yacht club, she and Jamie spent every available minute with each other, their appearance together at the coastal walk putting the seal on their relationship as far as the Pelican Crossing community was concerned.

The only cloud on Erica's horizon, was how Kieren and Briony would react when they discovered she and Jamie were in a relationship.

So far, Erica had managed to avoid mentioning it during Briony's frequent calls to check on her and give updates on Ava. These Facetime calls which occurred at least once a week were like a lifeline to Erica, allowing her to see her granddaughter's face and how it lit up at the sight of her. Maybe Briony had been right when she said Ava missed her.

Erica managed to put her worry about her family in Western Australia aside, as her relationship with Jamie flourished and she became more and more sure that she wanted to spend the rest of her life with him, amazed and thrilled he seemed to feel the same way about her.

Today was the day of the fundraising winter fair which, following Liz's suggestion, had become the Christmas in July Fair, and it promised to be a popular event. It had been widely promoted in *The Echo*, and there were fliers and posters all around the town.

Erica looked across the back yard where she and Jamie were eating breakfast. She had come to love this place and would be sorry when she had to leave. At least she would be able to spend Christmas here. In her last email, Livvy had written to say she was planning to spend Christmas with her family in England and return early in the new year, adding that she couldn't wait to enjoy an Australian summer again after the cooler weather in England.

Erica knew she would have to find somewhere else to live, but she hadn't mentioned it to Jamie yet, content to enjoy life here for a few more months.

After a leisurely breakfast, Jamie said, 'I need to pop into the office for a little while, but I'll pick you up at ten. Okay?'

'Perfect.' It would give her time to call Briony to check up on how she was doing and to see Ava again. Now six months old, the little girl was developing a personality and Erica loved to see the changes in her.

She accompanied Jamie to the front door, where he pulled her into a warm hug, before walking off humming to himself. Erica smiled then turned back inside. She showered and dressed in the jeans and shirt she'd wear to the fair, where she had volunteered to help on one of the stalls, then picked up her phone.

Half an hour later, Erica ended the call and stared into space. While Ava had seemed as happy and content as usual, Briony had sounded stressed. Erica bit her lip, wondering for what must have been the hundredth time if all was well with her son's marriage, but knowing it was no use to question Briony any further. She could only hope the younger woman would take her advice and leave Kieren if things became ugly. The only information Briony was willing to divulge was that Kieren was worried about the car yard, that his dad had left things in a bit of a mess. Erica had no idea what she meant by that, assuming there were more debts than had been apparent at first. But it had been eight months since Geoff died. Surely Kieren would have everything sorted by now?

She sighed and determined to speak with Kieren again. It was all she could do from here.

Jamie's arrival, and the hug he gave her pulled her back into the present and her own life.

When they arrived at the sports ground where the fete was being held, it was teeming with people. Leaving Jamie, who was rostered to help with the sausage sizzle, Erica made her way to where she could see Gill and Poppy manning a stall piled with all sorts of homemade goods, from cakes and biscuits to potholders and old-fashioned tea-cosies crocheted by some ladies from *The Haven*. Erica was carrying her own offering, a tray of the chocolate caramel slice she remembered her mother making.

The morning went quickly, the stall rapidly emptying of goods as shoppers, eager to spend their money for a good cause, picked up bargains. After two hours, Erica was ready for a break. Despite being accustomed to spending the day on her feet at the hospital, she was tiring, glad when Poppy said, 'Let's take turns for lunch. Why don't you go first, Erica?'

'Thanks.'

Erica weaved her way between the stalls, following the scent of fried sausages and onions which became stronger as she neared the sausage sizzle where Jamie, Cam and Finn were busy barbecuing sausages and dropping them onto slices of white bread topped with tomato sauce and onion strips.

Laughing at the picture they made in the Christmas aprons, featuring various Christmas slogans which she knew Poppy had provided, Erica joined the queue. The sausage was as delicious as it smelt. After eating a sausage sandwich and drinking from a bottle of water with Jamie in a corner close to the sausage sizzle, she returned to the stall where she spent the rest of the afternoon being polite to customers and collecting their money.

*

That evening, after dinner – a takeaway curry from the local Indian restaurant – Erica and Jamie were seated on her sofa enjoying glasses of wine and slices of Christmas cake which Erica had bought at the fair. With Jamie's arm around her shoulders, Erica was feeling relaxed and happy. After the day they'd spent surrounded by signs of Christmas and the strains of Christmas carols being broadcast through the loudspeaker – another of Liz's ideas, it was no great surprise to her when Jamie asked, 'What are you doing for Christmas? Will you be seeing your son and his family?'

Without thinking, Erica said, 'I'll be looking for somewhere to live and packing up.'

'What?' Jamie pulled away and stared at her in surprise.

'I've been meaning to tell you. Livvy plans to return after Christmas, so…' She looked around her present home with regret.

'You don't need to do that. You can move in with me.'

It was Erica's turn to be surprised. She gazed at Jamie, her eyes wide. He looked shell-shocked, as if he'd spoken without thinking.

'I mean it,' he said. 'I know my place isn't much. I haven't done a lot in the way of renovating, not like Livvy or Lou. Even Phil's cottage had a makeover when he moved in. You could have free rein to…' His voice trailed off, clearly noticing Erica's surprise and lack of response.

Erica's mind was swirling. It would be a big step to move in with Jamie and while she was comfortable in their relationship, it was still very new and she wasn't sure if she was ready for this, the thought of how Kieren and Briony would react uppermost in her mind.

'You don't need to give me an answer now but keep it in mind. You may find it difficult to find somewhere to rent at that time of year, and you have a home with me,' he said, hugging her more tightly than ever. 'You must know I love you, Erica. I want to spend the rest of my life with you.'

Erica stared at him, her heart pounding, as she was overwhelmed by a surge of happiness. Jamie Whittaker loved her! It was what she'd yearned to hear when she was eighteen, and to hear it now… 'I love you too,' she said, her breath catching as Jamie swept her up in his arms, first kissing the tip of her nose, then her eyes, then finally their lips meeting and sending shivers of delight through her.

Forty-five

She loved him! Jamie was so thrilled to hear Erica say those words, it wasn't till next morning that he realised she hadn't replied to his suggestion she move in with him. Surely, if she loved him, it was the obvious next step? But he knew Erica too well to make any assumptions. As far as he knew, she hadn't told her son and daughter-in-law about their relationship, and he was mindful of what Briony had said to her about it being too soon after Geoff's death.

As they sat in the courtyard of Livvy's cottage eating breakfast, Jamie was more convinced than ever that this was how he wanted to spend every morning of the rest of his life, but he decided to move cautiously, aware how quickly Erica's mood could change. While both of them valued family above everything, he was very aware how Erica's family members in Western Australia were very different from his two boys. They had been encouraging him to find someone else for several years now.

'What would you like to do today?' Jamie asked, when he had demolished the bacon and scrambled eggs Erica had cooked for breakfast and drained his second cup of coffee.

Erica stretched her arms above her head. 'What would you say to kitesurfing?' After several more sessions, they were becoming more proficient at the sport, but although Gary had judged they were now skilled enough to go solo, they preferred to be part of one of Gary's kitesurfing groups, finding the company boosted their confidence.

'Good idea. Let me check with Gary.'

'You do that while I clear the dishes.'

Jamie watched Erica gather up the dirty plates and cups, marvelling at how he had managed to snare this incredible woman, not once, but twice, and conscious of how much he wanted to put their relationship on a permanent footing. He picked up his phone to call Gary.

By the time Erica returned, Jamie had arranged for them to join one of Gary's kitesurfing groups which was due to set off in an hour's time. He had also called Joe and invited him and Gill to come along, knowing the pair weren't complete novices at the sport having taken part in several sessions with Gary the previous year. He hoped that seeing Joe and Gill and hearing more of their plans might sway Erica's thinking about moving in with him.

The kitesurfing was as amazing as before, though the four of them were older by far than the other members of the group. 'You need to have a special group for geriatrics,' Joe joked, when they were all back on the beach.

'Not a bad idea,' Gary said, laughing. 'What do you think, Dad?'

'None of your cheek,' Jamie said, but he was laughing too. 'Maybe we're ready to take the next step and go solo.'

'Your choice,' Gary said.

'We can talk about that later,' Erica said.

'Why don't you join us for lunch?' Joe asked, as the four of them walked out of the building containing Gary's dive and kitesurfing schools.

'Sounds good. Erica?' Jamie said.

Erica nodded. 'Where had you in mind?'

'*The Grand*,' Joe said, only to be howled down by the two women, who suggested they'd prefer the yacht club or *The Blue Dolphin*.

An hour later saw all four seated in the yacht club, having taken time to go home to shower and change. Hungry after their exertions, they all ordered large servings of fish and chips to be washed down with beer for the men and a bottle of sauvignon blanc for the women.

'So,' Jamie began, 'I hear we're going to be neighbours.'

Joe grinned and took Gill's hand. 'As soon as settlement takes place, but we've already been in taking measurements and getting quotes for the work we want done.'

'Drop by next time you're there,' Jamie said. 'It's time I did some renovating too.' He gave Erica what he hoped was a meaningful look, but she didn't appear to notice.

'We'd be happy to share our plans,' Gill said, smiling at Joe.

Erica said nothing, but Jamie knew her so well he could tell she was lost in thought. What was she thinking, he wondered, hoping it was about his suggestion she move in with him.

By the time lunch was over, Jamie had heard a detailed description of what Joe and Gill planned to do with their new home. It made him realise how slack he'd been. He'd done nothing to improve his cottage since he moved in, considering it wasn't worthwhile to spend money when he was living there by himself. Maybe if Erica joined him…

*

Despite seemingly being lost in thought, Erica was listening to the conversation. Although she'd heard Joe and Gill talk about their new home before, this was the first time she'd heard them describe in detail how they planned to modernise it. Her mind went to Jamie's cottage. How she'd love to update it. She'd tackle the kitchen first, she thought, change the dark brown cupboard doors to white and the surface to granite or marble. Then she'd work on the rest of the house, paint the walls white instead of the present cream, recarpet the bedrooms and tile the floors in the rest of the house. Then the bathroom – she'd go wild there. White cupboards and surfaces again, a double shower and a corner spa bath.

'Erica!'

'Sorry?' Erica snapped back to the present at the sound of Gill's voice, and the realisation that all those renovations would only be possible if she agreed to move in to live with Jamie. She didn't see how she could do that until Kieren and Briony changed their thinking. If they considered it too soon for her to have a relationship with Jamie, they'd definitely freak out if they learned she was living with him.

'I was asking you what the news was from Briony. Is everything okay with her and Ava?'

'It seems to be. She doesn't give much away, though she did appear stressed last time we spoke. I worry about her… but feel helpless.'

'You're doing all you can, keeping in regular touch, letting her know you're available to help. I wish more of my clients had family like you to support them, though I know many would refuse to accept it.'

'I know. I was one of them,' Erica said regretfully. 'I knew Joe would always have helped me… Barb too, when she was alive, but I was too pigheaded – or embarrassed – to ask them… until it got so bad. I hope Briony doesn't wait till things get to that stage for her. I wish she wasn't so far away.' Erica bit her lip, her chest tightening as a wave of guilt flooded her again. Could she have done more to help Briony if she'd given in to Kieren's demands and remained in Perth, or as she suspected, would he have managed to control *her* life too?

'You did the right thing, coming here,' Jamie said as if reading her mind. He squeezed Erica's hand. 'Think of all you've been able to do since you arrived. You're independent, working at the job you love… and you met me again,' he added with a grin.

'You're right,' Erica said, a warm glow enveloping her at the touch of his hand and the memory of their times together. None of that would have been possible if she'd stayed in Perth. She suspected Kieren would have taken over her life, just as Geoff had, and she'd have been powerless to stop him.

Forty-six

Jamie was chugging down his second coffee of the day and preparing to head out to meet the members of the day's fishing charter. His mind was on Erica who was spending the day in Bellbird Bay at the *Bellbird Women's Centre*, something she had evidently promised to do the previous year before events overtook her. The local radio was playing in the background when suddenly a news item grabbed his attention. There had been a shark attack. He turned up the sound but had missed the vital part of the announcement – the location of the attack. He drained his coffee and turned off the radio. It was probably in Western Australia, or the North Coast of New South Wales, where the last two attacks had occurred. Thankfully, there hadn't been one on this part of the coast in his lifetime, though he seemed to recall his dad talking about one when he was just a nipper.

He was halfway out the door when his phone rang. Seeing Gary's number, Jamie sighed. *What did Gary want now?* His group would be arriving shortly, and he wanted to have everything ready for them.

'Gary, I don't have much time,' he said. 'I…'

'Dad, you haven't heard?'

Jamie saw another call coming through. It was from Joe's number. 'Heard what?' He didn't have time for this.

'It's Rory.'

'Rory?' *What had Rory got himself into now?* Out of the corner of his eye Jamie saw Poppy's son-in-law, Gavin, walking purposefully towards him. He was in his police uniform. What the…? 'Sorry, Gary, I need to go.'

'But, Dad…'

Jamie ended the call, just as Gavin reached him. 'Something the matter, Gavin?'

'It's Rory, Mr Whittaker. There's been a shark attack…'

Jamie felt the blood drain from his face. He let out a strangled sob. It couldn't be true. Rory was in the office at *Pelican Marine* with Cam, where he always was at this time of day, where… 'How is he?' he managed to say, his heart breaking. He felt numb.

'He's alive, but critical, in the hospital. I can drive you there now. Gary's already there. They were surfing together earlier.'

'My…' Jamie looked around, trying to remember what he'd been about to do.

'We can let your charter group know you have a family emergency.'

'Right.' Jamie allowed himself to be led to the police car parked nearby.

By the time they reached the hospital, his mind had covered all possibilities. It was a relief to meet Gary in the emergency department and to see him looking relatively calm but tight-lipped.

'It's his leg, Dad,' Gary said. 'They think they can save it, but it's touch and go. They've taken him straight into surgery. Is…?' He glanced around as if looking for someone.

'Erica's not on duty today,' Jamie said, cursing that this could have happened when she wasn't there.

'They say it could take some time. Should we…?'

Just then, Cam appeared and gave Jamie a hug, but he was too numb to return it. 'I came as soon as I heard,' he said, 'closed the office. He's going to be okay?'

It was Gary who answered, 'So they say. We just have to wait till he's out of surgery.'

'You're in shock,' Cam said, taking charge. 'We can't do anything here. I presume someone will call when Rory's out of surgery?'

Gary nodded. 'They have my number.'

'Then let me take you to the café. What you both need is a cup of hot, sweet tea.'

Despite the seriousness of the situation, Jamie almost laughed. It was his mother's remedy for any sort of shock. Feeling helpless to refuse, he accompanied Cam and Gary to the hospital café, where

Cam ordered three teas, then produced a hip flask from which he added brandy to their cups.

As the numbness receded and Jamie gradually felt himself return to something approaching normal, helped by Cam's brandy, he asked Gary what had happened.

Gary shook his head slowly, his eyes partly closed. 'It all happened in a flash. One minute we were barrelling into shore, Rory was calling out that he'd beat me in, then…' he made no attempt to wipe away the tears now coursing down his cheeks, '… he let out a yell and… We all saw it, the fin, the blood. A couple of other surfers helped me get him out of the water, called an ambulance. It was too early for the surf lifesavers to be on duty. Joe was there too. He… I couldn't… I'm sorry, Dad.'

'Not your fault, son.' Jamie sighed heavily, his voice filled with anguish. He checked his watch. How long had they been here? He'd lost track of time. What was happening to Rory? He started to rise, gazing wildly around the café. He felt a hand on his shoulder.

'It's okay, Jamie. The doctor will call when there's news,' Cam said.

Jamie sat down again, knowing there was nothing he could do but frustrated at doing nothing. He wondered why Gary had mentioned Joe but now wasn't the time to ask.

'I called Mum,' Gary said, when they were on their second cups of tea, this time without the addition of brandy.

Jamie almost choked. 'Why did you do that?'

Gary shifted uncomfortably in his seat. 'I thought she should know. She *is* our mother.'

'And… what did she say?'

'She didn't answer. I left a message.'

Jamie relaxed. So what if Gary had called Cindy. She wasn't likely to turn up here… or was she? She'd always had the habit of doing the unexpected, turning up where she wasn't wanted… and he didn't want her here, crying crocodile tears and playing the distraught mother to the son she'd been happy to abandon in his teens.

They'd been waiting so long that the call when it came was a shock, Gary's phone blasting out the theme tune from *Star Wars*. 'Sorry,' Gary said again as he grabbed his phone. He listened for a moment then said, 'He's out of surgery.'

'And?' Jamie demanded, his stomach churning, worst case scenarios flitting through his mind.

'That's all he said. We can go up to the ward, but he's still unconscious.'

As they rose to leave, Jamie stumbled. He grasped the back of the chair with one hand. It was as if his legs had turned to jelly.

'All right, mate?' Cam's hand was on his arm.

'Give me a minute.' Jamie was embarrassed to let his weakness show but this was Rory, his firstborn son, the boy he'd cradled as a baby, had taught to surf, to sail, the one most likely to take over the business when he decided to retire. What if…? He couldn't contemplate losing him.

Joe rushed in just as they were about to leave. 'I thought I'd find you here. How is Rory? I came as soon as I could. I had to take Coco home first. I couldn't believe my eyes when I saw…' He shook his head. 'There hasn't been a shark attack here in my lifetime.'

'Joe!' Jamie grasped his friend's hand. 'Gary said you were there. You saw it happen?'

Joe grimaced. 'I did what I could, but it was the paramedics who saved him.'

Jamie stared at his friend. *What did he mean?*

'Dad?' Gary took him by the arm. 'We need to go.'

'Sorry, Joe. We've just heard Rory's out of surgery. You can come with us if you like. I don't know…' His voice trailed off. He had no idea what sort of state Rory would be in, how badly injured he was. But at least he was alive.

Forty-seven

Erica had a smile on her face as she drove down the highway to Bellbird Bay. It had taken her a long time, but she was glad she was going to keep her promise to Ali Wells to talk to a group of women at the *Bellbird Women's Centre*, to share her experience of coercive control. Geoff's arrival in town, followed by his untimely death had forced her to cancel her talk the previous year, but it was finally going to happen.

The trip passed quickly as she listened to the audio version of the book which was this month's choice for the book club, enjoying the trip to the French Riviera with *A French Affair* by Jennifer Bohnet and the story of second chances.

Erica hadn't visited the women's centre before. She'd met Ali when she had come to Pelican Crossing at Gill's invitation to talk to the local Zonta group, a group Gill was encouraging Erica to join. Her eyes widened as she drove through the entrance to draw up in a spacious car park close to two long, single-storey buildings surrounded by trees and bushes. When she got out of the car, she saw a sign pointing to the office and a board which showed a map of the centre.

The tall, elegant woman she remembered came out of one of the buildings to greet her. Her short, grey-streaked hair was brushed back from her face, and she was casually dressed in a pair of jeans and a loose, pale blue shirt.

'Welcome to *Bellbird Women's Centre*,' Ali said. 'I'm glad you finally made it, but sorry for what you've been through. Thanks so much for agreeing to share your story with us.'

Erica gave a tight smile. Now she was actually here, she wondered how she was going to feel talking to a group of strangers about coercive control, about how she had been subjected to it for years, how it had happened so gradually she was lulled into a false belief that it was normal behaviour, how she'd thought everything was her fault, how it hadn't been till Geoff hit her once too often that she found the confidence to leave. 'I hope it will help at least one person to realise they can escape,' she said, unsure exactly who her audience would be.

'I'm sure you'll do a lot more than that,' Ali said with a smile, her calm demeanour and confident expression helping Erica understand why she held the position she did. She knew from what Gill had told her that Ali had been a lecturer in Women's Studies in a university, coincidentally located in Perth. 'Now, how about a cup of tea before I throw you to the wolves?' Ali chuckled.

'That would be great,' Erica said, feeling calmer as the butterflies in her stomach settled down. She wondered if Ali had this effect on everyone. 'I've never done anything like this before.'

Over a cup of camomile tea with Ali, Erica relaxed even more as Ali told her more about the centre and asked her how she was enjoying being back in Pelican Crossing.

'I'm loving it,' Erica said, beaming. 'I've caught up with old friends.' She couldn't stem her blush as Jamie's image forced its way into her mind. 'The only drawback is that I miss my daughter-in-law and granddaughter. I worry about them. My son… he's a lot like his dad.'

'I bet she's glad she has you to turn to if things get too much for her… like you had your brother.'

'I hope so, but…' Erica bit her lip.

'You, of all people, must realise that's all you can do to help,' Ali said gently.

'You're right.' Suddenly, Erica felt better about Briony. It was one thing to know, to have Gill remind her, but the same words coming from this gentle woman who ran this centre was balm to her soul.

'Are you ready?' Ali asked, when they had finished their tea. 'The others will have gathered by now. As you can probably realise, it would have been difficult for many of them to come here today. There's nothing to be afraid of. They won't eat you,' she said, as Erica began to tremble.

'Of course not.' Erica straightened her shoulders. She could do this and if, as she'd told Ali, she could help one person, it would be worth it. Even if Briony wouldn't accept her advice, perhaps these women would.

Erica followed Ali through the building to a brightly decorated room where a group of around twelve women were seated. They were chatting quietly together and fell silent when Ali and Erica walked in. Erica felt her phone vibrate in her pocket. She had turned it to mute before she left the car, though she wasn't expecting anyone to call. Both Jamie and Joe knew she was coming here this morning, and they'd be too busy to call, anyway. She ignored it.

Ali introduced Erica, then she stood up and began to speak. It was easier than she'd anticipated. Although she'd brought notes, Erica found she didn't need them. She spoke from the heart and saw her words brought several of her audience to tears – Ali had explained that not all of the women here were suffering abuse, some wanted the information so they could help a friend or relative, just as Erica was trying to do with Briony. Remembering this, she made sure to point out that it wasn't always easy for a woman to realise what was happening to her, and important that the time had to be right for her to leave, even with support.

Ali invited Erica to join her for lunch afterwards and she gratefully accepted, glad to have her ordeal over, though it had gone better than she expected and there had been lots of questions which she found easy to answer.

It wasn't till she was back in her car, and turned her phone back on, that she saw the message from Joe. Her heart dropped as she read his words.

Rory injured in a shark attack. Jamie at hospital. Meet us there. Hugs.

Forty-eight

Jamie was relieved to see Erica arrive. He'd been in the hospital for what seemed like for ever. Cam and Joe had stayed awhile, then left with promises to return. Gary had stayed longer, had gone back to be with Mandy and fill her in on what was happening, returned and had now gone back home again. Although Jamie knew there was nothing he could do for Rory who was still sedated, he couldn't bear to leave him.

'How is he?' Erica whispered, joining him at Rory's bedside.

'The doc says he's holding his own. They managed to save his leg, but he'll probably have permanent mobility issues. He's lucky to be alive and to still have his leg.'

'Oh, Jamie!' Erica hugged him tightly, her eyes wet with tears.

As Erica's arms wound around him, Jamie felt an easing of the tension in his gut that had been there since he heard about Rory. 'Thanks, Erica. I'm glad you're here.'

'I'm sorry I couldn't be here sooner. My phone...' Her forehead creased.

'It's okay. Gary was here, and Cam and Joe. They've promised to come back, but they have families. They had to go home.'

'Well, I'm here now and I'm not going anywhere.' Erica hugged him again. 'Have you eaten?'

Jamie shook his head. Food had been furthest from his thoughts. He hadn't eaten since breakfast, and it must now be late afternoon.

'Why don't I go to the cafeteria and fetch something. You need to eat. You'll be no good to Rory if you keel over too.'

'I don't think…'

'Mr Whittaker…' a nurse appeared in the doorway, '… I need to check Rory's vitals. Why don't you and your friend get something to eat while I'm here? Rory's going to be fine.'

Reluctantly, Jamie followed Erica out of the room and down to the cafeteria, with its memories of him and Gary waiting there for news.

When they were seated with cups of coffee and sandwiches, Erica asked, 'What happened? Joe left a message about a shark attack. Here in Pelican Crossing?'

'Yeah. We didn't think it could happen here. Rory and I even had a conversation about it… when we were discussing the removal of the shark nets. He and Gary were surfing when it happened. As I said, he was lucky. The shark took out a section of his thigh and he lost a lot of blood. He may need more surgery.' Jamie felt his eyes moisten at the thought of what his son had gone through. 'Joe was there, he…' he swallowed, '… he used his dog's lead as a tourniquet to stop the bleeding. Without that…' He shook his head.

'Oh Jamie!' Erica said again, placing a hand on his arm. 'Poor Rory!'

'It could have been much worse. We could have lost him.' The thought of what could have happened brought back the tears that were never far from the surface. He brushed them away. 'Sorry, Rici. It's been the worst day of my life.'

When they got back to the ward, Rory was partially awake. 'Dad?' he murmured.

'I'm here, son.'

'I thought I was dying. I saw its eyes. It looked straight at me and…' his voice trailed off, then his eyes closed again.

'He'll sleep for a while now. Why don't you go home and get some rest? You can see him again tomorrow,' a voice said in his ear.

Jamie looked up at the nurse he'd seen before.

'There's nothing you can do here,' she added.

'But…' Jamie looked at Rory who now appeared to be sleeping peacefully.

'She's right,' Erica said, taking Jamie's arm. 'Rory's in good hands. He's getting the best care. *You* need to rest too. I'll drive you home.'

'Thanks.' Jamie took one last look at Rory and allowed Erica to lead him out of the room.

*

Neither Erica nor Jamie spoke much on the drive home. She was too shell-shocked to make conversation, and assumed Jamie was the same. When they reached Livvy's cottage, she stopped the car and turned to Jamie. 'Do you want to come in or would you prefer to go home?'

'Here's fine.' The fit, energetic man she knew seemed to have shrunk. His eyes were red.

Erica got out of the car, and Jamie followed her in, slumping into a chair as soon as he reached the living room.

'I think we both need a drink,' she said.

'Cam put brandy in a cup of tea, but that was hours ago.'

Glad his mate had had the sense to provide some sort of stimulant but realising it would have worn off some time ago, Erica went to the kitchen where she poured two glasses of whisky. She knew Jamie was a whisky drinker and she'd noticed the bottle hidden away in Livvy's pantry. She could replace it later.

'Here,' she said, handing Jamie one glass. Then, taking a seat opposite, took a sip from the other. She flinched at the remembered taste, but it did help. It seemed to help Jamie too.

'How did your talk go?' he asked, after a few moments of silence while he drained his glass, then rolled it between his hands.

'It was fine, it's why I didn't get Joe's message sooner, or…'

'You couldn't have done anything.'

'No.' Erica bit her lip, wishing there was something she could do now, but all either of them could do was wait.

'I think I'd like to lie down.' Jamie placed his glass on the coffee table and rose, stumbling a little as he made his way to the door.

'You can stay here.' Jamie didn't look as if he had the energy to walk along the road to his cottage, even if he wanted to.

'Thanks. You'll join me?'

'Of course. I'll be there shortly.'

After Jamie disappeared into the bedroom, Erica tidied up, then called Joe.

'Thanks for letting me know about Rory, Joe,' she said. 'Jamie is taking it badly. I've never seen him like this.' Seeing Jamie's distress over Rory had brought home to Erica the importance of family and made her vow to try harder with Kieren, to help him see Geoff for what he was and change his own habits before it was too late, before his little family was lost to him.

'It's bad,' Joe agreed, 'but the boy will pull through. It could have been a lot worse.'

'Thanks to you, it's not. Jamie told me what you did.'

'It was nothing. Anyone would have done the same.'

Erica could almost see her brother shrug. She knew it wasn't true. Not everyone would have had the presence of mind to act as quickly as he had clearly done.

'How is Jamie now?'

'We're back home, and he's gone to bed, though I'm not sure how much sleep he'll get. But at least he's resting. I have tomorrow off, and we'll be going back to the hospital, but I have to go back to work on Monday. I'm not sure about Jamie.'

'It would be best for him to go back to work too, but I guess it's up to him.'

'I'll talk with him about it. He can always visit Rory every day, and it can be wearing sitting by a hospital bedside day after day.' Erica had seen relatives do that and end up becoming ill themselves.

'Good. I'll drop in too, and I know Cam plans to. We all need to support Jamie. He'd do the same for us.'

'It's going to be a long haul for Rory, Joe. More surgery, weeks of recovery then rehab. But he's one of the lucky ones.' She shivered remembering all the news items she'd read about surfers who'd lost their lives in shark attacks.

When the call ended, Erica took a shower then joined Jamie in bed, surprised to see he'd fallen into a restless sleep. She cuddled up to him and closed her eyes, hoping the warmth of her body would provide the comfort he needed.

Forty-nine

The next few weeks passed in a blur for Jamie as he spent as much time at Rory's bedside as he could, besides conducting those fishing charters he'd been unable to cancel. He and Erica spent every night together, and her company and closeness were a great comfort to him. He didn't know how he'd have coped without her calm presence and her warm body close to his. She also managed to pop in to see Rory every day during her breaks, and it was a consolation to Jamie to know she was right there in the hospital should anything go wrong when he wasn't around.

After four surgeries, during which flesh from his stomach had been used to repair his thigh, Rory was making what the doctors described as *a good recovery*, though his leg would never be the same, and Jamie worried about his mental health after such an ordeal.

Today, like any other day, he'd popped in to see his son early, before heading out with his charter, and now the day was over he was home to shower and change before making another visit to the hospital. Erica had called in the middle of the day to tell him Rory seemed brighter, and he was looking forward to seeing him. She had her book club tonight and had promised to pop in again on her way to Gill's apartment where her meeting was to be held. The hospital staff were very flexible with visiting hours, allowing him and Gary to visit when they were able. Mandy often visited Rory during the day too, taking along Archie who was growing fast and whose presence helped cheer Rory.

Jamie was feeling optimistic when he pushed open the door to Rory's room. Gary was there, and the two men were looking at something on Rory's iPad. They stopped when Jamie walked in and put it down.

'Good news, Dad,' Gary said. 'Rory, tell Dad what the doc said.'

'Seems I'm ready to get out of here and go to rehab. I'll be up and about in no time.' He grinned.

Jamie wished it was true. He knew it would be some time before Rory would be walking again, and that he might never be able to walk unaided. Fixing a smile on his face to hide his heartache, he said, 'That's great news, son.'

'Only one problem, Dad.'

'Oh, what's that?' Were they going to send him off to rehab in Brisbane where Jamie wouldn't be able to visit?

'Mum's here.'

'Where?' Jamie glanced around the room, almost expecting Cindy to pop up.

It was Gary who answered. 'She's in Pelican Crossing, arrived this afternoon. There's no room at our place and she and Mandy aren't the best.' He coughed and reddened. 'She's staying in a hotel, says she's going to visit this evening.'

'How did she…?' Jamie remembered Gary saying he'd called her after the accident, but that had been weeks ago. He'd thought if she was coming, she'd have come then, not waited till now. But Cindy had never acted predictably.

'I've been keeping her filled in,' Gary said, flushing. 'She *is* our mum,' he added, when both Jamie and Rory groaned.

'Why now?' Rory asked. 'I wish you'd told me you were in touch with her, Gary. You know Mum and I…'

Gary shifted from one foot to the other. 'She wanted to know. I thought…'

'Does she have that slimeball with her?' Jamie asked. 'The one she brought to your wedding.'

'No, she's here on her own. Give her a break, Dad. Can't you forgive and forget?'

Jamie tensed. He didn't want to argue with Gary, not with Rory lying there, but Cindy had done nothing to earn his forgiveness. Gary might be able to forget how she'd abandoned him and Rory when they were in their teens, but he never could. And the way she'd behaved towards him at Gary's wedding… A leopard didn't change its spots. But he wasn't going to allow her to chase him away from his son's bedside.

'Look at this, Dad.' Rory held up the iPad he and Gary had been looking at when Jamie walked in and turned it so Jamie could see the screen. 'I'm famous!'

Jamie stared at the screen and read the article headed: *Shark Attack in Tourist Town. Man Saved from Untimely Death.* It went on to describe how local man, Rory Whittaker, had escaped death from a shark attack, saved by the local mayor who used his dog's lead to stem the bleeding. There was a photo of Rory with his surfboard, taken a few years earlier at a surfing event down the coast, and one of Joe with Coco. Jamie's blood ran cold as he read the details. Even though he was well aware what had happened, seeing it posted on the internet brought back the horror of that day.

There was no need to wonder where they had got the story. The week it happened, Finn had covered it in *The Echo*, along with first-hand accounts from both Gary and Joe. It had prompted another debate about the wisdom of removing shark nets, much to the annoyance of all those who believed they were harmful to other sea creatures. Rory himself was vocal among those, saying that the shark had more right than he had to be in the ocean, and it was just bad luck they were in the same place at the same time.

They were still discussing the article, with Rory speculating how he could capitalise on it, perhaps offer to be interviewed on the regional television channel, and Gary teasing him that he would go to any lengths for this sort of recognition, when the door opened, and Cindy walked in.

The atmosphere changed immediately, the happy mood disappearing to be replaced by an awkward silence. Then Cindy rushed to Rory's bedside to hug the reluctant man, saying, 'My poor boy!' in a tearful voice, while Jamie looked on, grinding his teeth.

*

Erica was feeling buoyant as she parked her little Mazda in the hospital car park. Rory was recovering, albeit slowly; she'd heard today that he was ready to be moved into rehab, she had her book club this evening, and she would be sleeping with Jamie afterwards. All was right with her world. She was even beginning to think she'd agree to Jamie's suggestion she move in with him. The thought of being with him every day, of waking up beside him every morning, was becoming more and more tempting. Maybe she'd tell him tonight and they could celebrate that along with the next step in Rory's recovery. She'd worry about Kieren and Briony later. Surely they'd accept her and Jamie were a couple when it was a *fait accompli*?

She was smiling as she made her way to the orthopaedic ward, to the room which had been Rory's home for the past few weeks, cheerfully greeting those of the nursing staff with whom she'd become familiar on the way. She pushed open the door to Rory's room and stopped in her tracks.

The sight which greeted her was such a shock she couldn't speak. Instead of seeing Jamie and Rory, there was what appeared to be a closeknit family group, not only Rory and his dad. Gary was there too, and… Cindy, who turned at the sound of the door opening and glared at Erica. 'Who are you?' she asked.

'I…' Erica gazed at Jamie who seemed speechless too. 'I'm sorry. I made a mistake.' Her eyes filling with tears, she turned and fled, unheeding of Jamie calling her name.

She didn't stop till she was back in her car, then she tried to process what she had seen. Why hadn't Jamie told her Cindy was here in Pelican Crossing? Had he invited her? It was only natural, she supposed. Rory was her son. If it was Kieren lying there Erica would have wanted to be by his side, regardless of what he might have done. She tried to remember what Jamie had said about his ex, about why they had broken up, but all she could recall was that she'd left when the boys were teenagers. But she had come to Gary's wedding, so they were still in touch. Why hadn't it occurred to her that Cindy would be here? Why had it taken her so long to come to see Rory? But she was here now and had more right to be here than Erica. But how could Jamie have hidden her arrival from her? Did he still hold a candle for her? Where did this leave Erica?

Although tempted to go straight home, drink herself into a stupor and go to bed, Erica pulled herself together and drove to Gill's apartment and the book club, determined she wasn't going to let another man ruin her life.

'Are you all right?' Gill asked, when she opened the door to Erica, clearly seeing her drawn expression.

'I will be,' Erica said with a tight smile. 'How are you, Gill?' she asked, hugging her.

'I'm fine, but you look as if you've seen a ghost.'

'Not exactly, just a family gathering, and family is so important, isn't it, especially in times of crisis?'

'I guess,' Gill said, seemingly mystified.

Erica didn't enlighten her but went inside to where the other members of the book club were already seated, and took a gulp of the wine Gill handed her. She immediately felt better, though it was as if there was a void where her heart used to be.

The discussion about the book began, as members took turns to give their impressions. When Erica's turn came around, she had trouble remembering what the book was about and merely repeated what some of the others had already said. The rest of the evening passed in a blur, with Erica castigating herself for being so foolish as to trust Jamie, to trust herself. Briony had been right. It was too soon. It might always be too soon.

The meeting over, Erica was about to leave when Gill pulled her aside. 'Stay for a bit,' she said. Reluctantly, Erica agreed and followed Gill into the kitchen, taking a seat on one of the high stools while Gill made coffee, and dreading the questions she knew were going to come.

'Now,' Gill said, when she had joined Erica and they both had large mugs of coffee – Erica was sure hers would keep her awake all night, but after what she'd seen at the hospital, she was unlikely to get any sleep anyway, 'tell me what's up. Don't say, "Nothing" because I know you too well. You haven't been yourself all night. You told me last week how much you were enjoying this month's book, but tonight you hardly said anything about it.' She peered at Erica and waited.

Erica knew Gill wasn't going to be sidetracked by some glib explanation. She sighed. 'It's Jamie. When I went to the hospital tonight, his ex was there. They all looked so close. I felt...' her eyes moistened, '...I felt so humiliated.'

'What happened? What did Jamie say?'

'I didn't wait to find out. I left.' As she spoke, Erica remembered hearing Jamie call her name, but she'd been too intent on getting away to pay attention. 'He didn't tell me she was in town.'

'Oh, Erica. You should at least have given him a chance to explain.'

Erica shook her head. 'No, it's best this way, Gill. I can't go through it all again, the lies, the deceit. I thought Jamie was different.'

'He is. Has it occurred to you that you may have misinterpreted what you saw, that the closeknit family might not have been as close as you thought? I didn't handle his and Cindy's divorce, but I heard a few things at the time. It wasn't as amicable as he likes to make out. I think he almost persuaded himself it was… for the boys' sake. But I do know from what Joe's said that there's no love lost between him and Cindy. I didn't think she and Rory got on well, either, so it's a bit odd for her to turn up now.'

'Well, whatever. She's here, Gill, and I have no intention of getting in the way if she wants to patch things up with Jamie. An incident like the one that happened to Rory can bring a family together. I see it often enough in the hospital. And family is so important. I need to focus on mine right now, work out how I can help Kieren and Briony, for their sakes and for little Ava.'

'How do you intend to do that? I thought you said Briony wouldn't listen to you?' Gill sounded weary, as if she couldn't believe Erica's change of heart. Erica could scarcely believe it herself, but it was what was going to get her through the next few days and weeks, until she could get Jamie Whittaker out of her thoughts.

Fifty

Jamie couldn't believe his eyes when Erica turned and left without even walking into the room. He called after her and was about to follow, when Cindy said, 'Don't tell me… you and Erica Harris…' and laughed. He turned to speak, only for Gary to say, 'Leave it, Dad. Mum didn't mean anything by it.'

'Oh, but I did,' Cindy said. 'I remember you and her at school. Love's young dream. You thought you were so clever, that no one knew. Everyone knew. It was sickening, the way you… Then she left, married, went to Western Australia, I heard. You were lucky I was around to pick up the pieces.'

'That's enough, Cindy. You don't know what you're talking about. It wasn't like that.'

'Wait on, Dad,' Rory said. 'You and Erica… back then… Wow!'

'It wasn't a secret,' Jamie said, 'but Joe didn't know about us. I was his mate. She was his little sister. He might have objected. Luckily for us, he was too occupied with Barb to worry about what we were getting up to… not that we were doing anything we shouldn't.' He glared at Cindy for bringing this up, for getting him involved in this discussion when he should have been chasing after Erica. By this time, she'd have driven off, gone to her book club. Or would she? Maybe she'd have gone straight home. 'Sorry, guys. I need to go. See you tomorrow, Rory. I want to talk to your doctor about the rehab. See you soon, Gary.' He didn't say goodbye to Cindy. He couldn't bear to speak to her, to be in the same room as her any longer. He hoped this was a flying visit and she'd be gone soon, back to the life she'd chosen when she left him and her two sons over fifteen years earlier.

Jamie was right. There was no sign of Erica or her car when he left the hospital. Cursing himself for allowing Cindy to delay him, he went to his car and drove home, hoping he'd find Erica in Livvy's cottage and be able to explain Cindy's presence, sure that was what had upset her.

Jamie's heart sank when he saw the cottage was in darkness. Deciding she must have gone to her book club after all, he had no option but to drive on home. Perhaps she hadn't been too upset. He'd check with her tomorrow, anyway. There was no way he was going to let Cindy's arrival in town spoil the best thing that had happened to him in years.

Next morning, Jamie wakened at his usual time, thoughts of Erica and Cindy at the forefront of his mind. After his morning coffee and as soon as he figured Erica would be awake, he headed down to her cottage. Taking a deep breath, and unsure of her reaction, he knocked on the door.

*

When she awoke, it took Erica a few moments to remember what had happened, but when she did, she felt as if her world had ended. She couldn't bear the prospect of seeing Jamie and Cindy together again. But that meant she couldn't go to see Rory either. Luckily, she had a few days off between shifts, so there was no need for her to be at the hospital, but… what about Jamie?

A text from Briony with a photo of Ava decided her. The little girl was growing so rapidly. Erica was missing so much of her life, and she needed to see what was going on in her son's marriage. She opened her laptop and booked a seat on a plane to Perth, leaving that morning. She had just pressed send when she heard a loud knock on the door. She knew it must be Jamie. She couldn't face him, knowing what she'd seen last night. Gill's words came back to her. Had she misinterpreted the scene? Had Jamie known Cindy was in Pelican Crossing? Whatever the truth of the matter, Erica knew she needed time away from here, away from Jamie, time to clear her head. She ignored the knocking on the door till finally she heard Jamie's steps as he walked away.

Resisting the temptation to throw the door open and run after him, Erica picked up her phone to text Briony about her arrival and Joe about her trip. Then she packed a small bag, ready to drive to the airport.

Gill rang as she was getting into her car. 'Don't you think you're overreacting?' she asked. 'Joe tells me you're going to Perth… this morning.'

'It's only for a few days. I have some time off between shifts and it's an opportunity to see my granddaughter and check in with Briony.'

'I know you said you were worried about her, but isn't this a bit sudden? Last night…'

'Last night I was in a mess. I can see things more clearly this morning,' Erica lied. 'It'll be fine. I'll be back in a few days and…'

'Have you spoken to Jamie?'

Erica's stomach churned. 'Not yet, maybe when I get back.' Perhaps by then she'd feel strong enough to hear what he had to say, to accept that he and Cindy were back together. Family was important. She knew that. She was flying to Perth to try to save hers. If she kept telling herself that, maybe she'd get through this.

*

Erica tried to relax during the seven-hour flight, but she couldn't dismiss what she'd seen at Rory's bedside. She knew Jamie had been trying to contact her and had turned off her phone after a flurry of missed calls and texts which she managed to resist reading.

Briony and Ava were waiting to greet Erica when she arrived in Perth.

'What a lovely surprise, Mum,' Briony said as Erica hugged her, then Ava, and commented on how much the little girl had grown.

'It's not the same on Facetime,' she said, laughing as Ava grasped a strand of her hair and pulled it.

'How is everything?' Erica asked, when they were driving to Briony and Kieren's home.

'Good. I think Kieren wants to speak with you about something,' Briony said. Her eyes were on the road so Erica couldn't read her expression, but her heart sank. Surely her son wasn't going to try to persuade her to move back to Perth?

For the first time since her impetuous decision early that morning, Erica wondered if she'd been too hasty in making this trip. Briony appeared happy and content. Perhaps her worry had been unnecessary. But she was still concerned about seeing Kieren again. Their last meeting hadn't gone too well, and she was all too aware of his disapproval of her move to Pelican Crossing.

To Erica's relief, there was no sign of Kieren when they reached the house.

'Kieren will be home later. He always stays at the yard till late,' Briony said apologetically.

Swallowing the thought that this was so like what Geoff had often done, before coming home and blaming Erica when dinner was spoiled, Erica smiled. It was fun to help bath Ava and put her to bed, relishing the softness of her granddaughter's cheek against her lips as she kissed her goodnight.

Kieren looked tired when he came home, but there was no sign of the temper Erica had expected. Instead, he hugged and kissed her, saying, 'Good to see you, Mum. Briony told me how much she enjoyed her visit to Pelican Crossing, a happier one than last time.'

'Good to see you too, son,' Erica said, discovering she meant it. Despite everything, he was her son, and the thought flitted through her mind that perhaps he had thought her life would have been better if she'd stayed here.

'Briony said you wanted to speak with me,' she said to him, when dinner was over.

'Yeah.' Kieren pushed his fingers through his hair in a gesture so like Geoff's that Erica got a sour taste in her mouth. 'Let's go into the study.'

'Briony?' Erica asked.

'I'm off to bed as soon as I clear up here. I'll leave you to it,' Briony said.

Fearing the worst, Erica joined Kieren in his study, surprised when he poured them both another glass of the wine they'd had with dinner.

She was preparing what to say to refuse his demands, when he surprised her again.

'I'm sorry, Mum,' he said, pushing back his hair again. This time, instead of reminding her of Geoff, it took her back to the times when he was a small boy, when he was in trouble.

Erica gazed at her son, seeing the small boy he'd been before life and work with Geoff changed him, the small boy who had always loved his mother, who she'd hugged and kissed goodnight just as she had Ava. She wondered what he was sorry for.

'I'm sorry,' he repeated. 'Since Dad died… I've been going through the books at the yard, finding discrepancies, debts. It's made me think, remember… I've come to realise how I idolised Dad, put him on a pedestal, tried hard to emulate him, but…' He shook his head. 'He wasn't the man I thought he was. After discovering how he screwed up the business, I started thinking about how he was at home. The more I thought about him, about how he treated you.' He met Erica's eyes. 'He was a bully, wasn't he? I couldn't see it, but now, thinking back, I started to wonder why you never went out to work, to meet friends, why we never had people over like my friends' parents did, why Dad always locked himself away in his study, why you often looked cowed, afraid.'

Erica swallowed hard. This was the last thing she'd expected to hear.

'I started reading about domestic violence. Is that why you left him, Mum? Did he hit you?'

Caught off balance by this outburst, Erica could only nod.

'I had no idea.' Kieren was silent for several moments then said, 'And he followed you, that was what he was doing when he had the heart attack?'

Erica nodded again. 'I'd taken out an AVO against him. He worked out I'd gone to be with my brother and ignored it. I wasn't with Joe. I was staying with Gill, his partner, who was also my solicitor. You met her. He barged into her office. That was where…' Erica shivered at the memory.

'Then I came along blaming you for his heart attack, accusing you of all sorts. I'm sorry,' he repeated. 'I didn't know.'

'How could you? He was your dad. You loved him, wanted to be like him. I hated how he tried to turn you into a carbon copy of him.

I could see it happening but there was nothing I could do to stop it. Then after he died, when you started trying to control me, I knew I couldn't bear to have it all to happen again.'

'I didn't realise. That's why you went back there?'

'It's why I left, yes. But I now know it was the right move for me. It's where I grew up, where my brother lives, my old friends…' Erica tried not to think of one old friend, of Jamie. 'At first I was worried about Briony…' She paused.

'Briony?' Kieren stared at her, then he seemed to realise. 'Is that why you said what you did to me to me about Briony, how I needed to consider her, to help more with Ava? Did you think I was like Dad? Was that what you were worried about? I'd never hurt Briony. I suppose it might have seemed…' he faltered, '… it might have seemed I was acting like Dad, but I only wanted what was best for her and Ava.'

'Your dad would probably have said that too, to excuse his behaviour.'

'I guess… But I'm not like him… am I?' Kieren looked so worried, Erica was tempted to throw her arms around him and comfort him as she had when he was a child.

'I hope not,' she said instead.

Then they did hug, and Erica went off to bed, comforted by the knowledge that all was well with her family.

Fifty-one

Jamie couldn't believe Joe, when he told him Erica had gone to Perth. Had she already been gone when he was at her door? He thought not, but if she'd been home, why didn't she answer? She hadn't responded to his calls and texts either. Was she coming back? Joe had said a few days, but it had already been three days since she'd fled from Rory's hospital room.

A lot had happened in those three days, the most important being Rory's move into rehab where he was hoping, with the aid of the staff, to gain movement in his leg. Jamie sighed, aware it would be a long time before Rory was walking again.

Cindy had proved worse than useless, crying as if she was the one who'd been bitten by the shark, flirting with the doctors, and irritating the nursing staff who all regarded Rory as a hero. Thank goodness she'd gone now, after Rory, unable to bear her presence any longer, told her he didn't need her crocodile tears and fake concern.

Jamie wished he could tell Erica she'd gone, that there was nothing between him and Cindy, hadn't been for years, and she was the last person he wanted to see in Pelican Crossing. It had been bad enough when she came to Gary's wedding, but this time with her snide remarks, her comments about Erica, she'd gone too far.

One good thing seemed to have come out of Rory's attack. Seeing the news of the attack on the internet, one of Rory's old school friends had come back to Pelican Crossing. Livvy's son, Dylan, had been crewing on a yacht sailing around the Great Barrier Reef. By a weird stroke of luck, the yacht had just docked in Cairns when Dylan saw the post, and he had dropped everything to visit his old mate, moving into Rory's apartment and visiting every day. Seeing the two together, Jamie wondered if this was the someone Rory had referred to, the one who'd moved away. He supposed time would tell but it was good to see his son more cheerful.

Glad he had a busy day ahead, Jamie welcomed his passengers aboard and set off to spend the day fishing, hoping the task of keeping the group happy would prevent him from thinking about Erica and worrying about her. But it was a faint hope, as being out in the bay where they had sailed together brought back memories of those special times with her, making him wonder if they would ever be together again.

*

Erica's time in Perth was drawing to a close. She was due back at work on Friday, and planned to return the day before. She'd enjoyed the visit more than she expected. After her conversation with Kieren, she'd been able to relax in his company, pleased he'd finally seen through his father and confident in the knowledge he no longer had any desire to emulate him. Given the troubles the car yard was having, she'd planted the seed of the idea of their moving to Pelican Crossing and hoped it might bear fruit. Meantime, Kieren and Briony had promised to spend Christmas with her, so she had that to look forward to.

It would be a wrench to leave Ava again, but the knowledge she'd see her in a few months helped soften the parting, though it did nothing to help Erica prepare for seeing Jamie again when she got home. She knew there was no way she could avoid him… and Cindy, who she had persuaded herself would have moved in with him… instead of her. If only she hadn't been so reluctant to take that next step, had agreed at once when Jamie had suggested it. But might that have been worse? If she and Jamie had been living together when Cindy returned, how would she have handled it?

Realising this way of thinking was self-destructive, Erica tried to put Jamie out of her mind and concentrate on the short time she had left with her family.

Wednesday morning was a confusion of hugs, kisses and promises to keep in touch, all with the prospect of seeing each other again in a few months' time. Although she didn't understand what was happening, Ava joined in the general melee. It was almost a relief to Erica to board the plane, but that was when her nightmare about Jamie and Cindy returned with a vengeance.

*

Pelican Crossing looked exactly the same when Erica drove into it the following morning. She was feeling weary, having been unable to get much sleep on the plane, the time difference having wrecked her internal clock. As soon as she got home, she intended to have a hot shower, fall into bed and hopefully sleep for the rest of the day.

It was a relief to open the door to the now familiar cottage and find nothing had changed. It felt like home, and she'd be sorry to leave it. But she'd be able to spend Christmas here with Kieren, Briony and Ava. And surely she'd be able to find somewhere else to live until she could afford a deposit for a home of her own.

She made herself a cup of the herbal tea she loved and was about to take it with her into the bedroom when her phone buzzed with a series of messages. She'd turned it on when she got off the plane in case the hospital tried to contact her. Checking the screen, she saw another message from Jamie – he was persistent, but she had no idea what he could have to say to her – one from Joe asking her if she was home and could she call, and one from Rhana to say Betsy's pups were ready for adoption and would Erica like to come and choose one. Ignoring the text from Jamie, Erica called Rhana first, and feeling a sudden burst of energy at the thought of a dog of her own, made arrangements to visit later in the day. Then she called Joe.

'Welcome back,' Joe said.

'Thanks. It's good to be back.'

'How was it?'

'Good. Better than I expected. Ava's such a delight. She's growing so quickly. I had a long talk with Kieren, and I'm satisfied everything's okay with him and Briony. He's finally come to his senses and seen

Geoff in his true colours. I'm sorry it's tainted his memory of his dad, but it's better all round. And they're coming here for Christmas.'

'That's good news. And Jamie? Have you heard from him?'

Erica tensed, her lips tightening. 'He's been calling and messaging me,' she said. She didn't want to talk about Jamie.

'You should call him.'

A burst of anger shot through Erica. Joe was treating her just as he had when they were growing up and he liked to tell her what to do. 'And you should butt out of my life. I'm not a kid you can order around. I'm old enough to make my own decisions, Joe.'

'I only want what's best for you, Erica. You know that. Gill and I…'

So he and Gill had been discussing her. Erica fumed, all the joy in her homecoming disappearing in a flash. 'That's enough, Joe. When I want your opinion, I'll ask for it.' She ended the call, wishing it was an old-fashioned phone, and she could slam down the receiver.

Still raging at her brother, Erica drained her cup and headed for the shower where the warm water cascading over her went some way to help improve her mood. She knew Jamie was a mate of Joe's, but for her brother to try to act as some sort of go-between when Jamie had… it was intolerable.

*

Erica was in a better frame of mind when she drove up to Rhana's home, filled with the anticipation of choosing her very own pup. For once, there were no dogs swarming around Rhana's ankles when she came out to greet Erica.

'Hey, good to see you.' Rhana greeted her with a hug. 'Why don't we have a cuppa first and you can fill me in on what you've been up to.'

Erica gave a forced smile. She was eager to see the pups, but it would be rude to refuse, and it was some time since she'd seen Rhana. She'd been too busy with Jamie, she realised. Well, no more. She'd have lots of time for her other friends in the future, starting right now.

'You've been away?' Rhana asked, when they were settled with cups of peppermint tea and slices of fruit loaf – Rhana had been baking again.

'I had a few days between shifts, so I flew over to Perth to see my family there.'

'Everything okay?' Rhana appeared concerned, and Erica remembered confiding in her about Kieren.

'It's all good. I was worried about nothing. They're going to join me for Christmas.'

'Oh, I'm so pleased for you. Have you heard anything from Livvy?'

'She's going to spend Christmas over there and come back in the new year.' Erica bit her lip, remembering she'd have to find somewhere else to live.

'Where will you go?'

'I'll find somewhere,' Erica said with more confidence than she felt. It had just occurred to her that not all landlords would be happy for her to have a dog.

'And Jamie?' Rhana raised an eyebrow.

Erica grimaced. She'd forgotten confiding in her friend about Jamie too.

'That's history.'

Rhana's eyes widened. 'But I thought…'

Erica's assurance crumbled. Her eyes moistened. 'I did too, Rhana, but… Cindy's back. He has a family and now, with Rory's injuries… There's no place for me in his life.'

'That's not what I heard.'

Erica stared at her friend in surprise. Rhana rarely left her acreage. What did she know that Erica didn't?

'Cindy didn't stay. It seems neither Jamie nor Rory wanted her here. She went back to the city where she belongs. So, Jamie…' She gave Erica an encouraging look.

'Oh!' Erica didn't know how she felt. Seeing Cindy at the hospital, she'd assumed… And she'd blamed Jamie for… She hadn't answered his calls, hadn't even read his texts, been so determined to move on with her life, a life without Jamie. She'd been a fool.

Seeming to sense her confusion, Rhana said, 'Would you like to see the pups now?'

'Yes, please.' Erica pulled herself together. She'd figure out what to do about Jamie later.

A few minutes later, Erica was standing beside Rhana outside an enclosure, staring at the most appealing collection of small spaniel pups gambolling around, watched jealously by their mother. 'Oh, Rhana, they're gorgeous!' Erica said, filled with a warm glow, her earlier turmoil forgotten.

'Aren't they? I've been breeding spaniels for years, but I never get over the miracle of these tiny creatures.'

Several of the puppies came over to the fence, curious to see who was watching them. One was black with a streak of white on its forehead. It was smaller than the others, who were pushing it out of the way.

Seeing Erica's attention on that one, Rhana said, 'He's the runt of the litter. The poor creature has to fight for attention.'

'That's the one I want,' Erica said, her heart going out to the tiny black puppy, with which she felt a sudden bond.

'Are you sure? He doesn't have the best conformation. Maybe one of the others?'

'I'm sure. Look!' As if understanding she'd chosen him, the little dog was gazing up at Erica with soulful eyes. 'I have to work tomorrow, but can I pick him up on the weekend? I'll need to buy food, a dog bed, toys… What else will I need?'

Rhana laughed. 'I have a list,' she said. 'I learned pretty early on that most new owners haven't a clue how to prepare for having a new pup in the house. You're no different from anyone else.'

Erica grinned. She couldn't wait to take her dog home, sure he'd be a wonderful companion. It was only when she was driving home, imagining the cottage with the little black dog in it, that the image of Jamie flashed before her eyes, and she recalled what Rhana had said. Cindy had gone. Jamie and she weren't back together. *What did that mean for Erica? Had she ruined her chances with him?*

Fifty-two

Jamie continued to go about his daily tasks, running his charter business and visiting Rory who was beginning to make progress. Dylan was often there too, and it was a delight to see the two young men together and to listen to them chatting. Dylan was filling in for Rory with Cam at *Pelican Marine*, but had assured his friend that it was only temporary, and he'd find something else when Rory was back on his feet. They'd both laughed at that, much to Jamie's distress, but he supposed it was good they could joke about what was to him a dreadful tragedy.

But despite his routine, Jamie couldn't put thoughts of Erica out of his mind. He wondered what she was doing in Perth, if her suspicions about her son's marriage were justified and if so, what she was doing about it. He also wondered when she intended to return and how he could contact her when she did.

When Joe told Jamie Erica had returned, he wanted to rush over there to talk to her, to explain about Cindy, to reassure her nothing had changed. But Joe advised that wouldn't be the wisest move, describing Erica's anger on the phone. 'Give her a few days to settle down,' he said. 'There's no point in aggravating her when she's in this mood. I remember what she was like as a child. When something upset her, she found it hard to forgive. Let her cool down before you try to speak with her.'

Although it was hard, Jamie decided to take Joe's advice, realising he knew his sister better than anyone, better even than Jamie.

Jamie had been cooling his heels for a week, hoping for a glimpse of Erica when he walked past Livvy's cottage on his way to or from work. But there had been no sign of her. He'd even contemplated joining the group of wild swimmers on the other beach, sure she'd be there every morning at dawn. But so far, he hadn't dared, knowing Gill would be there too and would report back to Joe. He respected Joe and knew his advice was sound, but it was so hard to do nothing when he ached to be back on good terms with the woman he loved.

He sighed when he returned from the charter group he'd led that day. Another lonely Saturday evening stretched ahead of him, and still no sign of Erica. Unable to face another solitary evening, he walked back to the harbour, in the hope of finding one of his friends in *The Grand* and joining them for a drink. But although the bar was filled with people, none of his mates were there. Feeling dejected, he left and headed for the beach. The sound of the waves and the scent of the sea always helped his mood. His dad used to tell him he had been born with the sea in his veins.

Jamie was wandering along aimlessly at the edge of the water lost in thought, when a dog ran up to him and shook itself, spraying water on him.

'Lady!' a voice called.

The dog stopped in its tracks as old Agnes appeared to grasp it by the collar. 'I'm so sorry,' she said. 'Lady doesn't normally do that. She must have…' She peered at Jamie, seeming to suddenly recognise him. 'What are you doing here on your own? Where's that lovely lady of yours?'

Jamie stared at her in surprise. How did Agnes know about him and Erica? But their relationship hadn't been a secret, not after they'd appeared together at the fundraising walk. Agnes might have seen them there or on some other occasion. 'She's not mine, not anymore,' he said despondently.

'Why not? You make a good couple.'

Jamie kicked the sand underfoot. He thought so too.

'I seem to remember you were a couple before, when you were in your teens. You let her go then. Are you going to let her go again?'

Jamie kicked the sand again. 'Her brother said…'

'Poof, what does Joe Harris know about relationships? I saw that he and Gill Dickson were made for each other long before he did. I may never have married, but I do know a thing or two about what makes people tick, and you and Erica Harris were made for each other. You need to talk to her, tell her how you feel.'

Jamie was about to reply he'd done that, and she'd said she loved him too. But that was before… But Agnes and her dog had moved on. For a few moments he stared at their figures disappearing in the distance, Agnes's long, white hair flying behind her, her long skirt flapping in the breeze. Then he straightened his shoulders. Old Agnes was right. What did Joe know? It was up to Jamie to decide what to do, and what he wanted to do right now was speak to Erica.

*

Erica was exhausted. Although it was Saturday and she wasn't officially rostered on, an outbreak of sickness among Emergency staff meant she'd been called in to work. She perked up when as soon as she walked into the cottage, she was greeted by Bandit, the black spaniel she'd picked up from Rhana only a week earlier and who had already made himself at home in the cottage.

'It's good to see you too,' she said, crouching down to cuddle the puppy. She was so glad she'd chosen to get a dog, though he did create more work. She eyed the path of destruction he'd managed to create across the living room floor, his toys scattered everywhere and what looked like yesterday's copy of *The Echo* torn to shreds. She must have left it where Bandit could reach it. 'You little devil,' she said affectionately. 'You missed me too, didn't you?' She picked her pet up and let him nuzzle her face. She still missed Jamie, but it was hard to remain sad with this little ball of fluff to take care of and love. 'I'll just have a shower then we'll go for a walk,' she said, wondering if all dog owners spoke to their dogs as if they were human.

After a hot shower which helped her feel more energised, Erica pulled on a pair of jeans and a lightweight sweater. She was about to take Bandit's lead from its hook when there was a knock at the door. Expecting it to be Joe who had still to meet her new furry companion and had promised to bring Coco along to make friends, she opened it with a smile, which faded when she saw Jamie standing there looking sheepish.

Wracked with conflicting emotions, Erica stared at him, speechless.

'Don't close the door on me,' Jamie said. 'I know what you must think of me, but it wasn't how it looked. We need to talk. Can I come in?'

Slowly, Erica opened the door wider to allow him to enter, then led him into the living room. They both remained standing. Erica folded her arms, determined to keep her cool no matter what he had to say. She remembered what Rhana had told her, but what if she'd been wrong?

Jamie seemed awkward, standing there without speaking. Finally, he said, 'How about we sit down, and could you make some tea?'

Swallowing hard, her heart racing, her stomach churning, Erica went to the kitchen where Bandit was wondering what had happened. Weren't they about to go for a walk?

'It's okay, Bandit,' Erica said. 'We'll go for our walk later. As soon as Jamie leaves.' She filled Bandit's bowl with water which he lapped up noisily, then turned on the kettle and made two cups of tea – camomile to hopefully help calm her – and the English Breakfast she'd bought for Jamie when they were seeing each other regularly, though he often preferred coffee. She'd been home for over a week. Why had he waited till now to come to see her? And why at this time on a Saturday evening?

When she returned to the living room, Jamie stood up to take the cup of tea from her then sat down again, seeming to be more relaxed than earlier. He took a gulp of tea, put the cup down and began to speak.

'I need to explain, Erica. I know what you saw, what it must have looked like. But I had no idea Cindy was in Pelican Crossing. It was all Gary's doing. He thought…' Jamie scratched his head. 'I don't know what he thought. He'd been in contact with his mother about Rory's accident and she'd suddenly taken it into her head to visit. I suspect it might have had something to do with an argument with the creep she brought to Gary's wedding. I left soon after you did to follow you. I thought you might have gone home, but the cottage was in darkness. I realised you must have gone to your book club, so maybe weren't too upset after all. But I needed to talk with you to make sure we were good. When next morning, you didn't answer your door, then Joe told me you'd gone to Perth… I couldn't believe it.' He drew his hand through his hair making it stand up in a way Erica had always found endearing.

She swallowed, but didn't speak. She wanted to believe him, but was he speaking the truth? She needed to hear what else he had to say.

'Well, that's it, I guess. I didn't want Cindy here. I made it clear to her. Rory didn't want her either, so she finally left. Then Joe told me you were back, but he said you were angry and advised me to let you cool off before I approached you. That's why… Anyway, I'm here now because I couldn't stay away any longer. I need to know you forgive me. I love you, Erica. My life is nothing without you. I lost you once. I can't bear to lose you again. Please say you forgive me.' He gazed at Erica, his eyes filled with pleading.

Erica thought irrelevantly that Bandit often had the same soulful and pleading look in his eyes, before finding her resolution weakening and her eyes misting. She had a sudden urge to feel his arms around her. 'Oh, Jamie,' she said. She started to rise.

Jamie did too. They met, their tea forgotten as he reclaimed her lips and crushed her to him. Erica trembled, an ache of desire welling up and filling her with longing. It was as if she'd come home, as if they'd never been apart.

Suddenly, a tiny black furry bundle tumbled between them, tail wagging furiously.

They both laughed as they drew away from each other. 'This is Bandit,' Erica said, still laughing, 'The latest addition to my family. I promised him a walk.'

'Hello, Bandit.' Jamie crouched down to ruffle the dog's ears. 'I've always wanted a dog. Why don't we walk him together?'

It was romantic, walking along the beach with Bandit in the moonlight to the sound of the gentle lapping of the waves on the shore, stopping from time to time to kiss, to remind themselves they were together again. Erica had already forgotten her annoyance, her anger, her suspicions, her doubts. Now she knew the truth, she couldn't believe how stupid she'd been to be fooled by appearances, by Cindy. She knew she had to trust Jamie, trust herself, and listen to her heart.

When they left the beach and Jamie said, 'My place?' with a raised eyebrow, Erica happily agreed. She couldn't wait to be alone with him, to be in his arms again.

When they stopped to allow Jamie to unlock the door, Erica looked up. Above the door was a plaque which read *Safe Harbour*. She hadn't noticed it before, and now it seemed significant.

As soon as they were inside, Bandit, seemingly feeling at home, immediately ran to a spot by the back door, turned around a few times, then settled down, his head on his paws.

'He's making himself at home already,' Jamie said with a grin. 'You are going to move in, aren't you?' Without waiting for a reply, he pulled Erica towards him, his arms encircling her. Her body tingled from the contact. She could feel his uneven breathing on her cheek as he held her close. Then his lips slowly descended to meet hers. Erica felt her knees weaken. Her emotions whirled and skidded. This is what she'd been waiting for all her life. She'd found her own safe harbour.

Fifty-three

It was Christmas Eve, the night of the fundraising ball. In spite of his objections, Jamie had caved in and gone along with the other men to hire dinner suits for the occasion. Erica thought he looked very distinguished in the formal outfit, complete with a turquoise bow tie and matching cummerbund.

Erica was aglow with excitement as she dressed in the black strappy dress she'd bought specially for the occasion. She smiled as Jamie helped fasten it and dropped a kiss on the nape of her neck, sending shivers down her spine, reflecting how at home she felt in his cottage after only a few months. Bandit was at home there too, having made the spot by the back door, where his bed now sat, his own.

A tall, decorated Christmas tree stood in the living room, a replica of the one in Livvy's cottage where Kieren, Briony and Ava were spending two weeks over Christmas, two weeks in which Erica hoped they'd decide to make Pelican Crossing their home. So far, they had managed to protect the tree from attacks by Bandit, but they didn't hold out hope of safeguarding it for the entire Christmas period.

'Ready, beautiful?' Jamie asked, his hands on her shoulders as he looked at them both in the mirror. 'We make a striking couple.' He grinned.

'As ready as I'll ever be.' Erica still had to pinch herself that she was here, living with Jamie in Pelican Crossing, just as she'd imagined all those years ago when she was eighteen. And now she had a son, daughter-in-law and granddaughter who were staying only a few houses away and with whom they'd be spending Christmas Day tomorrow, along with Jamie's two sons, their partners and his grandson, and her brother and his partner. It was like a dream come true. But first, there was the ball, the highlight fundraising event for Joe's special project. They were so close to achieving their goal and tonight's raffles and auction should clinch it.

The ball was being held in the hall at the sports centre, and it was already thronged with people, all dressed in their finery when Erica and Jamie arrived. The event had proved popular, and tickets had sold out rapidly as soon as it was advertised in *The Echo*. Erica had even heard on the hospital grapevine how some people were offering to pay outrageous amounts of money if Joe would arrange to have additional tickets printed.

Erica and Jamie pushed their way through the noisy crowd of happy revellers, accepting glasses of complimentary champagne on the way, till they reached their friends. Joe and Gill were surrounded by Gill's group of women friends and their partners, all looking their best and drinking champagne.

'To a successful evening, Joe.' Jamie raised his glass, followed by the others, who murmured their agreement. Joe grinned.

'Barb would be so proud of you,' Erica whispered into Joe's ear.

'Thanks, sis. I think she'd be proud of you too, of how you've managed to turn your life around. I know it hasn't been easy, and I may not have helped as much as I could have, but you did it all the same. To you and Jamie and a wonderful future together.' Joe raised his glass.

'Thanks, Joe,' Erica said, feeling Jamie's arm around her waist, and knowing that while a happy future was never assured, hers was in good hands.

After an evening of drinking and dancing, tired but happy, Erica was glad when the ball finally ended in the early hours of Christmas morning. As she and Jamie walked home through the silent streets, the stars twinkling above them, she gave thanks for everything in her life, for Joe, for Ava, for Kieren and Briony, but most of all for Jamie. A year ago, she would never have believed how much her life would change, how she would be in a new relationship with her first love, looking forward to spending the rest of her life with him in this town where she'd grown up, never have believed she'd find such happiness.

What had seemed like a disaster when her Perth home had to be sold, had proved to be a blessing in disguise.

'Penny for them?' Jamie said, when she'd been quiet for some time.

'Just counting my blessings.' Erica smiled, gazing up into his eyes.

'The spirit of Christmas,' Jamie said, 'and you're the best Christmas present I could ever have wished for.'

'You're mine too.' Erica said.

'Really? I thought Bandit might have that accolade.' Jamie chuckled.

She swatted his arm. 'Well, you come a close second, I suppose.' Erica said, wrapping her arms around his neck.

Their lips met, and Erica closed her eyes to the most wonderful feeling as they kissed, transported to a world she never thought possible. Despite the late hour, and the very busy day ahead, Erica felt energised like she'd never felt before.

The End

If you've enjoyed Erica and Jamie's story, I'd love if you could leave a review on Amazon and/or Goodreads. A few words will suffice, no need for a lengthy review. It will mean a lot to me and help other readers find my books.

I'm thrilled so many of my readers are enjoying this series set in Pelican Crossing and are making friends with my characters.

Do you want to know what happens when Livvy returns? The next book in the series, Waves of Change in Pelican Crossing, is Livvy's story.

Sad to leave her daughter and granddaughters behind in England where she has been visiting for the past year, *Olivia Grace* is excited to return to her hometown of Pelican Crossing and resume her life as a counsellor. But a shock awaits her, threatening to destroy her future and forcing her to make changes she'd never anticipated.

Dan Parker has moved to Pelican Crossing with his teenage daughter after the death of his wife, intent on making a fresh start. Now, having fulfilled his long-held dream of opening a Wellness Centre, he confronts an unexpected challenge.

Faced with an unforeseen situation and frustrated by her friends' relentless matchmaking, Olivia finally admits her attraction to Dan and agrees to a date. But real life isn't a romantic novel, and things don't go smoothly.

Can these two lonely people find a future together, or are they destined to grow old alone?

For fans of heartwarming small-town romances, this is a must-read. With vibrant descriptions of the charming coastal town and two endearing characters who struggle with loss and loneliness, this book will tug at your heartstrings.

You can order here https://mybook.to/Wavesofchange

From the Author

Dear Reader,

First, I'd like to thank you for choosing to read *Safe Harbour in Pelican Crossing*. I hope you've enjoyed visiting Pelican Crossing as much as I've enjoyed creating it.

Like all my other books, although it is part of a series, it can be read as a standalone.

If you'd like to stay up to date with my new releases and special offers you can sign up to my reader's group.

You can sign up here

https://maggiechristensenauthor.com/subscribe/

I'll never share your email address, and you can unsubscribe at any time. You can also contact me via Facebook, Twitter or by email. I love hearing from my readers and will always reply.

Thanks again.

Acknowledgements

As always, this book could not have been written without the help and advice of a number of people.

Firstly, my husband Jim for listening to my plotlines without complaint, for his patience and insights as I discuss my characters and storyline with him, for his patience and help with difficult passages and advice on my male dialogue, and for being there when I need him.

John Hudspith, editor extraordinaire for his ideas, suggestions, encouragement and attention to detail, and for helping me make this book better.

Jane Dixon-Smith for her patience and for working her magic on my beautiful cover and interior.

My thanks also to early readers of this book –Maggie and Louise for their helpful comments and advice, and to fellow writer and kitesurfer, Fiona Tarr, for her help and advice with the kitesurfing scenes. Any mistakes are my own.

And to all of my readers, reviewers and bloggers. Your support and comments make it all worthwhile.

About the Author

After a career in education, Maggie Christensen began writing contemporary women's fiction portraying mature women facing life-changing situations, and historical fiction set in her native Scotland. Her travels inspire her writing, be it her trips to visit family in Scotland, in Oregon, USA or her home on Queensland's beautiful Sunshine Coast. Maggie writes of mature heroines coming to terms with changes in their lives and the heroes worthy of them. Maggie has been called *the queen of mature age fiction* and her writing has been described by one reviewer as *like a nice warm cup of tea. It is warm, nourishing, comforting and embracing.*

From the small town in Scotland where she grew up, Maggie was lured to Australia by the call to 'Come and teach in the sun'. Once there, she worked as a primary school teacher, university lecturer and in educational management. Now living with her husband of over thirty years on Queensland's Sunshine Coast, she loves walking on the deserted beach in the early mornings and having coffee by the river on weekends. Her days are spent surrounded by books, either reading or writing them – her idea of heaven!

Maggie can be found on Facebook, Twitter, Bluesky, Goodreads, Instagram, Bookbub or on her website.

https://www.facebook.com/maggiechristensenauthor
https://twitter.com/MaggieChriste33
https://www.goodreads.com/author/show/8120020.Maggie_Christensen
https://www.instagram.com/maggiechriste33/
https://www.bookbub.com/profile/maggie-christensen
https://bsky.app/profile/maggiechriste33.bsky.social
https://maggiechristensenauthor.com/